W9-DES-315

WITHDRAWN

SEP 24 2008

DEAREST DOROTHY,
IF NOT NOW, WHEN?

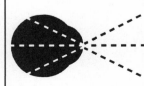

This Large Print Book carries the
Seal of Approval of N.A.V.H.

DEAREST DOROTHY, IF NOT NOW, WHEN?

CHARLENE ANN BAUMBICH

THORNDIKE PRESS

A part of Gale, Cengage Learning

GALE
CENGAGE Learning™

Detroit • New York • San Francisco • New Haven, Conn • Waterville, Maine • London

GALE
CENGAGE Learning™

Copyright © Charlene Ann Baumbich, 2007.
Welcome to Partonville Series #6.
Thorndike Press, a part of Gale, Cengage Learning.

Thorndike Press® Large Print Clean Reads.
The text of this Large Print edition is unabridged.
Other aspects of the book may vary from the original edition.
Set in 16 pt. Plantin.
Printed on permanent paper.

LIBRARY OF CONGRESS CATALOGING-IN-PUBLICATION DATA

Baumbich, Charlene Ann, 1945–
    Dearest Dorothy, if not now, when? / by Charlene Ann Baumbich.
        p. cm. — (Welcome to Partonville series ; #6) (Thorndike Press large print clean reads)
    ISBN-13: 978-1-4104-0612-5 (hardcover : alk. paper)
    ISBN-10: 1-4104-0612-1 (hardcover : alk. paper)
    I. Title.
PS3602.A963D426 2008
813'.54—dc22   2008014367

Published in 2008 by arrangement with Penguin Books, a member of Penguin Group (USA) Inc.

Printed in the United States of America
1 2 3 4 5 6 7 12 11 10 09 08

Dedicated to
Colleen Ann Baumbich

ACKNOWLEDGMENTS

This might seem like a strange way to open a list of acknowledgments, but I am truly grateful to the inhabitants of Partonville for continuing to talk to me. THANK YOU, folks, for helping me keep on circling the square in your lively company. Y'all took me on an AMAZING ride this time. I laughed and cried (with and for you), sent you hugs (when I felt sorry for you or just wanted to help you celebrate) and occasionally wished I could *smack* you. (Cora, Arthur, Gladys — you KNOW what I'm talking about.) You are all so dear to me. I feel like the luckiest woman alive to be able to hang out with such wonderful friends.

Thank you, God, for infusing me with Your creativity. The whole "watching the movie run in my head" experience is mind-boggling and awesome.

Thank you Real Life friends. Thank you for doing breakfast, lunch, dinner, snacks and/or beverages with me. Thank you for listening to hysterical phone calls and indulging me when I appeared at your doorstep begging for break time (BLESS YOU Burl & Ginger). Thank you for letting me know you were just thinking about me. Thank you for emotionally supporting me, even when I'm a brat.

Another big THANK YOU goes out to Nick Deones, who again helped me understand some of the many nuances of real estate. If there are any errors in this storytelling (sometimes I'm a numbskull), it certainly isn't *his* fault! Once again, Nick was kind, patient, informative and thorough.

To everyone who reads the series, and/or comes to see me when I'm book touring, and/or e-mails me notes of good cheer, YOU ROCK-O-RAMA. Each and every confirmation fuels me to keep writing. It seems that a note of encouragement always arrives just when I need one the most.

PENGUIN PEOPLE, YOU ARE THE BEST! Carolyn Carlson, you again helped me to live a dream while keeping me coherent and focused on the pages. (Readers, you have no IDEA how important her refinement is to your reading enjoyment!) Maggie Payette, this cover makes me CHEER! Maureen Donnelly and Ann Day, you two are part of a fabulous team. Sales and marketing, editorial assistants, copy editors, order fulfillers . . . way to go.

Danielle Egan-Miller, an agent with heart, guts and savvy, I raise my glass to you, again and again and again.

George, Bret, Brian, Katie, Bonnie, Bridget and Colleen, next to God, you are what makes my life worthwhile. All the "glamorous stuff" (writing, touring, speaking . . .) is wonderful, but nothing matters more than family. Nothing.

INTRODUCTION

*To be seventy years young is sometimes
far more cheerful and hopeful than to be
forty years old.*
— Oliver Wendell Holmes

And now, welcome to Partonville, a circle-the-square town in the northern part of southern Illinois, where oldsters are young, trees have names and the man in the moon laughs out loud.

1

Jacob poked the toe of one of his gray dress socks back inside the suitcase and jimmied the zipper around the last corner. "Phew!" In one frustrated motion he grasped the handle to the bulging carry-on bag, spun on his heels, tossed it onto the floor next to his briefcase, completed his 360-degree turn and plopped down on his bed where he rested his elbows on his knees and cradled his face in his hands. "Yes, you're going in circles," he muttered to himself. Bone tired, he suffered from ongoing jet lag and mental fatigue. These whirlwind — or whirligig, as his mom had taken to calling them — trips between Philadelphia and Partonville were about to do him in. But if everything went as planned, this would be his last round-trip flight before making his final journey, moving him — lock, stock and business practice — back to his roots.

In the little more than two months since

fifty-five-year-old Jacob Henry Wetstra had made the stunning announcement that he was moving to Partonville, the small town he'd left when he headed off to college, he'd sold his half of his Philadelphia law firm to his business partner Brenda Stewart and sold his condo, which he had to vacate in ten days. Even though he still worried about his decision, at this point the final transition couldn't come fast enough, if for no other reason than to end the weekly travel cycle: Tuesdays and Wednesdays working with bereft Partonville clients who had recently lost Rick Lawson, their dear friend, and, up until the time of his death, the town's sole attorney; the rest of the week in Philly wrapping up court cases and corporate documents, saying good-bye to longtime friends and clients, and packing a household full of items, much of which would go into storage for now.

Oddly enough, Jacob's decision to change the course of his life was prompted by a death. During Jacob's Christmas visit to his mother's home, Rick Lawson died in a car crash, leaving behind his invalid mother for whom he cared, and his only sibling, a brother, with no clue as to how to handle Rick's law practice. Jacob pitched in, lending Helen, Rick's longtime secretary, a temporary hand at trying to make sense of Rick's chaotic work piles. While sorting through the muddle and hearing so many touching accounts of Rick's caring presence in so many lives, Jacob awakened to a couple of truths: even though his life was successful professionally, it felt lacking in personal ways. And at eighty-eight, his mother, whom he adored, wouldn't be here forever. Perhaps it was time to make some changes. *If not now, when?* he'd pondered to himself. That simple question led him to where he was today: moving from upscale and big-scale everything to a tiny town of barely 1,400, a town striving to exist under the watchful eye of hungry developers who saw Pardon-Me-Ville, as it was often referred to, as nothing more than their next level-and-rebuild opportunity.

Jacob rubbed his eyelids with the heels of his hands while rehashing a question he'd asked his mom during his last trip. When could, when *should* he change the sign on what was now *his* office-entry door? "You'll know when it's time, son," she'd said. "For now, the words 'Rick Lawson, Attorney at Law' still serve as a sort of memorial marker for everyone who circles the square. Just trust God and your gut." She always made things like that sound so easy. *Right.* Jacob

15

pictured the worn RICK LAWSON, AT-
TORNEY AT LAW lettering on the dirty
glass window set in the shabby street-level
door. The door didn't even open straight
into the offices. Rather, it served as the
gateway leading to a rickety stairwell up to
his "new" second-floor, two-room professional digs. Quite the comedown from his
executive-everything suite of offices he'd
soon leave behind. Jacob decided that as
soon as Helen, who would stay on as his
secretary, could emotionally handle it, he'd
replace the entire door with something more
sophisticated, like solid oak with brass
fixtures and an engraved plaque bearing his
name. One more thing to add to his to-do
list. Too bad, he thought, a tired chuckle
rising in his throat, that he hadn't put
"check your sanity" on that list before making this remarkable — and surprising, even
unto himself — decision to uproot his life.

He shook his head and flopped back on
the bed. Clasping his hands behind his
neck, he stared at the ceiling light fixture,
the one with the rheostat, the one with the
hint-of-pink, frosted, decorative globe his
interior designer had insisted would help
calm and soothe him for a good night's
sleep. He'd dated the slim blonde for four
months before determining that apart from

Rita's obvious physical appeal, a talent for making his surroundings more aesthetically appealing and her aggressive pursuit of him — which grew increasingly suffocating and which he always found unattractive — they had absolutely nothing in common. The End. Another hopeful possibility down the drain. After Randy, his best friend, had inquired about Rita, Jacob had heard himself say "Life's too short to settle for a mediocre relationship." Well surprise-surprise. Randy married her, finding his relationship with Rita anything but mediocre. After Rita and Randy first paired up, the three of them found their get-togethers a bit awkward; but the past was soon forgotten and the friendship between all of them survived. Thrived even. For Jacob, Rita was more likeable as a friend after she belonged to someone else — a familiar pattern for him. Jacob even went on to become Randy's best man at their wedding. "Rita and Randy. All's well that ends well," he'd quipped to his mom during a phone conversation the day after.

His mom. She was starting to show her age. She seemed a little frailer each time he visited, and now she was taking that heart medication and popping an occasional nitroglycerin tablet. But some things remained the same about her, and one of them was her faith. "Just trust God and your gut," he again heard her saying, closing his eyes and letting out a weary laugh. "Good thing you didn't add *women* to that list, Mom."

Jacob hadn't grown into one of Philadelphia's most respected and sought-after trial attorneys (and one of its most eligible bachelors) because he'd trusted *anyone* other than himself. A relentless researcher, splendid orator and fierce competitor, throughout his career he'd learned to choose cases and clients wisely, work long, hard hours and receive handsome pay for his services. God and his gut? Nah. He trusted cold hard facts and was enough of a workaholic to prove them. But because of these very things, Brenda — and nearly everyone else who knew his Type A personality well — had asked, "Won't you be bored mindless in a small-town practice?" He wondered the same thing, although he never admitted it. Nonetheless, as long as his mother was alive, he was ready to ride it out and make adjustments as need be. Neither his conscience (she was so excited about his return she was nearly airborne, she'd told him) nor his emotions (he needed to pad his occasional lonesome heart with more of his

18

family's stories before it was too late) would allow him to live apart from her any longer, and he had Rick Lawson, a man he'd barely known, to thank for the opportunity. It would all work out, he kept telling himself.

First, though, he needed to *get* to Partonville. *One step at a time, Jacob,* he thought to himself. *One step at a time.*

He glanced at his bedside clock. 11 p.m. He needed to get to sleep. He sat up to set the alarm but rolled right back down, crossed his arms over his chest, then sat up and lay back a dozen times. No matter how tired he was, it never hurt to work the abs. He set his alarm for 4:30 a.m., shucked his clothes and sorted them between the dry-cleaning and laundry bags, which would be picked up the following morning outside his door and be delivered back fresh and ready to wear by the time he returned home. *Clean clothes for the permanent journey.* Always thinking ahead. From the abstract design on the tie draped over his neatly pressed shirt to his polished cordovan shoes on the floor, everything was in place for tomorrow's early morning get-up-and-go.

And go and go and go.

"I'll tell you, May Belle, I can hardly *stand*

it! Only ten more days," Dorothy said to both May Belle and Sheba, her mutt who trotted up for a head-scratch. Dorothy felt like a kid who'd been waiting for Santa to arrive for two straight months. Her firstborn son was moving back to Partonville! She never, ever, thought she'd see the day either of her boys would come home to roost. When Jacob left for Penn State so many decades ago, she knew in her heart he was leaving for good. He was a focused and ambitious young man with a do-gooder heart. Even as a little tyke he loved helping people. Vincent, Jacob's brother two years his junior, loved the country life, but he'd followed his ex to Colorado in order to stay near his teen sons, Dorothy's only grandchildren. She knew Vinnie wouldn't come back as long as his children were there, but she wouldn't want it any other way. The boys were blessed to have such a loving, involved dad living within miles of them. Oh, the prayers that flew for her faraway family. But now . . . now her Jacob Henry was coming home!

"Has Herb found Jacob a house yet?" May Belle asked the beaming Dorothy. Herb Morgan owned Morgan Realty, one of the few remaining independent Realtors in the area.

"Not last I heard, although I know Jacob's in pretty close touch with him. Anything is possible, but that son of mine doesn't tell me everything, thank goodness," she added with a chuckle. "As far as I'm concerned, I'm in no hurry for that to happen and in fact would be perfectly content if it never did. I told Jacob he could stay in my spare bedroom as long as he liked."

"To which he responded?"

"He didn't." Dorothy laughed and reached for another of the snickerdoodle cookies May Belle had baked. It was Dorothy's turn to host smorgasbord night, which meant both ladies gathered their leftovers, laid them out on the counter and, along with Earl, May Belle's forty-five-year-old mentally challenged son, helped themselves to the "splendor of choice," as Dorothy put it. Although either woman could suggest a smorgasbord night, it was usually Dorothy who made the announcement. In an unspoken rule, May Belle baked something for dessert, which was just fine with all of them since when *didn't* May Belle bake? Dorothy, sitting erect in a pink (her trademark color) sweat suit and white tennis shoes with pink curlicue shoe laces, dunked her cookie in her warm teacup of milk and took a bite. "Mmmmmm." She slid the bitten edge of

21

the cookie back into the cup and let it soak a moment longer than the last bite before smacking it down. "The perfect dunk is a wonderful thing, wouldn't you agree?"

"I reckon you're right," May Belle said, taking note that Earl was copying Dorothy's every move, although he held his snickerdoodle in his milk a little too long so that when he tried to bring it to his mouth the soggy mass broke off and plunked back into his cup.

"No problem," Dorothy said, launching herself out of her chair to retrieve him a spoon. "Here ya go. Fish away, Earl! Then again, it might make it easier if you drank the rest of your milk first, then there the cookie would be, ready for the pickins!" Earl gave his cup a thoughtful study before gulping down the milk, leaving only the doughy mass stuck to the bottom. He smiled at Dorothy before using the spoon she'd handed him to dig out the wet wad of cookie. Ever since he'd been a little guy, he trusted that his Dearest Dorothy had the right answers to just about everything.

"You know, May Belle," Dorothy said, a mischievous lilt in her voice, "maybe the reason Jacob didn't answer me when I offered him a home is because he might not find our cookie-dunking nightlife quite the excitement he's used to in the big city."

May Belle giggled, but not before covering her mouth with her hand, a habit she'd taken to when someone in first grade made fun of what they'd called her "carved pumpkin smile." She'd lost more baby teeth than anyone else in her class at that point and sported quite the look for a spell. Of course other children picked up on the teasing, each creating his or her own spin-off version, like "pumpkin face" or "pumpkin head," "May Belle, Schmae Belle" or "May-baleenie Hal-loweenie."

"When's Mr. Jacob coming again?" Earl wanted to know. Jacob had worked hard during his visits to continue gaining Earl's trust and friendship. Since he'd been away so long and only came for occasional visits, and especially since Earl was such a great help to his mother, Jacob hoped a sincere friendship with Earl could develop after he moved back. Not only that, but Earl was one of his mother's favorite friends, too, and not just because he was challenged or her best friend's son. Earl was kind, strong, considerate and child-like in so many wonderful ways. Of course he was also shy, slow to warm to people and opposed to loud noises. But everyone in town loved Earl (never referred to as retarded, but rather slow and particular), especially his Dearest Dorothy, as he always called her.

Jacob had scored big points with Earl by giving him a box of Cubs baseball cards for Christmas. Jacob knew Earl loved watching the Cubs on television and Earl had once, in a rare show of confidence and intimacy, taken Jacob to his bedroom to show him his collection of baseball cards his dad had given him as a child. The faces were nearly worn off those cards from all the arranging and rearranging. Although Earl's reading ability was limited, he knew enough to put names with faces and recognize team logos. He recited the first names — putting a Mr. in front of them, in keeping with the way he addressed anyone other than Dorothy — one by one as he flipped through the cards, turning each over as he went. "Time to add to your collection," Jacob said when he'd handed him the gift package. Earl opened it and without a word, disappeared to his bedroom to store them carefully with the crimped cards in his old cigar box. It was three days before he looked at them again, just to make sure they were still there. He'd get them out when the first season's game aired on television, see which players he could recognize. Now the baseball season was fast approaching and the box was right next to his chair in the living room where he'd sit to watch the games.

"Jacob Henry will be here tomorrow, Earl!" Dorothy said. "He'll be here for two days, then he'll fly back to Pennsylvania. Then next week he'll come here and never go back, unless he just wants to take a vacation. Your mom is so lucky to have had you right here under her roof all these years, and now I'll get to have one of my boys right near me again too. Won't that be grand?" Earl nodded and smiled. He loved it when Dorothy was happy.

May Belle stood to clear the dessert dishes but not before Dorothy snatched one more cookie off the plate. "Oh! I'm sorry," May Belle said, setting the plate back down in front of Dorothy. "I thought you were through."

Dorothy held the cookie in the air. "This is my last one," she said. "Do you hear that, stomach?" She set the cookie on her napkin and patted her rounded tummy. "Since I moved so close to you, dearie, I think my south forty has spread another three acres," she said, moving her hands to her rump and giving it a pat. "When spring officially gets here in another couple weeks, Earl, you and I should start taking a daily walk together, maybe go around the block a couple-three times. What do you say?"

"Good," he said, then gave her a nod. Since the cookies were right there and since Dorothy'd helped herself to one more, Earl grabbed another too. In a whisk, May Belle moved the remaining cache to the counter. "I think you two have had quite enough for one evening. You'll both be awake all night from the sugar high." May Belle, donning the festive spring apron with a colorful tulip pattern Dorothy'd given her for Christmas, opened Dorothy's drawer and retrieved a plastic bag to pack the cookies which she would, as always, leave with her sweet-toothed friend.

"Who do you think you are, bossing us around like that," Dorothy asked May Belle while winking at Earl. "Gladys?"

"Speaking of our mayor," May Belle said, "I ran into her at Your Store this morning. You'd think the election was next week rather than nearly, what, five weeks away?"

"I noticed the election falls on April Fool's Day this year. How perfect is *that?*"

"Really?" May Belle asked. Dorothy nodded, taking her last swig of milk. "She was telling me about the posters she's having made up."

"Posters?" Dorothy asked, glancing over at May Belle. "May Belle Justice, don't you

26

dare start washing those dishes! I've got nothing to do tomorrow but those dishes. Don't you make my services obsolete! Sit yourself back down here and finish your milk."

May Belle, her hand wrapped around the container of dishwashing solution, sighed, put the bottle back under the kitchen sink and did as she was told. There was never any use arguing with Dorothy. "Election posters, I guess. At least that's what I think she was talking about. She said she'd come up with a *brilliant,* and that is the exact word she used, slogan for this year's election, which, she reminded me, would be the first time she would be officially voted in." Jake McKern, Gladys's husband, had died in office. Since everyone knew she ran him anyway, the townsfolk just decided to let her officially take over the office after his death and ride out the rest of his term. "She didn't want to spoil the surprise so she didn't tell me what the slogan was, but she said to be on the lookout. I don't know why she's spending all that money on posters. No one's going to run against her anyway."

"Of this you can be sure," Dorothy said with conviction, "*nothing* is for sure but God."

2

Josh jumped off the school bus and waved toward the bus's back window as it pulled away. The same group of girls always sat in the back row of seats. He didn't know them other than by name, but they always launched into a sing-songy "Hiiiiiiiiii, Jooooooosh," when he got on the bus and waved to him when he got off. Kind of annoying but good for the ego. He'd be disappointed if they stopped, he decided.

He checked the mailbox. Empty. His mom must have picked up the mail already since she received tons of letters and big envelopes on a daily basis. He didn't know why he always checked the box anyway; there was never anything for him, aside from ten days ago, Valentine's Day. That day he'd opened the flap and lo and behold, there was a pink, square envelope addressed to Joshua Matthew Kinney, right on top of the stack. He recognized Shelby's handwriting immedi-

28

ately. Even though she lived in the same town and he'd seen her earlier in school, *and* they were getting together for a Valentine's date that evening, she'd still mailed him a card. It made him feel cheap for handing her one before second period. And embarrassed because he'd wondered why she hadn't thought to bring him a card. *Man, sometimes I'm just lame.* He held the envelope to his nose, gave it a sniff. Although it smelled pretty much like paper, he imagined he caught a whiff of the scent of her hair. Mm. He quickly tucked the card inside his backpack so his mother wouldn't see it, scooped up the rest of the pile of mail — bills, advertisements, a big envelope from the architect in charge of his mom's minimall project — and all but skipped up the lane, anxious to get to his bedroom to open what turned out to be a funny card (Shelby was not the mushy type) but nonetheless, she'd signed it, "Love, Your Shelby." AND she'd drawn three hearts and a long series of Xs and Os. "I'll collect on a few of those tonight!" he'd said to the card.

But today, like the rest of the days, there was nothing in the mailbox for him. He pulled his coat collar around his neck and trudged up the gravel lane, which was covered with a light dusting of snow. He was anxious to change clothes, fire up his truck and drive to town to his part-time job at the Lamp Post Motel. Yesterday, Jessica, pregnant and with a daughter nearing eight months old, told his mom she'd had a couple of check-outs and that she'd need some help to clean the rooms if Josh could make it by today. He worked "on call as needed" which, even though sporadic, at least earned him a little money every week.

Cleaning motel rooms wasn't at the top of his favorite things to do, but his mom had made it clear when she'd purchased him the used truck from Challie Carter, the guy who leased their farmland, that he'd have to earn money to help pay for gas and insurance. She'd even gone so far as to find him the job, and it didn't take him long to realize why: the V–8 engine guzzled so much gasoline he couldn't afford to drive to Hethrow to school every day, which didn't seem to disappoint his mother. Still, owning a truck with a V–8 was worth it. That thing could fly! Aside from the money, there were also a few other perks to his job, not the least being around Jessica Joy, the beautiful woman who owned the Lamp Post. And her husband, Paul, who also worked full-time in the Number Nine coal mine, treated him like a man rather than a kid. Jessica was extremely grateful for the much-needed help and lavishly praised him for every little thing he did, which caused him to work all the harder. Even though she was his mom's best friend, Jessica was about twenty years younger than his mom, and he couldn't help but take note of her soft hazel eyes, couldn't avoid sneaking a peek at her trim figure, feeling almost embarrassed by the ever-growing bump revealing her four-months-along pregnancy. Sixteen-year-old Shelby unquestionably owned his heart, but Jessica . . . even though she was already a mom, to a healthy sixteen-year-old male, she was a woman impossible to ignore.

You could keep time by Harold Crab's 2:30 appearance at the counter at Harry's Grill every Wednesday. It was one of the two days a week the *Partonville Press* rolled and Harold was not only the editor, but the rank-and-filer of typos and misquotes. Harold came at 2:30 because the grill was usually empty then and he could drink coffee with tons of sugar (never stirred since he liked discovering the sweet spot in the bottom) without someone's snide comment about having a little coffee with his sugar. Today was no different. At 2:30, there he was, paper sprawled on the counter in front of him, his red pen patrolling over each line, ready to dive-bomb and circle any error his eagle eye spied. After he read every story, editorial and advertisement from the headline to the back page, he counted the circles, turned back to the front page, folded the paper in half and gave the paper a grade. Today was a five-circle day. Pitiful. But then again, not too bad considering he and Sharon were, from reporting to printing, the only employees and currently distracted by a mammoth "other" project. The good news was that almost nobody in Partonville cared about the mistakes aside from Harold. And Gladys, of course, who thought errors in the hometown paper reflected poorly on the entire community and therefore herself.

Harold set the paper aside and took a sip of his lukewarm coffee. "I'll take one more topper, Lester. Anything to postpone going back to those piles of mini-mall entries."

Lester K. Biggs, proprietor and only employee of Harry's Grill, grabbed a clean mug, poured what looked to be no fewer than two heaping tablespoons of sugar into the bottom and filled it with coffee. "Here ya go," he said, setting it in front of Harold in exchange for his dirtied mug. "You deserve a fresh one. All everyone's been talking about in here the last two weeks —

present company included," he said, shooting Harold a smirk, "is that name-the-new-mall contest. From the sounds of it, every last soul in Partonville entered at least three times."

"You have no earthly *idea*, Lester. Why, we've even received submissions from Oregon!"

"The *state* of Oregon?" In a rare move, Lester poured himself a half cup of coffee, walked out from behind the U-shaped counter, sat on the stool next to Harold and swiveled his stool toward him. This sounded like it was going to be some story and his tired feet needed a break.

"Yessiree, Bob. Apparently folks are even encouraging their long-distance relatives to enter. I'll tell you, I've heard some of *the* most ridiculous ideas."

"For all the hard work you and Sharon have gone through, I hope you're at least getting some good laughs out of it."

"How's *this* for an entry — and I am not making this up, Lester — 'Mall of the Mind.' Now what in the *world* is that supposed to even *mean?* Katie Durbin wouldn't need to go through all the work of rehabbing the old Taninger Furniture building into a mini mall if people could just go shopping in their minds. Honestly. . . ." His

33

voice trailed off as he wagged his head and slurped a sip of the hot brew, then dabbed his mouth with a paper napkin. "You can't believe how many entries we've received that people forgot to put their names on. Thank goodness they haven't been any good, at least thus far."

"How many entries you reckon you've still got to go through before narrowing them down to the top twenty-five?"

"We haven't counted, but I'm guessing at least another hundred. And I bet we've already processed a good five hundred or so. Too bad we didn't keep count. Of course when you announce first prize is a one-hundred-dollar mall gift certificate good at any of the stores, and that there'll also be four twenty-five-dollar runner-ups, that's big incentive around these parts, what with so many people scraping for money and the threat of the Number Nine closing down. Our Ms. Durbin's obviously got deep pockets. Of course, another big draw, though, is that people are convinced the contest judging's going to be fair and square."

"How's it gonna work again?"

"Well, after Sharon and I narrow it down to our top twenty-five picks, then May Belle and Nellie Ruth, who everybody trusts, and Katie — who, as you know, still raises an occasional eyebrow — are each going to get a list of our selections which we'll type up for them without the entrant names so as to make sure nobody's accused of biases or partialities. Sharon and I will then tally *their* votes to bring it down to the top five." He stopped for a sip of coffee. "Then all five of us judges will have at it until we select the winner. Of course we're hoping we all agree, but like we said in the original article, if all the judges *don't* agree, a majority agreement of three will rule."

"This is some wing-ding. Sorry you got involved?"

"It wouldn't be so bad if entries were a uniform size and written in handwriting we could actually read without magnifying glasses and guessing. You should see some of the chicken scratch! While some good folks followed instructions, used the entry blank out of the paper, printed nicely and mailed it in, others have been dropping them off by the fistful and I mean to tell you they're written on all *sizes* of blank paper and envelopes, including, if you can believe it, the back of those skinny grocery register receipts from Your Store. We got four of those!"

Lester, who had just this morning finally had a chance to jot down a list of five possibilities on a napkin and was planning on giving it to Harold when he was done with his coffee, stuck his hand in his pocket and discreetly shoved the napkin to the very bottom. "I'll tell you," Harold continued, "our phone's been ringing off the hook for these last few days before the deadline. Seems like the minute anybody gets a bright idea for a mall name they just pick up the phone to tell us about it. We must be on their speed dials. Once the caller said, 'Oh, now that I hear that idea out loud, that's not any good. Never mind. Hold on while I think of something else.' You can bet your bippy I hung right up. The nerve. Some people are even calling wanting us to go through our whole pile to make sure we got their entries in the mail."

"Do ya?"

"Heavens, no. We tell them we're running a newspaper, not a confirmation service for the U.S. Post Office. Besides, we toss out the ridiculous ones right away. It's enough keeping track of the possibilities." He took his glasses off and rubbed the bridge of his nose before putting them back on.

"You allowin' the entries that didn't come in on the official entry blanks?"

"Sharon and I talked it over with Katie and decided that for better or for worse, we have to. Although we printed 'Official Entry Blank' on the form in the paper, we neglected to say that was the only way you could enter. And I suppose you saw last Sunday's letter to the editor from Cora Davis accusing me of just trying to sell newspapers — accused me of dreaming up the contest *just* to sell papers! — by implying one had to have an official entry blank for each submission."

Lester *tisk-tisked*, shook his head. "That sounds like Cora."

"You haven't had a chance to read today's paper yet, have you?"

"Liver day, you know. Been too busy chopping spuds and onions." The mere reminder caused him to gulp down the rest of his coffee, get back to the grill and take to finishing up the side dishes before the early-bird diners arrived.

"I wrote a piece telling everyone that as long as an entry gets to our office by eight p.m. tonight, it's in the running, but after that, never mind. Too bad, so sad, but it won't be considered no matter how much you whine or stomp your feet. Of course I didn't say it like that, but I'm sure they got my drift. I also let them know, and in no uncertain terms, that we would not be answering the phone after five p.m. tonight when our office officially closes. At five p.m. we're setting a shoebox outside the door and they can drop written entries into that until eight p.m. when we're picking it up and closing the contest, no ifs, ands or buts about it. We figure that'll give working folks who didn't have a chance to read the paper this morning one final chance to see the reminder and weigh in." Harold sighed, taking a quick look at the wall clock. "I better drink up and get back to the office to rescue Sharon. I tell you, folks have gone plumb nuts over this."

"Not all bad, the way I see it. At least it seems most everybody's finally rallying around the idea of the mini mall, *whatever* it ends up being called."

"Katie Durbin is as smart as a whip, getting people invested like this. And as far as I can tell, most of the controversy about the mall has died down."

Lester filled a couple of creamers, put them back in the fridge and got out a huge slab of bacon to fry up for the liver. "You gonna run a list of the worst entries, withholding names, of course? Maybe give out a few 'Thanks for the Laughs' booby prizes?" Lester chuckled, imagining talk around his counter if that should happen.

"Since I depend on subscriptions to keep

the paper afloat, I doubt that would be a good political idea."

"Right-o."

"Lester," Harold said, lowering his voice even though no one else was in the grill, "since I've never in all our born days known you to be a gossip, I *will* tell you the most obvious and preposterous laugh we've had, though."

"Shoot," Lester said as he tossed the slab of bacon on the hot grill, readying to pull the slices apart as they heated up. "I could use a good laugh today."

"McKern Mall."

Lester spun on his heels to face Harold. "NO!"

"YEP! Even though it was an anonymous submission, I would recognize Gladys's thick handwriting anywhere. She pushes so hard on the paper she leaves big indents in it. Can you imagine a mayor recommending a mall be named after her own self?"

"In Gladys's case, yes, I certainly can."

As if on cue, the door swung open and Gladys stomped in, the stomp being her natural gait. She was carrying a giant parcel. The two men clammed up and froze in place, which made them look highly suspicious if not downright guilty of something.

"What's going on here?" Gladys demanded to know when she noticed their odd behavior.

Harold stood and reached in his rear pocket to retrieve his wallet. "Nothing going *on,* but I'm going *out.*" He shot Lester a "Good cover, huh?" look and both men smiled, causing Gladys to puff herself up. "Sharon and I are *still* receiving mini-mall entries and as I'm sure you know, the winning announcement's scheduled for this Sunday's paper. We probably won't even have a chance to eat or sleep before then."

"No obvious winner yet?"

"Afraid not."

"I've been thinking about mall names myself," Gladys said, trying to sound casual while shifting the front seams to her winter coat slightly to the left, "thinking how appropriate it would be if we perhaps named the mall after a family from Partonville, you know, a family that's been influential in our community."

Lester coughed to mask his laugh, then coughed again, then cleared his throat.

"Interesting idea, Gladys," Harold said. "You mean like Wetstra Mall after Dorothy's family? I kind of like the sound of that. Wetstra Mall. After all, where would we be without our Dearest Dorothy? What do you think, Lester?" Lester could only grunt, go into a coughing jag and turn his face as far away from Gladys as possible. He was about to bust a gut. Everyone knew full well Gladys had always been jealous of Dorothy. Old Harold was really playing devil's advocate. "Or maybe Durbin Mall, since Katie Durbin's single-handedly investing her time and money into the project."

By now, Gladys appeared puffed up to twice her size. Before she could respond, Harold tossed his money on the counter and left with a "Gotta run!" The minute he cleared the building he burst out laughing, which he continued to do all the way to his office. He couldn't wait to tell Sharon.

Poor Gladys.

Gladys squinted and turned to give Lester, who still had his back toward her, a serious eyeball. He coughed yet again into the crook of his arm, cleared his throat and took a deep breath. "Can I get you something, Gladys?" he asked without turning to face her.

"Not if you're getting sick, Lester. Maybe you should be home in bed instead of here cooking cold germs into tonight's special."

"No cold. Just swallowed wrong."

She squinted and studied his back for a moment. Something still felt fishy, but she didn't have time to pursue it. "I'm just here

41

to put one of these posters in your front window."

"What poster would that be?" he said, finally looking over his shoulder.

Gladys laid her giant parcel on the counter and carefully opened the top flap. She proceeded to extract what could — and surely would — be described as a huge black-and-white mug shot of herself. The camera, wielded by her son, had been held so close to her face and she'd obviously worked so hard not to blink when the flash went off that Lester had to cough again. She looked plumb startled in the picture, as if somebody'd walked up behind her and said BOO! Gladys, on the other hand, felt that the up-close-and-personal angle, which she'd insisted on, made her look bright-eyed, alert and ready to step forward into the future, as she was fond of saying. Under her face, giant block lettering read MAYOR+MCKERN=MOMENTUM. *Well, you do barrel along, Gladys,* Lester thought. Without waiting for Lester's approval, Gladys propped the poster in the window right next to the front door.

"Thank you for your continued support, Lester," Gladys said as she barreled out the door to disperse the rest of her campaign materials.

Lester returned to his bacon and waited until he heard the door close behind that hurricane of a woman. "I don't recall ever giving it to you," he said aloud with a sigh.

"Don't recall giving me what?" a male voice asked.

Lester whirled around to discover Jacob seating himself on a stool. "Jacob! Good to see you again. Here to stay yet?"

"Not quite. But maybe that's because you haven't given it to me yet?"

"What?"

"No fair. I asked first."

Lester had to think for a moment. "Oh. I wasn't talking to you. I didn't realize you'd walked in."

"If you were talking to Gladys, she didn't hear you. She was already out the door and bounding toward Hornsby's Shoe Emporium before I came in."

"That was the general idea," Lester said, waving his spatula at the door. "I mean that she didn't hear me."

"I caught a glimpse of her poster on the way in."

"And?" Lester asked, turning the strips of bacon to keep them from crisping.

"Scary."

Lester laughed out loud, which felt good since he'd been holding in a guffaw since

Harold had caught Gladys in his crosshairs. "I quite agree. Now, what can I get you?" he asked, swiping his bacon-smeared hands down the front of his apron.

"The biggest, strongest cup of brew you got, and make it to go."

Lester grabbed one of the Styrofoam cups he used for large to-go soft drinks. "Okay?"

"I'll take it."

"How's things going for you up there?" Lester nodded to Jacob's second-floor office which was right next door.

"Helen and I are chipping away at it. One thing is for sure, I couldn't make this transition without her. I'm sure glad she's staying on to work for me."

Lester ran his thumbs around the rim of the to-go lid, sealing it in place. "Doesn't she want a coffee?"

"I asked her but she said no. She's been downing bottled water since Monday."

"You don't say. I just do *not* understand anyone *paying* for *water.* And say, don't you guys have a coffeemaker up there? Surely you do. You know, Rick ordered lunch from here just about every day, but come to think of it, I don't ever recall him asking for coffee and I know he drank the stuff."

"Yes, we've got a coffeemaker, if you can call it that. It looks to be twenty years old and the coffee tastes like it too. Sharon said Rick never wanted her to wash it. He said he'd done that once and the coffee tasted like soap for a week afterwards. It's on my list of things to replace. As for the water, Sharon's started some new diet — which she says is the fourth one she's tried this year — and she has to drink . . . I don't remember how many bottles of water it is a day, but plenty. Luckily I caught her on the second stair before she killed herself trying to lug a case of it up those steep stairs."

"Women can be so dern determined," Lester said, shaking his head. Jacob nodded in agreement.

"Since she's not drinking coffee, I'd rather do without than deal with that disgusting coffeemaker. I was going to pick one up, then I realized there's no longer an appliance store here in town. Guess I'll have to go to Hethrow."

"Wal-Mart," Lester said, his tone implying, *Duh!*

"Never been inside those hallowed doors. I'll have to go with Mom, I guess. I took her recently, but I stayed in the car to make a few phone calls. She can be my tour guide." Lester threw Jacob a puzzled look. For somebody so smart, Lester wondered how it was Jacob'd never been to a Wal-

45

Mart, but he kept the thought to himself.

"We sure are mighty glad to have you, Jacob. I don't know what we'd have done without you coming to our rescue."

Jacob looked thoughtful. "Thank you, Lester. You know, maybe Partonville's come to *my* rescue."

Even though Lester found that a curious statement, it wasn't his nature to ask personal questions. "Herb find you a place to live yet?"

"Not yet." Jacob set a couple of bucks on the counter. "See you next week. Who knows, you might start seeing me as often as you did when I came here after grammar school for French fries. Remember the mob of us kids you used to have in here every day?"

"I surely do. I miss the sounds and energy of youngens in here. They don't come around much since the town's schools closed and the kids all ride the bus to Hethrow. The bus drops them off right by their front doors now."

"Funny, my perception as a kid was that you never seemed too glad to see us."

"Is that so," he said more than asked. "Now you're starting to sound like one of my complaining regulars and you don't even live here yet," he said flatly, but a twinkle escaped from his eye.

Jacob chuckled, gave Lester a farewell nod and off he went. Just before he opened the door leading up to his office stairwell, he saw Gladys trudging into the front door of the old Taninger building, now under reconstruction for the new mini mall. His eyes scanned her obvious trail since one of her posters leered out of every window . . . except for Hornsby's. *Hm. Wonder what happened there?*

He'd noticed earlier from his upstairs office window, which was across the square from the Taninger building, that Katie's SUV was gone, but now he saw it was back. He took a sip of his coffee and mulled over whether or not to pop in and say hi, but then Gladys was there. He stayed put, rather enjoying the fresh air even though it was cold outside. His office always smelled . . . dusty, stuffy. Something. Maybe he'd have to get one of those air purifiers he'd seen advertised in the Sharper Image catalogue.

He stood sipping, thinking about how he hadn't seen Katie his last couple of trips. When he'd stopped by the Taninger building last week, he heard the construction guys banging away, but Edward Showalter came to the door and told him Katie wasn't around. Jacob'd left a message at the farm, but Katie hadn't called him back either. His mom said Katie'd gone back to Chicago for a spa day. That had been her routine when she lived in Chicago (born and raised there), before she moved to Partonville about six months ago. "Since it's a five-hour drive," his mom had explained, "she'll be gone two nights: one to make sure she's on time for her first treatment, then she stays the night at a hotel in Chicago to soak in the afterglow, as she puts it, and do a little shopping." *Ah, another city person finding her way, doing what needs to be done to stay sane,* he'd thought.

"I'm glad she took a couple days off," Dorothy said. "She's really been stressed. She ended up having to replace the boiler in that old building with forced air heat, quite the undertaking, what with also subdividing the interior into store spaces and incorporating that atrium. Yup, that heating issue was quite the expensive and time-consuming project — not to *mention* the whole asbestos surprise! Those things surely did set her budget and rehab schedule behind, which, as it turns out, were only the first in a string of glitches. Now there's some structural issue with the atrium; one of her anchor store lessees backed out when she told them the grand opening would be postponed until mid-April or possibly even early May; and about the time construction got back on track, the stomach flu ripped through her gang of construction workers, who, by the way, are quite the interesting lot." Jacob raised his eyebrows but Dorothy said no more.

"Surprising," Jacob had said.

"What?"

"That she's leaving Josh alone at the farm on two school nights." He wondered why Josh hadn't mentioned it in an e-mail. Not that they kept in constant touch since they'd started e-mailing, but something that big. . . .

"HA! She surely is not allowing that child to stay on his own, not with him dating Shelby and owning those hot wheels!" Dorothy chuckled. "I'd offered for him to stay here but she knew you were due in and didn't want to intrude so she got him a room at the Lamp Post, both of them knowing full well Jessica will report any tidbit of questionable behavior. I don't know if you remember or not, but Josh and Katie stayed at the Lamp Post for several weeks when they first moved here since school had already started and they were waiting to get into the farm after my auction and all, so it's kind of like a home away from home for him."

"I bet you miss our old Crooked Creek Farm more than ever, now that spring's not far off, huh, Mom?"

"Oh, I'm doing okay. And Josh and Katie have me out to visit as often as I like. But staying on topic, Jessica called to tell me it's working out *more* than fine with Josh staying at the Lamp Post a couple days since he's baby-sitting Sarah Sue tonight while she and Paul have dinner at the Wal-Mart and do a little shopping. She couldn't *remember* when they'd last had a big night out!"

"A big night out at Wal-Mart? Wal-Mart serves food?" Jacob asked, his face scrunched in a sour look. "No wonder Katie's staying an extra night in Chicago."

"Hey! Wal-Mart is one of Jessica's favorite places to eat, buster. Since when did you get too high and mighty for Wal-Mart?" she teased, sort of. He explained to her they didn't have Wal-Marts in the middle of big cities, at least not yet, and how she'd have to show him around one day, but not too soon.

Sometimes, Jacob thought, while taking another sip of coffee and reaching for his office door, Partonville felt like another world. How *would* he adjust after so many decades away? Something else to talk to Katie about on his *next* trip. Maybe she could give him a few pointers for transitional survival. But for now, he had work to do. *After next week, you'll have plenty of time to catch up with Katie.*

3

Sharon Teller loved her job at the *Partonville Press.* Harold, who'd hired her straight out of journalism school, telling her he was thrilled to have one of Partonville's very own coming aboard, respected and trusted her as a journalist, and yet treated her like a daughter when circumstances called for it. At twenty-six, Sharon's enthusiasm and curiosity rivaled that of any five-year-old, which made her a great reporter. These unwavering attributes — and several cups of highly caffeinated coffee — kept them both geared up for the onslaught of people stuffing fistfuls of entries into the shoebox outside the *Press*'s door.

"Sharon! For goodness sakes, stop looking out the window with that grin on your face," Harold pleaded many times, starting the moment she set the box out at 5 p.m., reentered the building, locked the door behind her and scurried to the window.

"People will think we're *enjoying* watching their tardiness!"

"Oh, but Mr. Crab, I *am!* I mean I'm enjoying the fact that so many people have such creative thoughts and that they're willing to share them. Isn't this whole thing just so *exciting?* I mean the contest, and the mall itself! Partonville has needed this kind of boost for years and now here it is." She was talking a mile-a-minute. "I just feel so blessed to be able to play a part in actually *naming* a *mini mall!*"

"Wonderful. At your age, you can probably stay awake after ten p.m., too, which is just what we're going to have to do this evening if people don't stop cramming their ideas into that box. It's likely we'll have to pull an all-nighter if we expect to narrow it down to the top twenty-five before tomorrow morning. We need to turn this over to the rest of the crew for a day and get back to the business of running a newspaper. That is what we do here, remember?"

"Oh, but I *am* thinking about the newspaper, Mr. Crab. Think about all of the *stories* we can write! I mean about entries and the contest winner, the grand opening, features on the new shopkeepers. . . . I was thinking just the other day about adding a new column alongside my 'Meet Your

Neighbor' column. It could be a 'Meet Your New Mall Neighbor!', but of course the column name wouldn't say 'mall,' it would have the new *name* of the mall and, OH! I can stop people in front of different stores and ask them where they've come from and what they liked best and. . . ."

"*Sharon.* SHARON! Slow down."

Sharon sprouted one of the reddest blushes Harold had set eyes on. "I'm so sorry, Mr. Crab. I was rambling, wasn't I? The new column idea wasn't really thought through. I should . . ."

"Sharon, *please.* Stop talking a minute." Sharon not only sucked in her lips but she clamped her hand over her mouth just in case words were still trying to escape. "I didn't say your column and feature ideas aren't good ones, and of course you're right in that the whole thing gives us plenty of new news. I'm just saying we need to *focus* here. We're going to pull that box in exactly . . ." he studied the clock on the wall . . . "two minutes, and I don't care how many people might be running down the street with papers in their hands. Then we're going to quickly rifle through them, pick out the best ones and line them up over there on the layout table alongside the others we've selected thus far, which, I believe at last count, was twenty-two, right?" She nodded her head. "Then we'll see how many we've added with this batch. Best-case scenario, it will only be three and we'll be done. Worst-case scenario — although I don't hold much hope for this, considering the pathetic masses we've already seen — there'll be several worth a second thought. In that remote case, we'll line them all up and start pushing strongest possibilities up and weaker ones down until we settle on twenty-five." (Sharon kept her hand clamped over her mouth since she still wanted to scream, "IT'S ALL SO EXCITING!") "Then you still have to type up the list, minus the entrants' names, remember, and make copies for Katie, Nellie Ruth and May Belle. We'll see what time it is when we're done and decide whether to drop those off tonight or tomorrow morning."

"Mr. Crab," Sharon said, lowering her hand only a few inches from her mouth, "I think May Belle goes to bed early. I'm thinking we should just put it in our plans to deliver the lists tomorrow."

"Good call. You're right about May Belle. And by the time we drive out to the farm tonight, Katie might be sleeping as well. I know that woman's been putting in some long hours. Plus, even if they don't get them until tomorrow, they'll still have forty-eight hours to pick their top five."

"Okay," Sharon said, trusting her mouth long enough to allow her to deliver a question, "but I keep forgetting to ask you something important. Do you know what time we're all meeting on Saturday to select the winner? The community band has band practice this Saturday out at the Park District building. You know, it's still so odd and sad not to see Mr. Lawson sitting there with his saxophone. . . ."

"You tell me what time practice is," Harold said, cutting her off before she got herself all off track again, "and we'll work around it, Sharon. But for now, let's get moving on those entries. I'll bring in the box. Better me than you, just in case people try to storm the place."

Jessica Joy was in the middle of changing Sarah Sue's poopy diaper when she was struck with her best mall-name idea ever. No matter she'd turned in seven other ideas, this one was brilliant! She checked her wristwatch. It was exactly 7:49. "PAUL!" she yelled from the baby's room to the front check-in office where Paul was finishing paperwork. "I HAVE A GREAT

56

IDEA FOR THE MINI-MALL NAME! THINK IT'S TOO LATE TO JOT IT DOWN AND GET IT TO THE *PRESS?*"

"WHAT TIME IS IT, HONEY?"

"SEVEN-FIFTY!" she screeched.

Paul tapped her on the shoulder and said, "No need to yell. I'm right here." Since he'd startled her, she yelped anyway. "Sorry, honey. Sorry," he said, in a soothing voice as he leaned over her, wrapped his arms around her waist, settled his hands on her bulging belly and kissed the base of her neck.

"What do you think, Paul? Think there's time to make it to the drop box? The newspaper said they weren't going to stay open one extra minute, and I'm telling you, I've got the winning idea. We could sure use that hundred-dollar gift certificate. Katie said she's negotiating with someone right now who wants to put in a baby store!"

"Here, let me finish our gal up," he said, giving Jessica a gentle hip-check to move her out of the way. "You write and then I'll run."

Through the darkness, Paul was already crossing the highway, blazing toward his target which, if he cut through a few back yards, was only about seven blocks away.

He, too, was sure he had the winner in his hand. Now all he had to do was deliver it in time.

He was absolutely flying. It brought back memories from high school when he used to run track. He still kept his letter jacket hanging in the back of his closet. For a family as poor as his to have managed to buy that jacket proved what a shining star his track letter was to all of them. With every stride, he remembered Jessica running toward him at the end of every meet, her arms outstretched, her face beaming with pride. They'd been high school sweethearts, their love never dimming. Zoom-zoom, adrenaline pumping, crowds cheering.

Only three blocks to go. He made a snap decision that this wide side yard looked like the best opportunity to cut through, especially since it was somewhat lit by a porch light. He hurdled a low fence and leaped a patch of newly turned black earth. Back onto the sidewalk he blazed. Even though it was cold, he was glad he hadn't put on a jacket, which would have only hindered his pumping arms. His work in the coal mines often left him craving fresh air and he was greedily gulping it down now! It felt so good to *run!*

One block to go. Was that Harold he saw

in the distance? NO! Faster, faster . . . almost there. . . .

BANG! Down he slammed onto the cement. He hit his head about the same time he registered the snap. He recognized the terrible sound from when he'd broken his leg nearly a decade ago.

Maggie blinked a couple of times before she recognized the heap. "PAUL! Are you *okay?*" He'd gone down right at her feet, just as Harold reached for the box to tell her she was the last entry. Harold had been in such a hurry to nab the box and get back inside, and Maggie was so intent on delivering her entry, that neither of them had noticed Paul racing toward them through the night.

"Harold! PLEASE!" Paul cried out. "I've broken my leg!"

Harold was stunned. How had this happened? It's like Paul had dropped from the sky and crash landed in front of the building. Paul rolled up in a fetal position and was grabbing at his leg. "Maggie," Harold said, trying to maintain a calm voice when he saw the blood on Paul's forehead, "you see to him while I call 911." He whirled on his heels.

"NO! HAROLD! *Please* take just one more entry," Paul said, groaning between the words. "I have no doubt this is your winner," he mumbled, sounding on the edge of passing out as he stretched his hand holding the crumpled entry toward Harold.

Harold bent down and took the paper. Paul moaned again. Seventy-two-year-old Maggie Malone, owner and sole stylist at Le Feminique Hair Salon & Day Spa, was now sitting on the sidewalk next to Paul, gently rubbing his back, her chartreuse parka fluffing up around her, its bottom edge and the backside of her green slacks in the small puddle of water gathered in the open area of the cracked and heaving sidewalk that caused Paul to go down. "Harold, have Sharon call Jessica and let her know he's going to the hospital," Maggie said in a calming voice.

"No!" Paul begged. "Don't call her. It'll scare her, and you know she's pregnant and. . . . She'll find out soon enough when I get home. And I don't need an ambulance. Can you two just let me catch my breath a minute, then help me get up? Please?" He studied Maggie for a moment, considering her age. "Or why don't you have Sharon come out and help you, Harold. No offense or nothing personal, Mrs. Malone, but I'm heavier than I look and I'm afraid I'll likely

60

be dead weight when you try to bring me up."

Maggie stood up, gave him one of her well-known head tosses, brushed off her hands and put them on her hips, which she cocked to one side. "Well, for an older woman, I'm stronger than *I* look, Mr. Joy," she said, grinning. She'd obviously read his mind. "You take as long as you want, honey, then let us know when you're ready to give it a go."

Paul smiled through his pain. "Yes, ma'am."

By now, Sharon was off the phone and running up behind Harold who handed her the shoebox full of entries. "I'm taking Paul here to the hospital, Sharon. You go ahead and start taking a look at these. I'll be back when I can."

Paul awkwardly brought himself to a sitting position, leaving his left broken leg extended in front of him. The pain was overwhelming. He felt on the verge of passing out. "Did you get Jessica's entry in the box, Harold?"

Harold grabbed Sharon's arm and stuffed the paper through the box slot. "Yup. Now, let's see what we can do about getting you up off that cold sidewalk."

■ ■ ■ ■

Hornsby's Shoe Emporium on the square had been closed for business for several hours, but a light was still burning behind the shoe storage area in a small back room that Tom and Frieda Hornsby had, shortly after they married and opened for business forty years ago, dedicated as their lunch and lounge area. Back in the day when Partonville was booming and Hornsby's Shoe Emporium was the only place within miles and miles to buy footwear, they barely had time to enter that room, other than to take turns sneaking back to wolf down a sandwich. But a lot had changed. Hethrow had spread into a metropolis, sprouting one mall after another filled with chain shoe stores. Partonville's schools had closed and kids went to consolidated schools. Now the Horsnbys had more time to spend relaxing in their lounge than they cared to. They mostly rested their aging feet, went through catalogues to order more miscellaneous items with a better turnover than shoes (shoelaces, shoe polish, socks — things Wal-Mart then started carrying when they moved into town) and fretted over how long they could stay in business.

But tonight the little room was filled with snacks, a punch bowl and people making merry under a handpainted banner that said GOOD LUCK TO OUR NEW MAYOR! At the center stood none other than Sam Vitner, owner of Swappin' Sam's, a salvage store at the edge of town. His campaign committee, secretly meeting since right before Christmas, consisted of Tom and Frieda Hornsby, George Gustafson who owned By George's filling station and Cora Davis, the town crier who dragged her husband along whether he felt like getting involved or not. Beulah Gustafson, George's wife, was not present, but she'd been sworn to secrecy about the meetings, none of which she'd attended since she'd told George in no uncertain terms that she'd be quiet alright, but that she was voting for Gladys! The only thing that worried Beulah, who had no doubt from the beginning of all this nonsense that Gladys would win, was that a miracle seemed to be taking place: for the first time in her life, Cora Davis *had* kept a secret.

4

Another long exhausting day, Katie thought as she attempted to tame her latest hot flash with a file folder, first fanning slowly, then quickly, then slowly again. She threw the folder down after deciding the act of fanning was making her even hotter.

She wished she'd just named the mall herself since everyone who ran into her — including, on a daily basis, nearly every single person in her work crew — wanted to know if she'd chosen her winner. Didn't people read? The contest wasn't over yet, not until Sunday when it would be announced in the *Press.* And why, in the name of sanity, had she *ever* told everyone way back in December that she would hold a town meeting to receive input about the mall as well as report on her long-range plans for more outreaching development? *That* meeting, rescheduled twice due to construction delays which left her short on information to even report, was now only two short weeks from tonight.

Maybe she should just run for the hills — or back to the city, as it were — while she could, she thought, slouching in her chair. But her pride and determination kept her moving forward, sticking close to the project to keep an eye on things, make sure they were on track — as on track as they could be after such derailment. She wiggled her fingers and admired her manicure. *Thank you, Dorothy.* If there was one bright spot at the moment, it was how right Dorothy had been to encourage her to keep her spa day last week. Too bad spa days didn't come with a month-long guarantee for continued well-being and a supply of hormone cocktails.

But Edward Showalter had not received the benefits of a spa day. He'd been relentless on the job since the day she hired him as her contractor. He was proving capable and surprisingly knowledgeable about many things, but sometimes it was clear that he, too, was in over his head, especially as it applied to people management skills — or lack thereof. Throughout his earlier working years, whether sober or drunk, whether working alone or as part of a crew pulled together for a specific job, he'd operated as an independent. He never before gathered the crews himself or served as boss. But here he was, as the official contractor, responsible for all such things. Edward Showalter was buddies (drinking buddies with some of them, back in those days before he joined AA) with most of the guys he'd corralled for this major task. But even though he'd only hired those he knew to be hard working and sober on the job, they, in turn, found it difficult to take him seriously when he pulled rank. This managerial flaw surfaced most when it was clear how glad he was to see Katie appear — no doubt drawn by the sheer volume of the voices — in the midst of yet another conflict between the workers.

The workers. Katie wondered if there'd ever been a motlier crew assembled by a more unusual character than Edward Showalter. As a hard-core businesswoman, for the first time in her life she thought she might just faint dead away when they showed up — that is once they *could* all finally show up following what came to be referred to around town as The Asbestos Debacle, a turn of phrase Edward Showalter, who adored turning his own phrases, transformed into The Arse-Beastos Dee-Backle Backup. "Ain't that the truth, Ms.

Durbin?" he asked, tickling his own self when he first used the goofy phrase to her face. Her lack of a smile, the immediate upshot of her eyebrows and her short lecture about how much this was costing her let him know *she* did not think he was as funny as *he* did.

But proving that looks — and nicknames (at least she *hoped* they were only nicknames) like Rooney and Moon Dog (also a guitarist), Smackman (yes, there was that one jail stint, but that was a long time ago) and Sherlock — could be deceiving, Edward Showalter's work crew turned out to be quite capable, hardworking and willing to put in whatever overtime was demanded of them. It was clear Smackman didn't much like taking orders handed down by a woman, but Katie only had to remind him once who signed his check. And in spite of the dagger tattoo on the side of Rooney's neck and his unruly, curly, bleached blond hair that stuck out from his ever-present red bandana, he was unquestionably a bull in terms of strength, a gentle giant when it came to respect for Katie and a wizard at reading blueprints, which is why Edward Showalter had hired him.

It was 7:45, past time for everyone, including herself, to go home. Her stomach was growling, her head was throbbing and her patience was gone. She scouted around the building until she found Edward Showalter, which was harder now that the individual store partitions were going up. More than once, she'd actually resorted to locating him with his cell phone, which she'd given him as a part of their business agreement. "Time to call it a day!" she yelled over the pounding, thinking how it might make more sense to invest in walkie-talkies, although she wasn't the walkie-talkie type. She detested that horrid ear-piercing sound they made before people talked. Then Edward Showalter said how much time it would save if he could pass a couple out to the guys and she relented, putting him in charge of the purchase and setup. She'd stick to her cell phone, thank you very much, so he better leave it on too.

"Oh, I'm glad you rustled me up!" Edward Showalter said. "I was planning on telling the guys to take off at seven-thirty! Kinda lost track of time." He gave her a salute, a habit he'd slipped into when she uttered what he perceived to be an order, and off he went. Within five minutes the place was cleared out.

She retreated to what would one day look like an office worthy of her position as Mall

Director but that was now nothing more than a framed-in square room with two sawhorses and a leftover TANINGER FURNITURE sign spanning the distance between them forming a makeshift desk. Funny, she thought, how she'd become oddly attached to that old sign, which read FAMILY OWNED AND OPERATED SINCE 1923. The boom of Hethrow's metropolis eventually drove the Taningers out of business.

Katie selected the rear second-floor corner location for her office because it felt like the best place from which to oversee the building project. After the mall opened, it would be the perfect lookout post. Rather than walling it up for total privacy, she'd ordered a full window to the mall side of the office that would enable her to view the second-floor shops from her desk. She could step outside her door to the atrium railing and see not only the shops on the first floor, but all the way down to the lower-level space located smack in the center of the floor plan.

She'd originally hoped to rent out more stores in that lower level, but after weighing several structural considerations, she tended to agree with the architect: put the money up toward the natural light in the tall building and save that center lower-level space for a store that can best be served by the exterior entrance on the side of the building leading down to it. Besides, most of the rest of that lower level was usurped by the heating system and utilities. The new phone and computer lines alone ended up needing their own control central, so what little space was left would be used for storage and for Edward Showalter's office, as Katie cut a deal for him to serve as permanent maintenance man and Building Manager once the mall opened. ("You'll know the building better than anyone else.") But what type of place would showcase well in that lower-level space from the balconies? She thought about locating the tea room down there but decided the openness wouldn't lend itself well to the cozy feeling she wanted for the tea room. And who would operate the tea room? Dilemmas like this seized her mind and kept her awake at night.

Then lo and behold, a new-to-the-business confectioner who'd heard about the mall through word-of-mouth contacted her. He said he needed a location that would allow him to split his store between penny ("well, nickel, dime, quarter, dollar") candies for the kids, fine chocolates and fudges for the adults, and a coffee bar specializing in chocolate coffees. He also needed room for a few tables so people could sit and enjoy his offerings. This answered another problem Katie'd been pondering: what to have in the mall for kids? It was the best of all worlds since they'd not only have a candy store they could afford and a place to hang out — but it would also give the kids their own side entrance, which would keep them from traipsing through the mall just for a piece of candy. Her hawk-eye view from just outside her office would allow her to oversee their behavior as well. The final plus: the heavenly smell of chocolate would no doubt waft up the atrium, enticing shoppers to make their way down. Perfect. Now if she could just land someone for the tea room. . . .

Walking her way around the atrium until she arrived catty-cornered to her office, Katie looked down the empty shaft that would soon house a very expensive elevator. She hadn't thought about an elevator until Carl Jimson, the architect she'd brought in from Chicago, queried her about a preferential location for the elevator, since a facility like this needed to be handicap accessible. After calling Jessica, Dorothy and May Belle (pregnant, older and bad back, in that order), they all agreed an elevator should be as close to the front entryway as possible in case a shopper needing to use it just wanted to pop into a store on the second floor or lower level. Katie's first inclination was to locate it at the back of the mall (anything to draw shoppers throughout), but her friends made perfect sense.

She rubbed her back as she tried to remember what she'd been told about fire codes. So many details. . . . Sometimes it was difficult to remember how she'd gotten involved in such a project to begin with. *No doubt lack of estrogen!* Retailing wasn't her thing. Buying and selling land for development was how she made her money. But now here she was. It just *had* to work. Partonville *had* to find new life, if for no other reason than to cause Colton Craig, the man whose goading had partially pushed her into this undertaking, to swallow his own smug face.

She walked into her office and grabbed her coat, then headed down the open stairs and made her way to the front window where she stretched again and panned the Partonville square, her eyes migrating toward Jacob's second-floor office. The two of them got off to a rocky start when they'd first met, but since she'd gotten to know him a little better over the Christmas holiday, she was surprised to find herself looking forward to his move to Partonville.

Just when she glanced at his window, she noticed his office light go off. She stared at his street-level door and thought about trotting over to say hello before he took off again tomorrow but quickly became distracted by a commotion inside Hornsby's Shoe Emporium.

Although the store was closed, a small gathering of people milled about inside. *What in the world?* Sam Vitner stepped to the foreground and then . . . right up into the display window! He fussed around with something, but due to the angle of her view, she couldn't tell what. Then the entire group, except for Sam who stayed in the window, walked out onto the sidewalk. One by one Katie made out their faces but she couldn't tell what they were clapping about, although it appeared to be a poster near which Sam was preening. *DARN!* She must have lost Jacob in the crowd. Since he drove a different rental car each time he came into town, she didn't even know what vehicle to look for, but then again he often walked to his office from his mom's. When she thought she'd missed him, a pang of regret ran through her already tired mind. She turned off her main interior lights, leaving a few work lights glowing, and watched out her window a couple of more moments in case

Jacob *was* still around. A short conversation with someone who could understand her city brain would feel so good. . . . *Oh, well.* The small crowd of people made their way back into Hornsby's, Sam stepped out of the window and they all disappeared toward the back of the store, turning off the showroom lights as they went. Curiosity getting the best of her, Katie swung on her coat and decided to take a stroll by Hornsby's window for a look-see before getting into her SUV and heading home. When she got there, her mouth flew open.

There was a poster with a picture of Sam Vitner, the owner of Swappin' Sam's, who had, over the holidays, tried to start a rebellion against her mini mall. Under his picture in large block letters it said MCKERN'S HAD HER TURN! / TIME TO SWAP! / VITNER FOR MAYOR! One by one her mind sifted through the gathering of faces, then it struck her: Sam Vitner, Cora Davis, George Gustafson . . . the very people who'd previously *aligned* with Sam to try and stop her development! But thankfully she'd maneuvered them around to her side.

A prickle ran up the back of her neck. *Or did I?*

"I buy everything I can from Richardson's

Rexall Drugs down on the square," Dorothy said as she quickly ushered Jacob through the cosmetics and drug departments at Wal-Mart. "I still get my prescriptions filled there too. The only time I came here for a prescription was for May Belle. It was a Sunday — the Rexall is closed on Sundays and evenings, you know," she said, pointing at her wristwatch, reminding Jacob it was 8:30 p.m., "and good for them! — but she was in terrible pain. Somebody told me I could get things cheaper here, but to be honest, I've known T.J. Winslow since he was born," she continued, stopping to study the price tag on her brand of denture soak. She raised her eyebrows at the difference in price from the Rexall but then moved right along. "I still remember how proud his dad was after T.J. went off to the school of pharmacy, came back and took over the business. It was hard enough to watch the Taningers close their doors, but I could only buy so much furniture to help support *them!*" she said, followed by a sad chuckle. "But I always need one thing or another from the Rexall. Besides, I don't have The Tank any more and Wal-Mart's too far on the outskirts for me to walk." Dorothy drove The Tank, her battle-worn 1976 Lincoln Continental, until it finally bit the dust after

an accident a year earlier. That was that —
although she still kept her driver's license,
just in case. "And Partonville doesn't have
any public transportation. And I'll tell you
what, it takes the cab service from Hethrow
way too long to get here and they charge
way too much and they don't want to wait
for you while you shop either unless they let
their meter run. Ask me how I know *that!*

"Hey!" she said, suddenly halting the cart
again. A look of mischievousness crossed
her face. "If your lawyering business doesn't
work out, maybe you could start a taxi
service!" Jacob raised his eyebrows. "Just
kidding!" He laughed while she started racing the cart forward again. "But seriously, I
hate to bother Arthur or Katie or Jessica for
a ride for every little thing, so I'd just as
soon walk the couple blocks to the Rexall
on the square — and walking is good for
me anyway — pay the price difference and
support our longtime local.

"And another thing about shopping at the
Rexall," she said, barreling them toward
kitchen appliances, a personal mission in
mind. "I can still look T.J. in the eye during
band practice without feeling guilty. You
know I taught that boy how to play the
clarinet when he was in grammar school,
don't you?"

Jacob laughed inside himself at his mom's use of the word "boy" for someone who was probably at least in his late sixties. "I'm not sure if I knew that or not, Mom, but I'll try to remember." For such a little town, he felt like he had a lot of personal things to learn about people.

Jacob was glad the sale of Crooked Creek Farm rendered his mom financially secure. But as much as he hated to admit it, he also understood why this store was so busy, although he was surprised by the huge amount of shoppers at this late hour. Times were hard here and people like the Joys — including many of the farmers — often worked more than one job just to make ends meet. They had to be careful with their dollars. The rub was, of course, that the lure of the lower prices, especially during hard times, made it even harder times for the local merchants who needed the people's spending dollars to stay in business. Yes, the friction between loyalties and finances was a complicated issue, one Jacob and his mom would discuss at length later that evening.

Dorothy stopped her cart in front of the coffeemakers and turned to face her son. "Now that you're moving back home, you can come to our community band concerts! We've been practicing Irish tunes for our

St. Patrick's Day performance out at the Park District building on the Saturday before the holiday, which I believe is actually on a Monday this year. But if you listen carefully, don't take T.J.'s talent, or lack thereof, as an indicator of my ability to teach, okay? He played *the* most horrid clarinet all through school, and he still sounds terrible. But you can't fault a heart that loves music," she said, turning to face the small kitchen appliances.

"Now, let's get you a new coffeemaker for your office. I reckon you can make your own coffee and still support business on the square by buying your lunches at Harry's!" she said with a wink.

"How did you know I needed a coffeemaker at the office? I don't recall mentioning that."

"I stopped in the grill today."

Jacob shook his head. Yes, everyone certainly did know everybody's business, including his already.

5

Jessica leaned into Sarah Sue's crib and gave her sleeping beauty a soft kiss on the cheek. She tiptoed out of the room, then scurried to the front office window, which had the best view of the street. Paul'd been gone nearly an hour-and-a-half now. It wasn't like him to leave her fretting. Best she could figure, it shouldn't have taken him more than twenty-five minutes max to get to the *Press* and back, even if he'd stopped to chat with someone. Harry's closed promptly at 6 p.m., so he wasn't there. She phoned the *Press.* No answer. But they'd said right there in the newspaper that they weren't going to be answering the phones after their regular hours. She went to the bedroom window just to make sure Paul hadn't taken the car. Maybe he'd been home and decided to run an errand or something. Nope, both cars were parked in their usual places. Honestly, if he didn't get home in the next ten minutes, she was going to rouse Sarah Sue, put her in her stroller and go looking for him.

Just then the buzzer in the office rang. She hurried to the lobby to find Harold Crab standing there, a serious look on his face.

"Good evening, Jessica."

"It's Paul, isn't it? Something's happened to him," she said, her voice cracking and rising an octave.

"Now, Jessica, don't you worry. I'm sure Paul's going to be just fine."

"*Going* to be?" Tears were already pooling in her eyes.

"He was in such a hurry to get your entry in that he sort of made a crash landing near the box."

"Oh, NO! OH! What's *happened* to him? Oh, it's all my FAULT! I asked him to hurry. . . ."

Her emotional frenzy obviously escalating, Harold said, "Jessica, honey, let's go sit down."

"I need to sit down to hear this?" she squeaked out. "Oh, *no,*" she moaned, as she began to rock herself. But she shucked him off when he tried to lead her to a seat behind the check-in counter.

"Jessica, honey, Paul is fine. Well, he has a broken leg, a couple stitches and a slight concussion, but other than that, he is just fine, honey," Harold said as he wrapped an arm around her shoulder.

"A *concussion?* A broken leg? What on earth. . . ."

"He was running and tripped on a crack in the sidewalk, right there in front of our building. I'm the one who should apologize, Jessica. That crack should have been fixed long ago." It was the first time it occurred to Harold he was ripe for a lawsuit here and that a big-city attorney had just moved to town. "Don't you worry, Jessica, the *Press* will cover all of his medical expenses." He hated thinking like that, but after all, what did he pay liability insurance for if not an occasion such as this? He'd already talked to Ben Malone about getting that sidewalk fixed — by tomorrow, if possible.

"Can you take me to him? Let me just wake up Sarah Sue." She was already turning on her heels but Harold grabbed her arm.

"Paul instructed me to sit with you until he gets home and to make sure you stay put. And stay *calm.* Maggie and Ben Malone went to the hospital to see how he was doing — he fell right at Maggie's feet — and they're with him now. They're going to bring him right home as soon as he's released. He would have been home a little sooner but Doctor Nielson wanted to keep an eye on him for a spell on account of the concussion. It was astute of Doctor Nielson to pick that up, considering we were all so worried about his leg." Jessica moved behind the counter and finally sat down. "That's a girl," Harold said, following her and patting her arm. "He'll be fine and he'll be here before you know it."

Jessica blew her nose, then steeled herself, swiped under her eyes and looked hard at Harold. "If he's not here in fifteen minutes, you're taking me to the hospital, do you hear me?"

"Yes, ma'am. I promise." It was clear Jessica was not going to truly calm down until she saw her husband with her own eyes. Thankfully, ten minutes later the Malones' big black Cadillac pulled up. Jessica was opening the back door of the car before Paul could even reach for the handle.

"Paul!" she whimpered as she leaned in and grabbed his face with both hands, her eyes taking note of the bandage. "Oh, *honey!* Are you *okay?* How's your head? And your poor *leg,*" she said. As soon as he was settled into his recliner, Ben told Maggie they should be going and Harold said the same, then added, "We'll let you get some much deserved rest now, Paul. And again, I'm sorry for that crack in the sidewalk. I'm seeing to it tomorrow. The *Press* will clear things with the hospital and I know Jessica here will take good care of you now that you're home."

"You let us know if you need anything, you two," Maggie said. "I'll call Dorothy first thing in the morning and have her get your Care Committee at church right on this." Although Maggie didn't attend First United Methodist, their Care Committee's reputation was known throughout town. "I'm sure you won't need to be cooking for a week or two, Jessica. You just save your energy to take care of your business, your husband, that beautiful daughter and *yourself.*"

"And Harold," Ben said, "I *will* be by tomorrow to fix that sidewalk." Ben owned his own hauling business and small cement jobs were right up his alley.

"Thank you," Jessica said, anxious for everyone to leave so she could hear from Paul how he *really* felt. As soon as the door closed behind their last visitor, she sat down on the floor next to the foot of his recliner and rested her head on his unbroken leg while she gently stroked the cast on the other.

"Oh, Paul, this is all my *fault!* Me and my dumb mini-mall entry, and asking you to *hurry!* I am so sorry." She began to weep again.

Paul reached his hand down and rested it on the top of her head. "Sweetheart," he said somewhat weakly due to the medications, "I'm going to tell you something now and I'm only going to say it once, and then I don't want to ever hear another word about it. Ever. Are you listening?"

She looked up at him through her tears and nodded.

"This was not your fault. I ran, and I loved the running. I ran because your entry was worth it and it made me happy to get it to the box. I didn't have enough sense to slow down before I got to that bad spot in the sidewalk near the *Press's* door. If I had, I would have seen — I would have *remembered* — that crack there in the sidewalk since it's been there for years. I ran. I didn't slow down. There was a crack. I fell. . . . This, Jessica," he said, pointing to the small bandage on his head, then to the cast on his leg, "is not your fault and that is that. Do you understand?"

She stared at him, wanting to confess the guilt that was consuming her, wanting to trade places with him. He saw it on her face.

"Jessica?" he said, resting his palm on the side of her face, his fingers gently moving over her cheek. "You have nothing to feel guilty about and nothing for which you need forgiveness. I'm the luckiest man alive to have a wife who is looking at me with such beautiful, giant, saucer eyes of love. I only had two stitches and my concussion is a small one, and so, thank You, Lord, is the break. We have *much* to thank God for, considering I was such a lughead, so let's spend our energy on that." But she *still* looked guilty.

He used his thumb to smooth her tears into her soft white cheeks. "Come up here and give me a kiss, honey. We're both done feeling bad about things now, okay? We're already concentrating on making things right, okay? Jessica?" She gave him a small grin. "That's my girl."

She stood up, hovering over him for a moment, taking extra care not to bump his head or his leg before she gingerly lowered her heart-shaped mouth to his. Their lips came together in a familiar, soft, assuring and loving way. A second kiss quickly followed.

"Jessica," he said, cutting the second kiss short and releasing a huge sigh, "I have one more favor to ask you."

"Anything, Paul. What is it?"

"I can't believe I'm going to say this, but no more kisses like that one, at least not right now, at least not tonight, dear, okay?" His voice waffled between husky — that husky she knew all so well, which is what got her in this too-soon-again pregnant condition — and laughter. His "not tonight, dear" line struck Jessica so funny that she let go a chuckle, which caused him to laugh too, then suddenly stop to hold his head between his hands. "And not too much more laughter tonight either, okay? I have a headache." At that, no matter how badly it hurt him to do so, they both laughed until they cried, she from seeing her handsome husband in such a terrible state, and he — although he was able to camouflage his hurting tears as laughter spillover — from the pain and painful truth of *all* of it, including the fact that they were already strapped for money, and now this.

6

With barely a lick of sleep, Cora arrived on the sidewalk in front of Harry's at 5:40 a.m., twenty minutes before the grill opened. People had taken to lining up outside and starting their visiting a little early since Lester didn't turn his CLOSED sign to OPEN until 6 a.m. straight up, not a minute before or after. Cora figured Lester probably wouldn't yet know about Sam's bid for mayor, since he lived right above the grill. He turned in early and came straight down to work when he awakened. Cora leaned toward the door to make sure nobody would get in before her. *Oh!* she thought. *This* is going to be *good!* Her adrenaline was pumping so hard she felt like one of those jitterbug lures her husband used to cast near the shore to catch bass.

Arthur Landers was next to arrive. He usually sat in his truck until Lester opened the door, but today he all but leaped out of his old Ford pickup for a closer look when he noticed Sam's poster in Hornsby's window, which was right next to the grill. Cora watched his lips moving as he read Sam's slogan aloud, which, as far as she was concerned, was brilliant enough to beat Gladys without one issue being brought up by either of them.

"Well I'll be *dad*gum!" Arthur said loudly. Just as Cora hoped, Arthur made his way straight toward her.

"It's about time for a *swap,* wouldn't you say, Arthur? Of course I've known about his run for mayor since December, what with him asking me to be on his election committee and all." She puffed herself up so much Arthur thought she was mimicking Queen Lady Gladys.

"I think old Sammy done swapped his brain for peanuts," Arthur said, shaking his head.

This was not the reaction she'd been expecting. "I'd say the only one who's *nuts,* Arthur Landers, is the one who doesn't recognize the best mayoral candidate when he sees one!"

"Ya say he asked *you* ta be on his ee-lection committee?"

"Yes, sir," she said, pride oozing in her words, her chin lifting when she spoke.

"Well there ya have it. Nuff said. Sam's nuts."

"Arthur Landers," Cora said through her clenched jaw, "you are an impossible old coot."

"I'd say tha only im-possible thing in this here conversation is tha notion of Sammy boy bein' a mayor." And then he smiled, which really made her angry. But the smile wasn't only because he'd said something clever, which he knew he had, but because he saw what Cora didn't see, and that was Gladys tromping her finest mayoral tromp right up behind her.

"Good morning, Arthur, Cora," Gladys said without looking at them. Instead she nudged Cora out of the way in order to put her hand up to the grill's window to block the glare and make sure Lester was stirring in there.

Cora spun around to find herself not a foot from Gladys's face. Due to her political alignment with Sam, Cora expected Gladys to unleash a tirade of hateful words her way, which caused her to instinctively back up, bumping smack into Arthur, who pushed her — and none too gently, she would say when she retold the story, although she made it sound like he'd launched her — off the top of his feet, which

89

she'd accidentally stepped on. Arthur's move cast her straight into Gladys, suddenly making Cora feel like the ball in a game of bumper pool. Arthur laughed at Cora's flailing arms and backed himself up another yard to clear the way for what would undoubtedly be her return trip.

"Cora Davis!" Gladys said, as she held her arms out and backed Cora off. "What on *earth!*" Gladys straightened her disheveled self.

Cora steadied herself, then went eyeball to eyeball with Gladys, who just looked at her like she was daft. It wasn't until that moment that it hit her: Gladys didn't know yet. *Priceless.* Cora's eyes ablaze with anticipation, she turned to face Arthur . . . who didn't say a word. His mouth, which had previously been open, clamped shut. He knew exactly what Cora was waiting for. With his index finger and thumb pinched together, he drew a line across his lips and mimicked throwing away a key. A storm flashed in Cora's eyes, which was immediately extinguished by what she saw over Arthur's shoulder: Sam Vitner. *Yes!*

Sam almost never frequented Harry's in the morning, what with opening his salvage business so early. But this morning he decided to open late, figuring he would chalk up his appearance at Harry's Grill as his first official campaign stop. On his way to the grill, he first sidled up to Hornsby's window to admire his poster in the daylight. He stood grinning at himself for a moment before turning to notice Arthur, Cora and Gladys staring at him. He straightened his spine and drew a deep breath. "Game on," he muttered to himself as a rehearsed — yes, in the mirror — campaign smile spread across his face. "Good morning, Arthur, Cora, *Gladys*," he said with vigor, pinning her with his stare.

"Sam," Gladys said, acknowledging his presence with mayoral dignity. She looked at Arthur and Cora, waiting for their "Good morning" to Sam, but they just stood there, both of their mouths agape as their heads swiveled from Sam to her, then back again. For the second time in three days, Gladys thought something was fishy at Harry's and it had to do with her. But before she could pursue it, next to arrive on the square was Harold Crab who looked like he'd been up all night, which he nearly had.

By the time he'd arrived back at the *Press* from the Lamp Post last night, it was after 10 p.m. Sharon was in a state. She'd been worried about Paul ("And as a *reporter,* Mr. Crab, I should have been at the hospital *covering* the accident! I did take pictures of the crack, though") and trying to select the top twenty-five mall entries since so many last-minute drop-offs were surprisingly strong contenders. Harold waited until she wound herself down before dropping the bomb about Sam's poster, which he'd discovered on his way back to the office.

The two of them yammered for an hour about the implications of a mayoral race, bemoaning it was too late to make phone calls. After coming up with a list of interview questions for both candidates, they had to put that topic to rest in order to focus on the mall names. They didn't leave until after 1 a.m. When Harold got home, he replayed everything to his wife, then lay there with his eyes open for an hour, his mind spinning like a firecracker gone wild. By the time he dozed off, his alarm was ringing.

The morning plan was for Sharon to head out to Swappin' Sam's to interview Sam and find out if he had a platform in place. She was on her way there right now. Harold agreed to cover the grill, which they knew would be the day's first opportunity for reactions from Gladys. When he'd left home, he wondered if Maggie had spread the word about Paul's accident last night. If she had, he considered all the chiding he'd likely have to endure about sidewalk neglect, especially since Sharon seemed intent on running her picture of the crack. He hoped the whole topic would be overshadowed by Sam's announcement.

Harold didn't notice the little gathering outside the grill because he was writing on his reporter's tablet as fast as he was walking, something folks around town had witnessed for decades. When he finally slammed the pad closed and looked up, he saw Sam, Cora, Arthur and Gladys staring at him. He whipped out his pad again, wondering if he would ever be able to keep track of all the heated words undoubtedly already flying. But before approaching them, he quickly grabbed his cell phone and called Sharon.

"Get over to Harry's, NOW!"

Jessie Landers usually got up shortly after Arthur left for Harry's in the morning. She wasn't one to sleep in or loll around in a nightgown and robe. In fact, she wore pajamas and got dressed as soon as she awakened. She didn't understand anyone wearing night clothes any time other than when they were ready to go to sleep, since that's what they were for, for goodness sakes. This morning's attire was the same as almost every other outfit in cool weather: jeans and a flannel shirt. Nothing frilly for Jessie.

She cleared her plate from the table and set it in the sink. She only washed dishes once a day, and that was after supper. Sometimes she didn't get around to that either. "They're not going anywhere," she'd tell Arthur if he happened to mention the pile — which, after nearly six decades of marriage, he'd pretty much learned not to do since Jessie didn't take kindly to criticism and she was likely to throw something at him, like the dish soap, the wet dishrag or a Brillo pad, while reminding him that if the dirty dishes bothered him so much, *his* hands weren't broken.

Jessie threw just about anything any time to keep her pitching arm in shape. The Wild Musketeers, Partonville's mostly senior citizens softball team, would start practicing around mid-April and she could hardly wait. Winter was hard on Jessie since she was a woman of get-up-and-go. She took another sip of her coffee while adding "skip rocks in creek" to her mental list of things to do today. If she could believe the radio weatherman — the radio her preferred mode of entertainment over that mindless and endless television Arthur watched — it could get up into the mid-fifties today.

Before heading to the creek to warm up her pitching arm, however, she needed to pay bills. She hated that chore, but in all the years they'd been married, Arthur simply would never do it. A genius at car mechanics his whole life, he couldn't add up rows of numbers correctly for the life of him, so she'd taken over paying the bills, although like the dishes, she let them pile up until they *had* to be done, and today was the day. Forty-five minutes later she was done with the dreaded reminder that money was too tight. Aside from her long-ago semi-pro baseball days, Jessie never worked a paying job since she'd married. When Arthur retired from running his automotive repair shop out in the shed, they had to tighten their belts, which it seemed they had to take in another notch every year. Challie Carter leased their land, but that was a modest and unpredictable income. Although it would be better for their pocketbooks if Arthur didn't eat at the grill every morning, she enjoyed her quiet time too much to complain. Honestly, the man needed to find more to do besides hang around and torment *her* all day! Their financial situation was the over-riding reason they'd accepted the option deal Katie offered them. But then, that needed to stay confidential, at least for now. It said so in the contract.

Jessie put on her jacket and walked the envelopes down the lane to their mailbox. Since their farm was next to Crooked Creek Farm, first she heard, then saw, the back end of Josh's new truck go fishtailing down the gravel road toward Hethrow. Jessie'd heard Katie's SUV pass by some time ago. *He must be late for school today. Good thing his mom isn't home to see that!*

7

Harold stuffed his cell phone back in his pocket, grabbed his pencil and poised it over his pad. "Mayor McKern, what was your reaction when you heard Sam Vitner here was running against you?"

Everyone's eyebrows flew up in the air as their eyeballs shot toward Gladys. "Running against me for what?" she asked, as she looked at Sam, waiting for him to clarify the question. And what *was* that ridiculous giant button he was wearing? she wondered.

Sam looked perplexed. Surely Gladys knew, right? He looked at Harold who shrugged his shoulders. Even if she didn't know, a mayoral candidate didn't have to make his own announcement, did he?

Harold took a deep breath. "He's running against you for mayor, Mayor." Gladys took a closer look at the button. TIME TO SWAP. VITNER FOR MAYOR. She gave Sam a good hard stare, as though daring him to say it was true.

Sam pasted his campaign smile back on his face and tapped the button twice with his index finger, which he then pointed at her. "Here's to a fair-and-square race between you and me," he said, turning his finger back toward himself. Then he held out his hand to shake, which Gladys was momentarily too stunned to take.

"You saw it here, folks." He quickly withdrew his hand as he spoke to everyone gathered around, including Jacob who'd stopped by to pick up one of Lester's large coffees to drink on his way to the airport. He and his mom had stayed up late chatting and he told her not to get up early. "Our *current* Mayor, our current *Acting* Mayor that is — and wouldn't it be nice if she *did* act like it! — won't even shake to a fair-and-square campaign," he said, looking toward Harold. "Did you get that, Harold?" he all but whispered out of the side of his mouth. Harold grimaced but nodded while Sam reached into his pocket. "If any of you think it's time for a SWAP, start wearing you one of these!" He withdrew a fistful of buttons which he held out on his palm. Cora grabbed one and pinned it to her coat. Arthur shook his head when Sam passed the buttons his way. Harold explained that official press members could not wear anyone's campaign buttons, especially while on duty.

Gladys was momentarily saved by the bell when Lester unlocked the door and she could be the first to duck in — everyone right on her heels.

Jessica nursed Sarah Sue while she talked to Katie in hushed tones so as not to awaken Paul. She'd watched the clock and made herself wait until 8 a.m. to call Katie on her cell phone. Jessica knew the construction crew started at 7 and Katie liked to be on-site to make sure everyone checked in. Jessica at first thought she shouldn't bother Katie, but she knew Katie wouldn't want to learn the news about Paul from someone else, and moreover, Jessica *needed* to talk to her best friend.

Paul had barely slept last night and neither had she. Even though he tried to convince her to go to bed, she insisted on camping out on the couch in case he needed anything. "If you don't want me to worry, then don't make me leave your side tonight," she said. He muttered something about emotional blackmail but smiled and shut his eyes. In reality, she was worried about his concussion and wanted to keep an eye on him for at least twenty-four hours.

"You should see him, Katie. Both eyes are black and swollen, his nose has a scrape, his head has a bandage and his leg's in a blue cast, if you can imagine that. I could just kick myself for sending him racing off like that, but I promised him I wouldn't bring it up again."

As badly as Katie felt for Paul and Jessica, she was somewhat distracted. She'd just said good-bye to Sharon Teller, who, tape recorder in hand, asked her how she felt about the uprising against Gladys — and therefore herself, since Sam's platform included promises to stop Partonville from becoming Durbinville. After Sharon left, Katie instructed Edward Showalter to lock the front door and not let anyone else in unless they were delivering materials. She needed to think. She'd started her day by arguing with Josh and it had gone downhill from there. And now here her best friend with her own serious problems was on the phone. She just didn't have the heart to interrupt her with her issues, at least not right now.

"I've noticed that crack in the sidewalk, Jessica. I can picture just where you're talking about. To be honest, you have a lawsuit on your hands, no doubt about it. Maybe

100

you two should talk it over. I know you told me Harold said his liability insurance would cover the hospital costs, but what about Paul's missed work? Pain and suffering? *Neglect?*"

After a long period of silence, Jessica quietly said, "We're just not the suing type, Katie. We adore Harold and we know how hard he works too. The town's too small to cause trouble over a stumble. Yes, financially this isn't good, but we'll make it. God always sees us through. And you know. . . . Oh, never mind."

"What?"

"I don't think I should say what I was thinking. *You're* the one with the good business head."

"Jessica, I thought we'd moved past the phase in our friendship where, aside from decorating matters where we both know you excel, you assume your opinion isn't as valid as mine. What? What are you thinking?"

"I'm thinking that if somebody sued Paul and me over a fall, we'd probably lose our motel. I'm thinking you're about to open an entire mini mall with stairs and railings and . . . and . . . I'd hate it if somebody sued *you* because they tripped."

Katie's sigh was so loud it sounded like a wind tunnel. "I hate it when you're so nice."

"Oh, Katie, I'm *sorry.* I didn't mean to . . ." Katie cut her right off.

"Jessica! Stop apologizing for being *nice!* I don't *really* hate it. That was just a phrase. I was more chastising *myself* for defaulting to the sue mode. I'm still wearing my City Slicker, big business hat, I guess." *And my own urge to strike out against a senseless group of backwards people who don't recognize a helping hand when they see it!* "Things are just different in a town this size." *Now* there's *an understatement.* "But just the same, please tell me you'll consider *all* your options if money gets too short because of this. Promise?"

"Promise. But in the meantime, we'll need to tighten our belts here again for a spell. I hate to take money out of Josh's pocket, but I wouldn't feel right having him come when we're down a paycheck ourselves and business is so slow right now anyway."

"I don't see how you can afford *not* to have him come. He could at least take out the garbage and carry your groceries, watch Sarah Sue when you have errands to run or need to take Paul to the doctor, get you caught up on some of the maintenance issues, like cleaning the motel laundry room. Remember when you were talking about that the other day? You have *everything* to take care of right now and I can already hear a tired tone in your voice." *Takes one to know one,* she thought, the old childhood taunt popping into her head. "And remember, we traded Josh's help for your decorating expertise on all the aesthetics for the mall. Don't think for a moment you got the good end of this deal, because when we get the mall to the decorating point, I'll keep you more than busy." *I need all the help I can get to make this mall irresistible.* "You'll wonder why you ever made such a rotten deal. Do you have any idea how much work it's going to take to achieve the *wow* factor I'm after when people walk in and see that atrium?"

"I don't need to see the atrium to feel my own personal *wow* factor right now, Katie. I'm still not sure I'm up to that task and. . . ."

"Not another word. I'm telling you that you have the talent. I'm promising you right here and now that I won't wear you out, or I know I'll have Paul to answer to. But we made a trading deal and I plan to hold you to it, friend of mine."

"Banners!" Jessica suddenly yelled into the phone, causing Sarah Sue to snap her head back from Jessica's breast and pucker up. Jessica smiled at her baby girl, who unpuck-

ered, smiled back and latched back on. Jessica was afraid her happy yelp might have awakened Paul, but she didn't hear him rustle.

"Excuse me? Did you say *banners?*"

"Colorful banners hanging from the atrium railings! Oh, *Katie!* That would be *perfect!* They would have movement and eye appeal. We could change them with the seasons! Put wreaths on the exterior doors with ribbons to match the colors of the banners!

"You know, Katie, Dorothy once told me when we use our God-given gifts that it's like pumping fuel into our souls. She was so *right!* THANK YOU for helping me to continue to do that! It's so *energizing!*"

Katie wished she could mine Jessica's sudden gust of enthusiasm. She wanted to ask her more about the banners. She wanted to tell her about Sam's bid for mayor and the apparent list of people who wanted her to fail.

She wanted to ask Jessica what she thought *her* gifts were, if any — aside from causing commotion in town.

But instead, Edward Showalter walked up, obviously needing her attention. It was time to hang up.

Thursdays were one of Maggie's busiest day at La Feminique Hair Salon & Day Spa, and busy made Maggie happy. She was booked hair-root-to-hair-tips solid for the day, and she always made sure her wardrobe and accessories had enough pizzazz to keep her energized.

With St. Patrick's Day only two-and-a-half weeks away, she was already into her green theme, which immediately and annually followed her red Valentine's theme. Maggie adored holidays, which gave her reason to celebrate, not that she needed a reason. She sported a sweeping up-do held in place by two green chopsticks complete with dangling plastic shamrocks, leprechaun drop earrings, a green-and-white silk Irish scarf tied around her neck (souvenir given to her by a client who visited the Emerald Isle), a white blouse onto which was pinned a small gold replica of an Irish harp (another client gift), green stretch pants, green knee-high hose, and comfy green gym shoes with white laces. Her green pumps would have looked nicer with this ensemble but they were too tight this morning to make it through a busy Thursday. "I should have skipped the potato chips last night," she'd told Ben on his way out the door. "My feet feel like water balloons."

Before she even put the coffee on at 8 a.m., she popped her Chieftains CD into the expensive boom box one of her daughters gave her two Christmases ago and twirled herself around a few times during the first track. Coffee percolating, hot pot, tea bags and an array of chocolate mints set out, she had just enough time to phone Dorothy before her first client arrived. She grabbed her cordless phone, settled into the styling chair, looked in the mirror and shook her head while she listened to the rings. The shamrocks and leprechauns, who appeared to be dancing as they bobbed this way and that, displayed *marvelous* action, which fueled her to face the long day. She smiled at herself, lifted first her right eyebrow and lowered it, then her left. Maggie was one of the few people with ambidextrous eyebrows, which delighted her. Just another of her special talents.

"Hello," Dorothy said, her voice sounding craggy as though she hadn't yet spoken this morning. And she had a vague lisp.

"Dorothy! Maggie here! I didn't wake you, did I?"

"Goodness me, no — although I did sleep

in some this morning since Jacob and I didn't get to Wal-Mart until late and then we talked until, oh, I'd say midnight or after. Sheba and I are just lying here relaxing, thinking about how we ought to get up. I don't even have my partial plate in yet! Maybe the sounds of my tongue flapping through the gap between a couple back teeth is why you thought you woke me up." The image tickled Dorothy so much she broke out in a laugh, causing Sheba to scoot up and lick her cheek. "Jacob slipped out of here without making a sound," she said after her laughter died down. "When we turned in last night, he told me not to get up, but that surely wasn't my plan. I couldn't believe it when I woke up and saw the time. I *hate* I didn't get to kiss him good-bye before he left for the airport. But just think, Maggie, when he comes back in a week, he'll be here for *good!*"

"Think you should try a new hairdo this afternoon just to celebrate?" Maggie asked, using her fingers as a squeegee to swipe lipstick from the corners of her mouth. She looked at the little bit of lipstick color on her fingers, then looked at her lips. Funny, she thought, how much the color of her lips changed the shade of the lipstick. She should have gone a tone darker wearing *this* shade of green in her scarf.

"If you can find a new way to coif my pink scalp, I'll tip you extra." Both of them chuckled, knowing full well Dorothy's ultrathin hair left them no choice but her old-lady "round do." At least that's how Dorothy referred to it. "What can I do for you so early this morning, Maggie?"

"I don't know if you heard or not, but last night Paul Joy had a little accident."

Dorothy tossed the covers back, sat up, swung her legs around to the floor and stood, which she realized made her a little lightheaded, so she sat back down on the edge of her bed. "Accident? What kind of accident? He's okay, isn't he?"

"He fell down in front of the *Press*. He was running — literally — to get Jessica's last-minute mall entry in the box and he forgot about that broken cement there, you know where it is, and did he ever crash to the sidewalk, and right at my feet! Turns out he broke his leg and has a mild concussion. Harold took him to the hospital since Paul wouldn't let us call an ambulance."

"Is he still in the hospital?"

"No. Doctor Nielson set his leg and made him stay for awhile, just to make sure he was going to be okay from that head bang. Ben and I took him home. Harold went to the Lamp Post to notify Jessica and stay with her until he arrived."

"Oh, I bet that poor child was a wreck."

"That is an understatement."

"How bad was the break?"

"Bad enough, but Paul said he hoped he wouldn't be off work more than the six weeks he'd have the cast on. Actually, he said he hoped he could go back *before* the cast came off, but I don't hold much hope for that since he works down *in* the mine, unless they give him an office job for a spell. Have you ever heard tell of them doing that?"

"He broke his leg once before, but that was so long ago I can't remember. Those poor kids. They've had more than their fair share lately. Have you called anyone from the Care Committee yet?"

"I figure I'd just turn it over to you, Ms. United Methodist Church Activator. You're the one who gets things done. I would have called you last night if I'd known you were up late kibitzing, but there wasn't really anything that could be done right then anyway."

"I better get my teeth in place and make some calls, get some food sent over there. I imagine Jessica's got enough on her mind without thinking about dinner. I'll take a walk over there later, too, see if I can help them with anything." Dorothy heard a familiar tinkling sound in the background. After Christmas, Maggie, who loved shopping and hit every closeout rack, table and display in the county, had purchased herself a half-price door chime that rang when someone came in. "Sounds like Wilma Anderson just arrived anyway." All clients were familiar with the La Feminique Hair Salon & Day Spa Thursday lineup.

"You win the million-dollar prize! Tell Jessica hello for me when you see her, and tell Paul that old Mrs. Malone is working a nine-hour day today."

"Old Mrs. Malone? Since when did our one-and-only Maggie Malone become *old?*"

"He'll know what you mean!"

Dorothy finished her morning bathroom duties, dressed, ushered Sheba on a quick walk around the block and pulled out her Care Committee roster complete with "Dishes to Be Taken" chart. (Before the Care Committee made use of a chart, one poor family found itself with enough sloppy joes to last a month!) Of course she'd start by calling May Belle, who could come up with good easy menus at the drop of a hat.

"Howdy Doody, dearie!" Dorothy said

110

when May Belle answered her phone.

"Now don't you sound perky for so early in the morning."

"You wouldn't have said that if you'd heard me awhile ago. Have you ever heard me talk without all my teeth?"

"How would I know?"

"I reckon I sound like a lizard."

"I can't say as I know what a lizard sounds like, Dorothy."

"Neither do I. But I can imagine, can't you?" May Belle chuckled. She adored Dorothy's humor. "But my teeth aren't why I called. I don't know if you've heard or not, but if not, Paul Joy fell in front of the *Press* last night. He suffered a mild concussion, from what Maggie tells me, and a broken leg. We need to crank up the Care Committee."

At the sound of the words *Care Committee,* May Belle turned the dial on her oven to 400. She would adjust the temperature after she figured out what to make. Since baking was her joy and her ministry, her oven was seldom a cold one. "Is Paul okay?"

"Maggie said he would be. He fell right. . . . You know, let me give you the details later, since the little I know is secondhand. I'm going to stop by Jessica's and I'll give you a call after I get it from the horse's mouth, see Paul for myself. In the meantime, let's get them fed for the next couple weeks."

8

Eleven-thirty and the lunchtime crowd at Harry's Grill had grown by leaps and bounds since word spread about Sam's run for mayor. Everybody was talking at once and a few were even yelling.

Cora Davis sat on the edge of her usual seat at the table in the front window, from which she could overhear anything in the tiny restaurant, seating capacity twenty-five. She'd been lit up like a Christmas tree since the morning lineup tumbled inside. In order to maintain her high-alert listening mode, she didn't dare speak since she wanted to make sure she captured every hot word in order to relay them to those poor souls who couldn't be there this morning — especially Maggie Malone, whom she would see later today during her hair appointment. Now that the posters were up, the contested mayoral race bomb had dropped on Gladys and word was spreading, the election race

— and all that implied — was on.

Nellie Ruth McGregor hung up the phone in Wilbur's office. Wilbur owned Your Store and Nellie Ruth was the assistant manager. When Wilbur tracked her down in the frozen food section to tell her she had a phone call, it unnerved her. Although she was sorry to learn about Paul's misfortune, she was relieved to find out ES (aside from Johnny Mathis — no, not that one — she was the only person to call him ES rather than Edward Showalter, which was how everyone referred to him) had not been injured on the job. She started fretting about that possibility when he told her late one evening — when he *finally* called her — that he'd been working on scaffolding around the atrium most of the day. Since she'd waited more than six decades to fall *in* love, she certainly wasn't ready to have him fall three floors *out* of her life!

Dorothy'd phoned Nellie Ruth, a member of the Care Committee, to ask her if she could pick up a few jars of baby food for Jessica and drop them off on her way home. Nellie Ruth said she was taking a late lunch hour and that she had another errand to run anyway, which was to pick up the list of mini-mall finalists, then she'd get right on it.

Nellie Ruth was happy to have things to think about aside from how disappointed she felt that she almost never got to see Edward Showalter these days. He worked late almost every night and at least a half-day most Saturdays. Since Katie got him that cell phone, it seemed like she always had something to ask him after hours, the ringer interrupting the few conversations she and ES did manage. He hadn't even had time to come over and see how much Morning and Midnight, the kitties he'd surprised her with, had grown the past couple of weeks. The little rascals were getting into everything, but they sure were entertaining. At least she had them for company, she thought, as she drove around the square hoping to catch a glimpse of ES through the Taninger window. But no such luck. She did, however, see one of Gladys's "interesting" posters, is the way ES had put it, which she thought was very kind considering Gladys looked nothing short of stupefied.

The election race. That's all anyone had been talking about in the grocery store. She'd even heard raised voices in the produce aisle already! She hated politics.

"Prayer accomplishes more than all the politicians put together," she told ES one night after they watched the early evening news together and listened to yet another riff between the Republicans and Democrats. Of course watching television together was a thing of the past, she thought, now that Katie Durbin had stolen her beau's time.

Forgive me, Lord, for such a selfish thought! ES is so proud of his position and I'm proud of him too. It's just that . . . I miss him. There's a season for everything, and this is the season for getting the building done. I'm sure after it's open and he starts his new permanent job, his hours will be steady and predictable. Give me patience, Lord. Just give me a little patience. Amen.

When Nellie Ruth walked into the *Partonville Press*'s office, she found Sharon banging away on her keyboard like there was no tomorrow. "Hi, Nellie Ruth," Sharon said, glancing Nellie Ruth's way.

"I'm here to pick up my copy of the mini-mall finalists," Nellie Ruth said, glad to find her enthusiasm had returned, reminded once again of why she was such a prayer warrior.

"If there *is* a mini mall to be named," Sharon said, then made a few more key-

116

strokes before she stood, stretched and handed Nellie Ruth her sealed envelope.

"What do you mean?"

"You haven't heard about Sam Vitner's run for mayor?"

"I'd say you can't work in a public place today and *not* hear about it." She almost sounded disgusted, but then realized so and added a chipper "Right?"

"I'm transcribing my notes from an interview I did with Mr. Vitner earlier today and his platform is definitely against Mayor McKern, which means he's against anything she's for, which means he's against what he perceives to be Katie Durbin's attempt to . . . let me give you a direct quote which will appear in Sunday's *Press.*" She sat back down at her computer and began scrolling through her notes. ". . . her attempt to steal our town right out from under our noses, all for her own financial personal gain. And Mayor McKern has played right into her web."

Jacob's first flight of the day was a small jet that took him out of Hethrow Regional Airport to Chicago. "Fast puddle jumpers," he told his mom. "We spend more time waiting to board and sitting on the tarmac than flying." Even though the flight wasn't very long, he was glad to deplane so he could stretch his long, weary frame. *Only one more of these miserable trips,* he thought as he strode along at a fast clip, having booked a connecting flight with little time to spare.

When his brother, Vinnie, had phoned recently and asked, "So, how goes the countdown to moving day?" Jacob told him the thing he was most anxious to finish was folding himself up "like origami to fit into the cramped and noisy tin can of an airplane."

Just when he'd begun to believe he'd handle the transition from Philly to Partonville with flying adult colors, he came across that scene in front of Harry's this morning, an event that reminded him how much Partonville seemed nothing like the rest of the world. *A handshake on a fair-and-square campaign? Is that really what Sam Vitner was carrying on about?* Of course it made Jacob chuckle to picture presidential candidates performing that ritual, then sticking to it. Down and dirty campaigning was more like it these days. *Where have integrity, honesty and representing the people gone?* On the upside, he mused, perhaps those very questions served as part of the catalyst to move him back to Partonville. It's not that he'd lost *his* honesty and integrity, but in the long run, helping fat cats get fatter had eroded his sense of mission. He felt a kind of purpose that stirred his emotions when he thought about helping the people in his mom's little town. *Mom's little town. Will it ever feel like mine?*

He flipped a few more pages, read a travel piece, then shut the magazine, stuffed it back in its compartment and closed his eyes. He was tired. Not enough sleep — again. His mind drifted to the fact he hadn't seen Katie. He had this niggling feeling she was somehow going to be caught up in this mayoral ruckus. He recalled Sam Vitner leading a personal charge against her mini mall once before. But then he'd watched Katie work her magic at the annual Happy Hookers (rug hookers turned bunco players) Christmas party out at the farm, heard the verbal blow-by-blow presentation she'd given to thwart the enemy, so to speak. She'd followed a plan his mom had played a hand in scheming. *What a pair of headstrong, determined and clever women.*

His mom. He was going to keep focused on her. No matter what kind of trouble the people of Partonville seemed to be stirring up, he simply would not allow himself to be sorry about this move. Besides, if Katie did get caught up in the strife, he was glad to imagine he might become her ally, of sorts. He smiled thinking it might be the City Slickers against the locals. *Brother! Sounds like the Hatfields and the McCoys!* But the odds were always better when there were two against . . . however many.

Then again, how bad could it *really* get in Pardon-Me-Ville? He smiled and nodded off, all but shaking his head at the ridiculous notion of a feud.

9

Colton Craig held the receiver to his ear
with his left hand; the thumb and index
finger of his right hand were wrapped
around an expensive imported cigar. He
took a slow drag, then watched the smoke
curl into the air after it passed through his
lips. He was leaning back in his ergonomic
leather chair, gazing out his office picture
window onto Hethrow, in large part a
metropolis created by Craig & Craig Developers' own careful planning, business savvy,
shrewd dealing and hard work. (Colton and
his brother's firm had helped develop Hethrow from a small town nearly off the map
into a major city split by the interstate
highway.) He was engaged in a relaxing
early afternoon chat with one of his old
Chicago friends, Carl Jimson. Their friendship had been limited to Christmas cards
the past couple of decades, but when Carl
started making occasional trips to Parton-

ville and realized he'd be within a short distance of Colton, he gave him a call and the two had dinner a couple of times, maintaining somewhat closer phone contact after their reunion of sorts.

Since both men were in related fields (Carl an architect and Colton in commercial real estate development), their conversations usually wandered around to their latest interesting architectural discoveries. Today was no different. After breezing through casual personal chit-chat, Colton recapped the unusual design features he appreciated in the new, privately held hotel he'd stayed in during his recent vacation to Jamaica, saying that management had made wonderful use of what he could only describe as octagons throughout. "Lobby, rooms . . . it was like walking through a clever puzzle."

"It's wonderful when aesthetics marry purpose," Carl said, then added that one of his clients had just announced a chocolate shop would complement an element of *his* design.

Unbeknownst to Carl, word of the confectioner coming to the mini mall had already spread throughout the greater Partonville area. The confectioner's sister, a freelance journalist, had immediately sent out press releases announcing that Sheldon Prescott had finally found a space for his long-time vision, Alotta Chocolatta.

"Carl," Colton said, leaning back a little farther in his chair, "this is interesting news, especially on the heels of the phone call I received yesterday."

"Oh?"

"Even with a chocolate shop, it sounds like Kathryn Durbin's going to have a run for her money, which she's spent plenty of already." Nobody in the commercial real estate business referred to her as Katie, most not even knowing that Katie, not Kathryn, was her given name. When she'd thrown her hat in Chicago's cutthroat development arena decades ago, she believed Katie sounded too . . . casual or flip or something, so she'd printed her business cards with Kathryn Durbin and that's the way she remained. "I'm still hard-pressed to understand what's driving her with this . . . what's she calling it? A mini mall?"

"Yes, a mini mall, soon to have a name. But how'd you know I was talking about Kathryn?" Carl usually held client information close to his vest.

"Wild guess helped along by a recent press release I read in our *Daily Courier*."

"Oh. Well, you said you couldn't figure

out what's driving her and I'd say it's a keen mind for business. And don't forget, she has a brilliant architect on the job, so you can be sure her interior building design is going to be noteworthy on its own." Colton heard the smile in his friend's voice.

Carl Jimson's reputation as an architect was excellent. And he was glad to have an opportunity to finally work with someone often referred to as Kathryn Durbin, Development Diva. Katie contracted him from Chicago thinking her plans would be more secure from the likes of Colton Craig, a man who'd played a hand in her losing her position in the windy city. She didn't know Carl and Colton were old buddies. Throughout the years Colton had occasionally mentioned Katie's name to Carl, but Carl had no idea the two had become Big Gun adversaries down here in the northern part of southern Illinois. Carl also had no idea his shrewd friend started taking notes the minute Ms. Durbin's name came up.

In its day, Partonville had been the center of attention in the area; but once the interstate and automobile plant came to Hethrow, the boom was on and Partonville suffered. After a couple of decades of huge growth, west was now the only direction left for the Craig brothers to expand. Dorothy's

Crooked Creek Farm had been their target. They'd made Dorothy a silent offer, hoping to buy her out, annex the property and keep their expansion marching clear through the Partonville square, which was dying out anyway. But then Katie bought Crooked Creek Farm out from under them — and moved onto it. Colton and Katie had always played the same cutthroat game, each beating out the other over the years. But up until the last twenty-four hours, he couldn't figure out *what* she thought she was up to, moving onto a farm, acting like the Lone Ranger, pretending to save Podunk Partonville from evaporating into extinction by investing in a long vacant building on a dying square. The only thing he knew for sure was that big money was her target, and after that surprising phone call, he finally had the proof.

Colton didn't want to shut off Carl's information, which was, at least thus far, known by him anyway, but now that he'd acquired the under-the-table news, he forced himself to stay casually inquisitive so as not to raise any suspicions. "Oh, that's right. She's running a contest, isn't she? Kathryn Durbin running a contest. I never thought I'd see the day."

"That contest is more than it appears.

She's rallied the residents with it. Good business, if you ask me. And honestly, I think her endeavor's going to have a big payoff. She's a shrewd businesswoman, Colton, and when the rehabbing finally comes to an end and the shopkeepers get set up, she's going to have a good drawing card there, a draw I think might help sell the whole town — which," and he stopped to chuckle here, "might one day rival the likes of Hethrow." Of course he was kidding, but even the insane notion of it irked Colton.

Or had Kathryn drawn Carl, one of the best in the business, into some bigger plan Colton didn't yet know about and perhaps *he* was being baited? After all, Carl had a reputation for getting involved with major expansion projects.

Colton took another draw on his cigar and this time blew the smoke out the side of his mouth. "She's a worthy opponent, but then that's no surprise. Truthfully, I've always found her fortitude quite attractive." Since Colton was known as a twice-divorced womanizer, Carl had no doubt about that. "Maybe you're not aware of it, but Ms. Durbin and I have gathered a few decades' worth of dueling history in the commercial real estate game. Although when she left

Chicago I'd won the last round, I believe she's positioning herself to try to best me here in my own territory, or at the very least give me a run for my money." Sounding unsure for the moment was better bait.

"Come on, Colton. I hardly think a mini mall in a town of fourteen hundred people is going to rival Hethrow."

Maybe Carl *wasn't* in on anything bigger than that one project. Either that or he was very shrewd. "I wasn't going to say anything, but I'm sure by this morning it's already become public knowledge."

"About?"

"Seems our Ms. Durbin's aligned herself with Gladys McKern. She's quite the . . . character. You familiar with her?"

"She's the mayor of Partonville, right?"

"At least for now."

"And that means?"

"I received an anonymous phone call yesterday — at least the caller thought it was anonymous, apparently never having heard of caller I.D., which doesn't surprise me for a Partonville resident — advising me that not everyone in Partonville is happy with the new mall, and furthermore, they're ready to do battle against the way *Katie,* as he referred to her, has been sewing up properties in and around Partonville."

"And?" Carl was clueless as to what Colton was driving at, and why should he care anyway? He wasn't even from the area and he was hardly her confidant. She'd hired him to work on a building and he did. End of story. Still, his curiosity was piqued.

"And the caller went on to say somebody needed to put a stop to it."

"By?"

"By ousting the mayor — who was clearly in Ms. Durbin's pocket, according to my caller — this coming election and getting someone in who had their own deep pockets and connections. Somebody who could come up against her, so to speak, is the way my caller put it. Somebody who could keep Partonville from becoming Durbinville."

"You're kidding me, right? They think she's trying to turn Partonville into Durbinville?"

"I kid you not. But most importantly, they think she's a shyster and they want someone to help stop her."

"And that savior would be?" As if he hadn't guessed.

"The caller perceived me to be the money machine and himself to be the new mayor, although like I said he didn't identify himself right off, since he was," and he stopped here to chuckle, "trying to be

128

anonymous, remember."

"And the caller was?"

"Sam Vitner, the guy who owns Swappin' Sam's. You familiar with him?"

"Not that resale place on the edge of Partonville with the toilets sitting out in the front lawn?!" If there was one key thing about Swappin' Sam's, it's that it was impossible to miss. But the chaos of its appearance had indeed lured Carl right in for a look-see and a brief chat with Sam. The place reminded him of a junkyard his dad used to take him to when he was a kid. Oh, how he loved prowling through that place with his dad, watching him pick up this and that, then listening to him tell all about what it was for, how one relative or another used to have one, or what it was replaced with when progress came along. He adored his dad. He'd have listened to him talk about *anything* just to spend time with him, feel him reach down and grab his hand, playfully bonk him on the head, tuck him in to say his prayers.

"Exactly that place."

"And this guy thinks he can beat out McKern for mayor?"

"He said he already has a base of solid supporters and that his posters were going up last night. He said I should have a look in the window at Hornsby's Shoe Emporium today. He said once people knew he was running against — and this is a direct quote — 'Mayor Turncoat, it would be easy pickens from there on in.' " Colton's spot-on imitation of Sam made Carl laugh.

"Kathryn doesn't know about this yet?"

"If those posters did go up last night, I imagine every-body in Partonville knows. Like all two-bit towns, they have quite the grapevine." Carl didn't like the tone in Colton's two-bit dig, especially not when *he'd* just tangentially invested his reputation in a piece of Partonville. But then, that was Colton. He'd always been smug. "What she doesn't know — at least not to the best of my knowledge, unless Vitner felt the need to brag about our possible alliance — is that now *I* know what she's been up to regarding all those *surrounding* properties. And Carl, I'm assuming this conversation we're having is confidential."

Carl didn't respond right away. He didn't like the odd turn of events here and felt himself to be in a hard place between a client, who was paying him and whom he rather liked, and a friend, who he also knew could be somewhat snaky to get what he wanted. He hoped Colton hadn't just played him. Then again, what did he have to lose anyway? "Of course," he finally said.

"Well, since you're working with Kathryn, at least until the building is done, I know you well enough to understand — and respect — your loyalty. And by the way, how could you *not* be on the side of a smart, beautiful, leggy woman like that?" They chuckled in agreement.

"How, by the way, did you respond to Vitner's proposal?"

"I told him what I tell anyone who says they'd like to join forces with Craig & Craig Developers, which is of *course* I'm interested."

"So he's going to be like . . . a snitch? Or, what?" As far as Carl could figure, Colton would have no interest in *saving* Partonville, not when there was more money to be had mowing it down and turning it into a Hethrow subdivision. He doubted Vitner had thought about *that* when he'd made his alliance.

"Let's just say he vowed to try to break the tentacles of trust the townsfolk have with Morgan Realty, Katie Durbin, as he *kept* referring to her, and Gladys McKern in order to get people to let *him* know — and therefore let *me* know — when they're thinking about selling. People should have some fair-market competition for their

properties, which, up until Sam's thoughtful meddling, the whole dumb lot of them
hadn't considered, it seems."

Carl's stomach was swiftly sinking. The
whole dumb lot of them? He'd grown to
admire Ms. Durbin's tenacious attempt to
help the people of Partonville take a stand
against what — *who* — he now understood
to perhaps be one of their aggressors. He
recalled the homey feeling and courtesies
he'd enjoyed at the Lamp Post motel on
each of his stays. Even though he found
Lester K. Biggs, the crotchety guy at Harry's Grill, a tad terse, he hadn't missed the
collection jar Lester kept out on his counter
for one local family or another, or the way
the locals gathered around the U and, for
better or for worse, shared pieces of their
lives, teased each other, stood together in
the end. He happened to be in town around
Rick Lawson's death and had witnessed an
entire population grieve the loss of one of
their own. City life had its advantages, but
who in *his* gated community would truly
miss *him* if he were gone? Carl was raised in
the country, his father, now deceased, was a
second-generation dairy farmer in Wisconsin. Partonville had made him lonesome for
that sense of oneness he used to know as a
kid, and that had given him a feeling of

132

protectiveness and satisfaction in investing in such a place, no matter how small — or remunerative — his contribution had been. "If I may ask, how does this all pertain to the mini mall, Colton?"

"How does all this pertain to the mall? you ask, Carl. Well, I'll tell you what Vitner told me. Through her alliance with Herb Morgan's long history as a trusted independent Realtor, Kathryn's been purchasing any and all properties as soon as word-of-mouth reaches Morgan that somebody's thinking of selling. Vitner said she's paying Morgan a finder's fee, using him as a buyer's broker. She's been buying old houses within the town itself, reportedly having some vision to morph some of those old homes surrounding the square into 'quaint shops nobody can afford to shop at,' is the way Vitner said it.

"But here's her loophole . . . or my gift, I should say: I just learned through Mr. Anonymous that she's also secured four out of the six farms she needs to tie my hands from *ever* expanding in that direction, unless I one day pay *her* a fortune for it, which I'm sure is her *real* game. Honestly, Carl, the woman is all smoke and mirrors. A few months ago she had me convinced she was talking to farmers about a Preservation

Easement Program or some such nonsense. Instead, she's been buying and tying! She's temporarily sewn up those four farms through an option to buy them at a later date, and with upfront money — and with a *confidentiality* clause in it while she goes after those last two farms. Now I know why my land scouts have been getting the cold shoulder, which I might never have known until Vitner told me. He knows about it because the landholder of one of the biggest farms — and a key piece she needs to lock me out — didn't like her offer the way it stood and figured he could probably hold out for more. Then the guy got a little big-mouthed about it to Sam one day, who'd already decided he'd had enough of Ms. Durbin, and Vitner became determined to shut her down — shut the, and I again quote him here, 'whole dang lot of them down.'

"Of course *nothing's* usually guaranteed in real estate until a deal's signed and money passes. Gone are the days of handshakes and trust, even among the backwards." Colton's snicker bordered on menacing. "That's why she's paired with Morgan, the local known and respected factor, approaching the farmers through him rather than doing it herself, which is very smart. Of course they'd picture me to be the big bad wolf too — unless Vitner, their mayoral hopeful, convinces them otherwise, which maybe he can do, and maybe he can't. Anyway, on Kathryn's behalf, Morgan proposes the idea to the farmers — and Carl, it's prudent — that if they want to keep farming for awhile and yet have the assurance of a comfortable retirement when they're ready, why wait? Why not option now for the possible sale and hopefully have the best of both worlds?"

"Why doesn't she just buy the places outright?" Carl asked, sounding livelier than his heart was feeling. But after all, what would it hurt to find out a little more information himself, especially if Colton had played *him,* which by this time he felt pretty sure of.

"She didn't get wealthy in this game by being stupid. No sense emptying your cash drawers before you know if you can lock up *everything* you need to make your plan work. With the purchase option, if things don't go her way the most she can lose is her earnest money. So it goes like this: Morgan tells them his buyer — which everyone knows is Kathryn, or Katie, or whoever she's calling herself to the townies — needs time for something, which he doesn't tell them is to secure *six* properties before she will exercise her option to buy. If they agree to her terms and timeline for the option, she gives them earnest money with the contract — since tying up any other possible sale of your land has to be worth something — and then she includes a confidentiality clause." He laughed. "*Whoops* on the confidentiality, huh? Anyway, during this option period, they continue farming their land and selling their crops while she reaps the benefit of possible land grabs for the future at today's prices, although I'm sure she uses an escalation per acre as the timeline increases."

"I still don't get something. If these farmers *do* sell, where are they going to live?" Carl thought about his folks, who ended up going straight from their farm into a modest prefab home in a retirement community when they could no longer care for the land or themselves. His dad couldn't bear to watch anyone else farm the land.

"If they want to stick around, there's a thing called a life estate agreement, which means they'll get to stay in their home and a few surrounding acres — you know, in case they want to keep their chickens or goats or whatever — until they're dead. That's how you end up seeing an occasional farm house in the middle of a housing development."

"Who's the guy, or at least one of the guys, holding out?" Carl asked.

Colton went silent for a long spell. "Now that, my friend," he said, his voice shifting tones, "you don't need to know."

Carl took Colton's sudden reluctance to play all his cards as a sign of a shift in trust. Well, then, that made them even.

10

Josh leaned over and gave Shelby one more kiss on the lips before she said, "I *have* to go, Josh. Don't look, but my mom just appeared in the front window." Shelby nodded her head sideways to indicate which direction he shouldn't look, which he immediately did. She giggled. "I'm really not in the mood for her Lecture Number 273 again," she said with a sigh, "the one where she reminds me what too much kissing can lead to," she paused to deliberately cross her eyes, a familiar gesture she sprang on him to make him laugh, "so I better get inside before she's knocking on your truck door."

Josh's heart skipped a beat and his neck reddened at the mere thought of too much kissing, which personally he didn't think was humanly possible. But he knew exactly what her mom was worried about since he thought about *exactly* that a bazillion times a day, even right this moment, even though his girlfriend looked ridiculously silly — but *still* oh so cute.

He wondered how much different Shelby's mom's lecture was from the one his mom delivered. Every time he was going to be at the farm alone his mom deemed it necessary to say, "And do not bring anyone in the house named Shelby. And not in the barn, either, you hear me?" What did she think he was, deaf? "And you treat her like a *lady.* This is a small enough town to count on the fact that somebody is always watching you." *Moms and their scare tactics. Could be a reality show.* But how dumb. He knew about the Fire Pit hidden in the woods at the end of a dirt lane on the outskirts of Partonville, the one their parents didn't know about — or so he thought, since the Fire Pit had been the preferred necking spot for generations. When Josh had first overheard a portion of a conversation about it, he'd enthusiastically said, "Oh! Do you have bonfires there? We have a fire pit down by the creek!" Kevin, Josh's best Partonville friend, rapped on Josh's head with his knuckles. "Hel-*lo! Fire* Pit, Josh-o. Couples in parked cars? Get it?" Sometimes Josh felt so dense.

Kevin pointed out the entrance to the

secluded wooded area one time when they were out cruising in Kevin's car. When they passed right by the turnoff that looked to be nothing more than a two-lane cow path, Josh asked him why he didn't take him back there so he could see it. "You and me? At the *Fire Pit?* I wouldn't be caught dead driving back there with a guy! You don't go to the Fire Pit unless you're with your woman and . . . on *fire,*" he said, winking. The first thing Kevin said when he saw Josh's new wheels was, "Josh my man, that truck bed is a Fire Pit magnet!" Josh's heart raced again just thinking about it. He awakened from his momentary spring-fevered trance just in time to notice Shelby, who had uncrossed her eyes and was reaching for the door handle.

"Wait! Let me get your door!"

"That's okay," she said, opening the latch. "I already know you're a gentleman."

Not if you knew what I was thinking. . . . One of these days maybe he'd just casually mention the Fire Pit to her, see how she'd respond. She leaned toward him and gave him a quick peck on the cheek before she slid out of the truck.

Her mom greeted her at the door, then waved to Josh. After several volleys of waving, he finally made himself pull away, deciding that for now he'd just have to be happy with the warmth she'd left at his side and the lingering scent of her hair. He was so revved up it was all he could do to keep from tromping on the gas pedal and laying a patch of rubber, but her mom was probably still at the window and . . .

Yes, his mom was right. Somebody was always watching.

At least his day was winding down better than it started. He went to bed late last night after working on his physics homework for three straight hours. He was usually good about getting up on his own, but he forgot to set his alarm before he dozed off with his bed light on and the book still in his hands. He overslept by forty minutes. His mom didn't realize he wasn't up until she was ready to leave for work and she yelled up the stairs for him to have a good day — and he didn't answer. She barreled up the steps, blasted his door open and shook him out of a sound sleep. The minute his eyes sprang open she was right in his face. All he'd asked her to do was to back off a little until his eyes focused, but she'd misinterpreted his "back off" request and a brief yelling match ensued. His mom had accused him so many times lately of mouthing off that he'd all but been silent around her the last two days. Once she got on her roll this morning, she said she was tired of his pouting and accused him of just trying to push her buttons. He couldn't win. The last thing he heard when she flew out of his room on her way to work was, "And you *better* not miss your *bus!*"

Oh, well. Some things couldn't be helped. After all, he hadn't missed the bus on purpose. He'd scrambled as fast as he could to gather all his homework, which he'd left around the room in a disheveled mess when he'd climbed in bed last night to finish studying. He'd even skipped his shower trying to beat the clock. But when he heard the bus toot the horn at the end of the lane and he wasn't even finished dressing yet, he knew his efforts were in vain. The bus driver waited for nobody longer than thirty seconds after the toot. "No way, José," he said to his reflection in the small dresser mirror. "Might as well take a shower now," he muttered, shucking his unbuttoned shirt off his shoulders. Even though he barely ever got to drive to school, one of the things he liked most about doing so was that he could leave later and still make it to his first class on time since his home was near the beginning of a very long bus route.

The day had passed quickly and spring

had arrived, he mused as he passed by a farmer plucking rocks out of his field and a woman inspecting her flower bed. He rolled down his window and sniffed the fresh spring air, something he'd seen Dorothy do countless times. Although his route didn't require that he circle the square, nearly everyone did whenever they could, just to see what and who they might see. He'd gone halfway around when he realized he'd rather not see his mom — or have her see him. It would be humiliating if she bolted into the street and flagged him down, which he wouldn't put past her since she had been so mad this morning.

He veered off the square and wove his way around the side streets until he found himself in front of United Methodist Church. He remembered his Uncle Delbert — Pastor Delbert Carol Jr. — mentioning on more than one occasion how Josh should stop by the church some time, kidnap him, he'd joked, and take him for a ride in his truck.

"Josh!" Pastor said, when his nephew appeared suddenly in his office. He stood up and scooted his chair so quickly that it rolled back and banged into the wall behind him, a habit he just couldn't stop. The wall looked like he'd been chipping away at it with an axe.

"You know what I've heard, Uncle Delbert. 'Pastor writing a sermon. Please interrupt.' " In fact it was his Uncle Delbert who'd told him that. "Not only am I interrupting you, I'm finally kidnapping you — at your very own request — for a ride in my truck!"

After they buckled up, Josh drove toward the hard road, as Dorothy always called it, that headed out of town in the direction of the farm. "Hey! Let's circle the square a couple times," Delbert said.

"No can do, unless you'd like to risk running into my mom's warpath."

"Oh?"

"Long story, but trust me. We're better off not circling the square today. Maybe next time." He cranked the radio up just one more notch and gave the engine a little goose.

"So what can she do?" Delbert asked, patting the dashboard. During his senior year in high school he'd worked as a pit crew member on his buddy's stock car out at the raceway. Even though these days he drove a minivan (maybe especially because he drove a minivan), he still loved speed and the rumble. He thought the picture of him standing next to his Buick Wildcat with his shirt unbuttoned nearly down to his navel was the best picture ever taken of him and his hotrodmobile, as his friends called it. Recollections of back-road drag races awakened latent memories of headlights flashing through the darkness, squealing tires, giggling girls. . . .

Josh goosed the engine again, causing the truck to lunge ahead. "How should I know?" He glanced at his uncle and gave him a devilish grin.

"Because you're sixteen and this thing has a V-8 — not that I'm advocating anything illegal, mind you, but there is no law about how fast you can *get* to the speed limit!"

It was all Josh could do to keep from flooring it, his desire to do so lingering since he'd dropped Shelby off, thoughts of the Fire Pit still coursing through his brain. "Hang on!" he said, hesitating only a moment before mashing his foot on the gas pedal. He watched the speedometer race to sixty-one miles per hour, causing Delbert to let out a very unpastorly "Yeee-haw!" Josh let up on the gas and flipped on his blinker to turn onto the county road that led to the farm. Once they were past the ninety-degree bend in the gravel road, he yelled "HANG ON!" and pushed the pedal to the floor. The truck bed shimmied back and forth as

rocks pelted the undercarriage. He understood all the more now why Dorothy used
to love flooring The Tank on this strip of
road, and the experience was made all the
better by having his uncle, whom he so
much wanted to get to know better, riding
shotgun. He felt like a modern-day cowboy
— until he heard the siren behind him.

When Dorothy heard a knock at her door,
she'd discovered Katie standing there looking like she was ready to cry, which was saying something since Katie was about as stoic
as they come. "I couldn't talk to another
living soul about this besides Jessica, Dorothy, and she's got her hands more than full
right now. She doesn't need *my* sob story."
The two women sat at Dorothy's kitchen
table where Katie had been talking nearly
nonstop since she arrived.

When she'd let Katie in, she knew God
answered at least a portion of her prayer by
sending Katie to her house for shelter.
Dorothy's phone had been ringing off the
hook since early this morning, everyone
sharing their opinion about the big news,
wondering what Dorothy thought about it
and who she would vote for — although
most believed it would be Gladys since Dorothy was so tight with Katie. After each new

call, Dorothy shot up another of her Bazooka Prayers telling God to just DO SOMETHING about this situation before a civil war broke out in Partonville.

"I just *had* to get out of that building," Katie said, scurrying in and closing the door behind her after looking up and down the street, "and go where nobody could find me. I didn't even move my car. I snuck out the downstairs side door of the mall and zipped over here as quickly as I could, hoping nobody would see me. I don't know whether I'm more mad, frustrated or just . . . dumbfounded by this turn of events. I thought we had put these issues of mistrust behind us."

When Edward Showalter came to Katie's office to tell her he'd turned away no fewer than four people who'd come calling for her that afternoon, at first she just thanked him for doing a good job. Then he told her who they were. She understood why Herb Morgan and Gladys would come, and she in fact felt badly she hadn't given Edward Showalter instructions to allow them in. She'd have to call them tonight and apologize, which made her slightly curious as to why they hadn't already called her. (Actually, they were too busy calling each other, trying to figure if they had anything serious to worry about due to their alignment with Katie.) But Frieda Hornsby? Why would she want to see Katie? The clincher, however, was what Edward Showalter told her Sharon Teller said when he'd told *her* Katie wasn't accepting visitors. "I'd hate to have to report in the *Press* that Ms. Durbin couldn't be reached for *further* comment after she learned about the conflict surrounding her this morning." Katie stared at him in disbelief for a moment, then thought about marching herself straight to the *Press*'s office and giving Sharon a piece of her mind. Were they all *insane?* But that, she knew, would be a huge tactical, political and personal error. You don't antagonize the press. Instead, she decided to just escape until she could calm down and gather her thoughts. "If anyone asks where I went," she told Edward Showalter while she was gathering her green file box and handbag, "tell them you don't know, which will be the truth. And I'm turning my cell phone off," she said, doing exactly that. "I'll see you in the morning. Let everybody knock off at five tonight. We could *all* use a break." Edward Showalter's mouth was still hanging open when she walked briskly past him and flew down one stairwell after another — him leaning over the atrium rail watching her until she disappeared from his sight.

"Now, honey," Dorothy said, "just settle down, have another sip of water. Here, let me get you a fresh glass," she said, noticing Katie had nearly drained the first one.

"It just does *not* make sense! How did I get to be the villain by pouring my time and money into. . . ."

"*Enough,* Katie," Dorothy said sternly as she placed the fresh glass of water in front of her and sat back down. Katie was stunned and her face and stiffened posture showed it. "You have a right to be upset, honey," Dorothy said, lowering her voice and patting Katie's shoulder, "but sliding into a pity party never gets a body anywhere. I know that because I'm an expert at flinging myself down that slippery slide. Thank goodness God usually gets my attention before I crash land! And I'm sure nobody's thinking you're a *villain.* Goodness me!"

Katie gulped down another half glass of water, then grabbed a paper napkin out of Dorothy's napkin holder, dipped the edge of it in her glass, wrung the extra water back into her glass and patted her upper lip with the cool, damp wad. "I detest these hot flashes," she said when she finally spoke. "And you're right. Pity parties are unbecoming and unproductive. Thank you. I'm behaving like a child. One of those in my household at a time is almost one too many right now," she said, sitting back in her chair and dabbing under her eyes.

"Oh?"

Katie thought about launching into her morning, but truthfully, it would sound trite in light of the rest of her day and just fuel her ire. Besides, Josh was always so good about getting himself up. Why had she flown off the handle the one time he accidentally slept in anyway? She flashbacked to the state of their relationship when she and Josh moved to Partonville. Thankfully, there'd been mending and growth on both of their parts. But all her hours on this mall project — and working too many hours was mostly what had broken their relationship in Chicago — was causing her to fall back into old workaholic patterns, which led to a disconnect with her son and a shortened temper. She sighed, vowing she would make it up to him tonight.

"It was nothing, really. Or just one more thing, or. . . ." She sighed again, set the napkin on the table. "To be honest, I could use one of your prayers."

"You got it! And to be honest with you, I'm kinda frustrated with the Big Guy since I thought He already took care of this mini-mall mess, so I guess I'm ready to give Him a good what's-for anyway!" Now it was Dorothy's turn to sit back and sigh. After Katie finished digesting the fact that anyone would be bold enough to give *God* a lecture, both women closed their eyes.

"Well now, Lord, I guess Katie and I *both* need to take a deep breath here, don't we?" She stopped and inhaled, as did Katie, each woman slowly releasing her breath with intention. "There now, I can think straight and talk calmly. But just the same, You need to know *we don't get it!* We do *not* get why Katie here is trying so hard to make things right for people who are determined to make things hard on her. No Sir, we do not get it." A rather long silence passed, which Katie was actually glad for, finding herself silently parroting Dorothy's words.

"But then I guess the truth is we don't need to get it, do we? We just need to get You on our minds since You're the one who's really in charge here — even though *we do not get it!* Sorry. I just can't help myself! But God, You can help us, so get on it. Work Your mysterious ways in us so we can work Your will in this here town. Keep us clear thinking, especially Katie. Send her signs of hope and cheer to let her know that there are people who are *for* her. *For* her projects. Help those voices rise up and be heard. And while You're at it, keep the fine folks in this town from spewing unkind words around about each other like poison spitballs. But most of all, no matter who is mayor or what we're doing, help us keep our eyes on You. Amen."

11

After Carl Jimson and Colton Craig hung up, Colton decided to take a drive to Partonville to circle the square himself, see if Vitner's bid for mayor had indeed hit the streets, see if he could get a feel for just how strong a bid it might be, considering the guy's place of business had toilets in the front yard, which he'd forgotten about until Carl brought it up.

As he approached the outward edge of Hethrow, he drove along wondering exactly how many pieces of property Kathryn had sewn up throughout Partonville and its eastern outskirts. He'd never before underestimated the sheer guts, will and slickness of that woman, but this time he had. It was time to gather more information and strategize. If he played his cards with the wrong partner, he might end up . . . on the sidelines.

Not that long ago, he would have bet cold

hard cash that Partonville would be dug under by now. But then Development Diva arrived on the scene and blocked his bid to land contiguous Crooked Creek Farm, the gateway to his conquest. *Surely* she wasn't doing all of this just to get *even* with him. But rivaling that thought was one other: surely she hadn't lost her mind and actually *become* one of them! No, he could not fathom the thought that that sexy, kick-butt woman had morphed into a Pardon-Me-Viller with some sappy vision to play Robin Hood.

He decided to take the back roads into Partonville, especially the gravel road that passed by Crooked Creek Farm. Although he hadn't caught wind of any rezoning proposals regarding the subdivision of Kathryn's property (which he'd fully expected), in light of what he'd learned from Vitner, it was time to get a firsthand look himself. And what about Wetstra's twenty-acre land grant to the conservation district for the development of Crooked Creek Park? Was that underway yet? Kathryn had no doubt won the farm's sale out from under him by writing that sentimental little ditty into the deal. He didn't remember reading any more about it since the original reporting. Then again, he didn't often see that rag of a Partonville paper either. Maybe it was time to subscribe. He grabbed his mini-recorder out of his suit jacket pocket and left himself a message to give the conservation district a call. If the mall and the park received grand opening publicity at the same time, Partonville might draw more attention to itself than he cared to read about.

Then again, nothing wrong with using the press. In fact, there were two people he needed to hook up with: that cute little reporter Sharon Teller who'd once come to his office about a year ago to find out his "intentions" for Partonville, and Sam Vitner. Possibly in that order, possibly not. He wondered if he should also stop by Challie Carter's farm, see if he could catch him at home, see if everything Vitner told him was true about Challie holding out. After all, Carter owned, leased and farmed more land than anyone else in the area.

When he passed by Crooked Creek, where he noticed no physical signs of any changes, the sight of the fields birthed a delicious thought. He hoped Carter, whom his scouts had approached numerous times but who loudly dismissed them, was the one who leased and therefore farmed Kathryn's land. Just one more thing to find out.

■ ■ ■ ■

"I noticed you trimmed Ms. Durbin's hair again," Cora said to Maggie while Maggie readjusted Cora's plastic drape, both of them knowing darn well that Katie had left for her spa day in Chicago with longer hair than that with which she returned. "It looks nice." Cora'd been relentlessly working to present "due cause" to anyone she might be able to persuade to cast their vote for Sam.

"No. I've only cut her hair one time, and that was right before Thanksgiving. And a splendid makeover it was, if I might say so myself." It hadn't escaped Maggie's attention that although Katie had kept the new short hairstyle she'd given her, it wasn't La Feminique Hair Salon & Day Spa that got the business for those trims. Yes, it rankled Maggie some, but she wasn't about to let Cora know that. "After all, just like you always come to me, I'm glad Katie stays loyal to her stylist, since she has that monthly chance."

Maggie slid her fingers up the short length of Cora's hair and began snipping, reaching for another section and repeating the process around the right side of Cora's crown.

"That's an awfully generous attitude to

have, especially since you're working so hard to make a living."

"Not generous. Just realistic. Why, look how many years I've been traveling to Yorkville to have Marjorie trim *my* hair! I can't imagine trying to train someone else how to best handle my natural curl. You know, not everybody knows how to deal with curly hair." Cora raised her eyebrows. She'd known Maggie Malone since their school days when Maggie's hair was as straight as a board, which it had been most of her life. She'd obviously received a perm last week, which wasn't her first cycle of curls. "Keep your eyebrows down, Cora," Maggie said, grabbing her comb to slick Cora's bangs straight down her forehead. "I'd hate to have you end up with bangs a half-inch long because that's where I thought your eyebrows *belonged.*" What she really wanted to say was, "And please keep your mouth shut too." But then that wouldn't be very professional or kind. Then again, it wasn't very kind of Cora to intentionally goad her over Katie's hair, which was something she'd been trying to forget. Maggie literally bit her tongue while she finished Cora's bangs and spun her around to face the mirror again. Cora could just be *impossible!*

"I'm just saying that for someone who says she's trying to keep a town alive by getting people to come here and spend their money, she's willing to drive . . . how many hundreds of miles elsewhere to spend her own? And she never gets gas from George." Their eyes locked in the mirror. Maggie knew Cora was trying to read her reaction, so she spun her chair back around until she faced the center of the room, Maggie moving herself behind the chair. She hated that Cora did have a point here, especially since she'd recently overheard George complaining that Katie drove right by his filling station when she went to get gasoline. And he was the only station in town.

"Maybe," Maggie said, a note of sternness in her voice (snip-snip went her scissors), "if George Gustafson would turn loose a little of that money he socks away — and I'll tell you, pretty soon we aren't going to be able to afford to drive our own cars if he keeps raising his gasoline prices — and upgrade his pumps to accept credit cards, like the ones I used last time *I* went to Chicago for the hair show, he'd give her a convenient reason to stop in!" (Snip-snip-snip.) "People from the city aren't used to some of our backward ways, and why should they have to be?" Maggie was always one for progress, which is why she closed her shop every couple of years, painted it with new colors, renamed it and had a grand re-opening with dollar-off coupons in *The Partonville Press*. "If this town wants to up-grade," (snip-snip-snip-snip), "that needs to include George Gustafson! Why do you think I turned my shop into a day spa the last time I remodeled?"

Cora reached up and grabbed Maggie's hand to stop the cutting for a moment, which seemed to become more frenzied and erratic the faster Maggie spoke. "Turn me around, Maggie Malone," she ordered, which Maggie did. Cora wanted to look her straight in the eyes. "And what is it again that makes this place," she hesitated, cast-ing her eyes around at the small two-chair establishment with only two hair dryers, a rack of aromatherapy products, whatever *they* were, and a playpen for her great-grandchildren in the corner, "a day spa?"

Maggie placed her hands on her hips and cocked them. "I've said it before and I'll say it again. *I* make this a day spa, Cora. *Spas* offer more than *haircuts,* you know." She briskly leaned in so close to Cora's face that Cora could feel her breath on her cheeks, making Cora feel pinned in her chair as she reared her neck back. Maggie's eyes slowly scanned from Cora's hairline to her chin. "In fact, if you'd like to make an appointment for a moustache waxing," she said, stopping to run the end of her pinky finger across Cora's upper lip, "I'd be glad to oblige you in my *day spa*."

"I have no such *thing!*" Cora spurted in disgust. "And I also have no reason," she said, launching out of her chair and nearly crash landing, forgetting Maggie had pumped her up, "to keep coming to a beauty shop that pretends to be a spa just to be insulted!" She yanked at the Velcro neckband until it released, wadded the drape into a ball and tossed it onto her vacated chair. "And on second thought, perhaps I understand why Ms. Durbin travels all the way to Chicago for her services!" Without offering to pay Maggie a cent, she stormed out and slammed the door behind her, leaving Maggie's chimes wildly jangling.

Maggie picked up the drape, gave it a shake, wadded it back up and tossed it in her clothes hamper as though shooting a basket. She sat down and swiveled her chair toward the mirror, taking stock of her face to see if it looked guilty. It wasn't good business to tick off a regular, no matter how many times said regular customer crossed the boundaries of good behavior. But nope, not a trace of guilt. In fact, her face appeared rather satisfied.

Just after the door chimes finally settled down, they began to tinkle again. It was May Belle. "Did Cora get a call her house was on fire?" May Belle asked as she shucked off her worn trench coat and hung it on the bentwood coat rack.

"No. Why do you ask?" Maggie queried, although she could guess.

"She was all but running down the sidewalk with wet hair that only looked half cut."

"Really?" Maggie asked, but not really, studying her smug smile in the mirror, then grabbing her eyeliner and carefully adding a tad more under her bottom row of lashes. She stood up and motioned for May Belle, who always arrived early, to take a seat. Although other customers started at the shampoo bowl, Maggie always spent a few minutes brushing May Belle's hair, the gift of touch pure grace to a woman who no longer had a man in her life to wrap his arms around her, something Maggie was thankful for each time Ben reached for her. "Well, whatever it was," she said, snapping out a fresh folded drape and securing it around May Belle's neck, "it gives me a chance to spend a little more time with you today, dear." Although May Belle was grateful for the extra attention, she couldn't help but wonder what on earth. . . . It was obvious, however, that Maggie wasn't going to talk about it.

Maggie plucked May Belle's long black hairpins from her hair and lined them up on the counter. She picked up a brush, but then set it down and instructed May Belle to sit tight for a moment. She walked to her aromatherapy display and ran her fingers down the new line of air-freshening products until she spotted the sage. She picked it up, held it at arm's length and gave it a few spritzes as she turned in a slow circle. "There, that should do it," she said aloud, although she didn't say what it was she was trying to do and May Belle didn't ask — nor had she noticed any offensive odors when she'd arrived.

Maggie rhythmically began brushing May Belle's hair, allowing the brush to glide to the very ends of her long silver strands before lifting it to her crown again. After a few cycles, she stopped for the briefest of moments, inhaled a deep breath of sage and slowly exhaled through her mouth. "There now. That's officially *better*," she said, returning to the careful, beautifying art of brushing. In a voice as serene as a gliding swan, she added, "The ancients were right. Sage purifies, no doubt about it."

12

"May I see your driver's license, Josh?" Sergeant McKenzie asked in a stern voice. Mac, as he was known around town, knew everyone by name. It was his business. Josh undid his seat belt, which he was happy he'd been wearing, leaned forward and retrieved his wallet from his back pocket. He rifled through it until he found his driver's license and passed it through his open window. Although when he'd first been pulled over his instinct was to get out of the car, Mac officially ordered him to remain in his vehicle, causing Josh's heart to race all the faster, if that was humanly possible. Mac looked the driver's license over, then asked to see his insurance card and registration. Josh fanned through his wallet again until he found the insurance card, his hands shaking so badly he dropped his wallet twice into his lap before accomplishing the simple task. His mom made him put his registration card in the glove compartment the day it arrived. "Excuse me, Uncle Delbert," he said as he leaned across the seat to pop open the glove compartment in front of his uncle's knees.

"Uncle Delbert?" Mac leaned down to look across the driver's seat. Although he'd noticed the latched seat belt on the passenger's side (ready to ticket said offender should it not be fastened), he hadn't taken note of the passenger, figuring it was one of Josh's buddies. "Pastor Delbert?" Mac looked stunned.

Pastor Delbert Carol Jr.'s face turned crimson. It was one thing to be a bad influence as an uncle. But the *pastor!* "Hi, Mac . . . Sergeant McKenzie. This is not only embarrassing, but you know, this whole incident is really *my* fault. I . . ."

"No disrespect, Pastor," Mac interrupted in an officially firm voice, "but you're not the one behind the wheel." Delbert hushed, sitting back like a scolded child.

"You got that registration there, son?" Josh had momentarily quit thrashing through the glove compartment in hopes his uncle could pull some kind of holy rank with either Sergeant McKenzie or God — or both — to get him out of this mess. No such luck.

"Here you go, sir," Josh said after he

retrieved the document.

Mac went back to his patrol car and stayed there for an excruciating amount of time. "What's he doing back there?" Josh asked his uncle.

"Calling the county jail to make sure they've got a cell open."

"WHAT?" Josh's voice went up an octave and the blood drained from his face.

"Josh, I'm just kidding, but it wasn't funny. Sometimes I say dumb things when I'm nervous. He's probably just checking your paperwork to make sure it's in order, even though he knows it's not a stolen vehicle and you're not on the run." Josh hung on his uncle's every word when he wasn't freaking out over what was sure to be the utter wrath of his mom. How could her half-brother (or half of a brother, as Josh referred to him) have such a good sense of humor about something like this when his mom would likely go berserk shortly before selling his truck and grounding him for life.

"Listen, Josh, I'm so sorry about this. I feel like it's my fault for egging you on. After all, I'm the adult here."

"Not to mention the *pastor*," Josh said, the hint of a smile approaching his lips . . . until Sergeant McKenzie shoved his license and registration in front of him, causing him to jolt back to attention.

"Sorry. Thought you heard me coming."

"No, sir. I didn't." Josh started to put the documents away but then said, "Here, Uncle Delbert, would you please hold these for me until we're through?"

"Sure." It was the least he could do.

"Son," Mac said, tipping his hat back with his index finger, "I started following you today when you revved 'er up back there on the highway. I couldn't have pulled you over for that, since you only got to about five-miles-per-hour over the limit. You know, I was hoping you would prove me wrong, but this feeling I got in my gut — call it natural-born police instincts, if you will — usually serves me well, and something told me you were heading for trouble, so I followed you. Still, I kept hoping that maybe since you'd made it this long without getting into trouble with Challie Carter's big old V-8, you might be more sensible than most sixteen-year-olds. But sooner or later, I guess temptation wins out." Josh looked at his hands, his embarrassment not ebbing. "When I saw that truck bed shimmying this way and that, I had no choice but to put a halt to what will officially be termed reckless driving." Yes, this was bad and getting worse by the moment, Josh thought.

But putting his ticket, grounding and mother aside, if there was anyone he hated to have disappointed, it was his uncle. Ever since Mom and Uncle Delbert found out less than a year ago that they were related, he longed to get to know the man — whom he even somewhat resembled — better. Because Josh's dad wasn't around, and when Josh *did* visit him his dad spent more time talking about his daily kids (as Josh referred to his dad's children from his second marriage) than his firstborn child, Josh longed for a relationship with a strong male. He especially hoped to make his uncle feel proud to call him "my nephew." And now . . . *What's wrong with me! I thought after that dumb Christmas stunt I'd be smarter!* During his first solo trip to Chicago after receiving his driver's license, he'd gotten a little careless and caught himself weaving lanes without even checking side- or rear-view mirrors. He was just lucky he didn't sideswipe anyone. *If only I'd have checked my mirrors today!*

"Are you listening to me, boy?" Sergeant McKenzie asked as he reached for his citation pad.

"Yes, sir," he said, although his mind had wandered, causing him to chew on his lip just to stay focused. When he let up on it, he found himself spewing a speedball of words. "To be honest, sir, I'm guilty. As much as my Uncle Delbert said it's his fault, you are exactly right: I am behind the wheel."

Sergeant McKenzie's jaw dropped. Not many people — young or old — owned up to their antics behind the wheel. He cleared his throat, looked at the citation pad and cleared his throat again. "Here's what I'm gonna do. I'm gonna let you off this time, this . . . *one* . . . *time.* But consider yourself forewarned: I'll be watching you extra careful, young man. Understood?"

"Yes, sir," Josh said, reaching his hand out the window to shake Mac's. "And thank you, sir. I promise you I will not disappoint you."

"It's not about disappointing me, son, it's about staying safe. Do you have any idea how many one-car accidents — rollovers — we have on these gravel roads due to reckless driving? Even the most experienced gravel riders occasionally get themselves in trouble. Just ask your friend Dorothy Wetstra about *that* some time!" Delbert swallowed down a smile. He'd known about Dorothy's well-deserved reputation for wild driving since he was a boy. She'd been towed out of a ditch on more than one oc-

169

casion. He, for one, was not unhappy when The Tank went to scrap metal heaven.

Sergeant McKenzie disappeared back into his squad car and drove on down the road. Josh looked at his uncle with pleading eyes. Okay, so he didn't get a ticket. Maybe Uncle Delbert had prayed them out of it. Now the only question that remained was, will he be able to save me from the wrath of my mom — by keeping quiet?

Nellie Ruth was doubly excited when she opened the door. She was grinning and clapping and gave Edward Showalter such a short peck on the lips that he almost missed it, but she didn't want him to miss what was waiting behind her. Morning and Midnight had followed her to the door and seated themselves right on her heels. She stepped aside and said, "Look who's come to greet you!"

"Well I'll be darned if they haven't grown another inch!" Edward Showalter said as he squatted down to pet the kittens. Midnight, the black female with startling green eyes, bolted away and disappeared down the hallway, but Morning, a somewhat larger and completely white male, arched his back as he slipped toward Edward Showalter's outreached hand. "For someone who never

had a pet before, I'd say you're a natural mother, Nellie Ruth."

Nellie Ruth's eyes welled with tears. He couldn't have said anything more reassuring. Less than ten weeks ago Edward Showalter had presented the kitties to her as a surprise gift, along with everything they'd need to get along for the first month. Although they'd gotten off to a rocky start by getting into all kinds of trouble and disrupting Nellie Ruth's perpetual order, Nellie Ruth had finally relaxed a little after figuring out how to avoid most of the mishaps. She couldn't imagine her life without them. "They are the best kitties," she all but purred. "And don't take Midnight's disappearing act personally. She often does that with me, too, which is why I was so pleased she came to greet you at the door. For two kitties from the same litter, they sure do have different personalities."

"Just like humans, I reckon. And come to think about it, Midnight's the perfect name for a cat who disappears."

Nellie Ruth squatted down next to her beau. They took turns stroking Morning's back as he wove a figure-eight around their ankles. "You must be bone tired," she said, turning sympathetic eyes his way.

He reached for her hand and kissed her

fingertips. "I'm feeling better now that I finally have a chance to spend a little more time with you. What a surprise to get off early — or, well, on time — for a change! And something smells awful good. I hope you didn't go to any trouble, though, since I did call at the last minute with that dinner invite."

"I was going to cook for myself anyway, which is never much fun, and it just seemed like we'd have more quiet time to visit if we didn't have to drive somewhere. I put three frozen chicken breasts in the microwave to thaw instead of one, breaded them with a simple mixture of cracker crumbs and parmesan cheese and I'm sautéing them in butter. I'm browning some mushrooms and onions on the side, though, so I bet the onions are what you're smelling."

"Yup. I reckon it's the onions, although heated parmesan might be it. Couldn't say. All I know is I'm good and hungry and happy for the company, and not in that order." He winked at her, which openly delighted her heart. "You could open me a can of cat food and brown it and serve it, Nellie Ruth, and I'd probably shovel it right down since you made it."

She crinkled her nose. "Obviously you haven't smelled cat food for awhile!" She

stood and told ES to make himself comfortable while she finished up dinner. He followed her right into the kitchen. Their time was so limited he didn't dare miss a minute of it. Cats were nice, but it was Nellie Ruth he came to see. He watched — and admired — her every move while she stirred the onions and mushrooms, turned the chicken, made some instant rice and set the table. He stared so intently she became self-conscious and began to feel everything she did was clunky.

"Is my shameless admiration making you nervous?" he asked, after noticing she rearranged the forks a few times until they were perfectly parallel with the knives on the other side of their plates. She was a perfectionist alright, he thought.

"No. Well, yes. Well, not really. It's lovely to be admired," she said, her cheeks reddening. "It's just that after you live alone most of your life, you're not used to thinking about how you do things until somebody's watching you do them."

"I hear ya. When Katie Durbin stares at me, I can barely hammer a nail straight without bending it. Might have single-pounded a hundred other nails straight to the board before it, but when the boss lady's looking over my shoulder, it seems I either whack my own thumb or bend the nail."

"Are you still up on that scaffolding?"

"Not for now. In fact, we're probably done with that until we have to paint. We're already putting drywall in some of the stores!"

"Have you heard her mention a grand-opening date yet?"

"Your guess is as good as mine. Even when our work is done, there'll still be lots of movin' in for folks to do. I'm guessing I'll be pretty busy during that time, too, helping proprietors get their electrical and phone lines and computer wiring where and how they want it. We're installing more than plenty of jacks and everything, but I'm sure we'll have to move a few things around to accommodate their setups. One good thing about that building is the shipping dock the Taningers had put in for their furniture business. Between that and the elevators, the actual moving in of stuff should go okay. But to be honest, I think that candy man on the lower level is going to take some doing. He wants to cook fudge in one of those big copper pots and we're already considering special venting. You ever see them pour that hot fudge out onto those marble slabs?"

"FUDGE! Yummy. And the answer to your question is Yes, I did see one of those big pots on my one and only vacation to the Wisconsin Dells. My one and only vacation away from home, period."

"No. Please tell me you are not saying you've only had one vacation in your entire life!"

"I *am* telling you that. But don't feel bad. I've enjoyed my time off right here in Partonville. It's nice just to have the freedom to sleep in, stay up late and watch television if I want, get some deep house cleaning done . . . practice my music and do some crafting. . . ."

"Who'd you go to the Dells with, if I might ask a personal question?"

"My parents. When I was about eight, I'd say. I still remember those Duck Boats! And a rock that looked like a piano or something, and the fudge. Mmmmm." She filled their plates and set them on the table. "Would you give the blessing, please?"

"I'd be delighted," he said, first spreading his napkin on his lap, lowering his head toward his plate and inhaling the fineness of Nellie Ruth's labors. After he finished the blessing, he asked her how long they stayed at the Dells and if she remembered if she got her a pair of beaded moccasins for a souvenir. She told him no, no moccasins, but she remembered a tiny coin purse with

175

beads on it. She said they were there just one night, then her face clouded over and she stopped talking. It wasn't the first time he noticed that when she talked about her family she often stopped midstream. There was something she wasn't telling him, but he wasn't going to press. When the time was right, she'd open up. He hoped.

Nellie Ruth's father had violated her in unspeakable ways and memories of her family's night in a motel room momentarily shut her down. Thanks to the grace of God, Edward Showalter was the first man in her life to show her what being treated like a lady felt like. She hoped this bout of flashback would not upset her for the evening. *Lord, do not let this get a hold of me!* After dinner, Nellie Ruth washed the dishes and ES dried. Silently working side by side was comforting to her as she reminded herself that ES had nothing to do with the likes of her dad.

Midnight decided to show her face in the kitchen for a little while, which further comforted Nellie Ruth, even though the kitty didn't move in too close. When the dishes were done, Nellie Ruth and ES sat next to each other on the couch and held hands while they watched a little mindless TV. *Thank you, Lord. This is good and right.*

It wasn't long before Edward Showalter started yawning. "I'm sorry, Nellie Ruth," he said between yawns. "Please don't take this as any indication of my lack of joy in your company. We've just been putting in a lot of hours, and after such a fine meal," he said, patting his belly, "I feel like a lazy lugnut."

"Actually, I need to get busy with those mini-mall entries anyway. I picked them up today but haven't even had a chance to open the envelope. We're having our meeting this Saturday morning to select the winner!"

"Let's see, the day after tomorrow is Saturday, isn't it? When you work six days a week, it's easy to get your days mixed up. Can I help you with those entries?"

"NO! Aside from the judging committee, it's top secret, remember?"

"Can you just tell me if *my* entry is in the running?"

"You entered?"

"You betcha! Who wouldn't want to win a hundred-buck shopping spree, especially when they have the most beautiful woman in Partonville to share it with!"

Share. He said he'd share it with her. That was so romantic and generous that she leaned in and gave him a proper kiss, which he followed right up with another — and then another yawn. "Well now you *know* I'm tired," he said, shaking his head, causing them both to giggle like little kids.

"About your entry, I won't even know if you're in the top five. We're judging this round without names."

"Fair and square, huh?"

"Fair and square. And now, you have to go home and go to bed and I have to get busy. But wait! I can't *believe* we haven't even talked about the upcoming election! All of Your Store was buzzing as soon as word spread. From what I heard, more people than you might expect are upset about the mall. Is that why Katie let everybody off early today?"

"Maybe we haven't talked about it because we're *already* tired of the politics! That's definitely another reason I can barely stay awake, I'll tell you. She had me lock the door to anything but construction deliveries after Sharon Teller showed up bright and early this morning. I had to turn a bunch of people away, and they were none too happy about it."

Morning appeared cautiously and crawled up on Nellie Ruth's lap, and they listened to his purr. "Do you mind if I ask *you* something personal now, ES?"

"Fire!"

"Do you like working for Katie? I mean, is she good to you, what with making you work so many hours?"

"She's always paid me handsomely for my labors, even back when I worked on her Aunt Tess's house before Dorothy moved in."

Nellie Ruth stroked Morning a few more times. "But aside from the money, is she *good* to you? Does she treat you well?"

"Why do you even ask? You know Katie Durbin. You're both Hookers!"

"Which reminds me again that it's my turn to host bunco this month and I can't wait for the ladies to see my new Splendid Rose paint and meet the twins," as she'd taken to calling her meowing babies.

Edward Showalter stood, stretched, kissed Nellie Ruth one more time and asked for his coat. "You've got entries to read and Kornflake's waiting for his dinner."

"Tell him his cousins said hello, okay?"

"I'll do that."

While Nellie Ruth waved at him from her upstairs window as he pulled out in his camouflage van (or cammy-van, as ES liked to call it), it hit her that he'd never answered her question. *Was* Katie good to him? She certainly hoped so.

13

Carl Jimson had always been a night owl, so the fact that he was up alone at 11:30 p.m. wasn't unusual. Like clockwork, right after the ten o'clock news his wife kissed him goodnight and told him she loved him. As always, he switched the television in their spacious family room to the History Channel, picked up a biography from the top of his stack of books near his favorite lounge chair and propped up his feet on the matching ottoman. What *was* unusual, however, was that at 11:15 he'd closed the book and turned off the television. He sat in the dark staring into space, only the glow of their built-in, fifty-gallon aquarium lighting the room. Aside from the gentle bubbling of the aquarium's filtering system, the house was silent. But his mind wasn't.

Quietly, so as not to awaken his wife, he placed the book back on its stack, scooted the ottoman out of his way, stood, stretched and walked to the large glass sliding door, which he unlocked, opened and passed through onto the stone patio. He stood in the dark a few minutes allowing his eyes to adjust before flipping the override switch on the garden walkway lights, which the timer had automatically turned off at 11.

When he'd designed this home, he made sure it not only possessed every bell and whistle that tickled their fancy, but that it was equipped for all their aging needs. They found as they passed fifty-five that things like no stairs and brighter lighting became the priorities rather than the sweeping open staircases, lower-level recreation rooms and subtle ambient lighting in their two previous homes, each of which he'd designed for their growing family's needs. But now the kids were gone, the reading glasses a bit thicker and their knees occasionally let them know they were no longer thirty. The night he and Glenda moved into this home, complete with grab bars in the tubs and showers and wider doorways should the need for a wheelchair ever arise, they'd opened a bottle of fine champagne and toasted to the last house they would likely ever own.

The sprawling ranch was situated on the private and premium two-acre location at the very rear of their gated community, their lush backyard rimming a county arboretum. The Jimsons' groundskeeper kept everything immaculately trimmed and tidy. The only thing more beautiful than their estate, he'd once told Glenda, were the pastures on his childhood farm.

He decided to stroll the flagstone walkway through the gardens, the full moon casting a moody glow throughout. As he walked the lighted path, even though he was wearing an undershirt, turtleneck sweater and a fleece pullover, he wished he'd thought to grab a jacket, the night air undoubtedly colder here than it was in Partonville this time of year, which although not *that* far south had a surprisingly different climate.

Partonville. There it was, he mused, the reason for his broken evening ritual, his jitterbug brain. This was the first time since his afternoon conversation with Colton he'd had a chance to meditate on why he was feeling so . . . what? Unsettled? Used? And why did he care that much about Colton's motives or agenda anyway? Yes, he, the architect, had accepted a long-distance job. He did it well, he got paid handsomely and it was almost over, aside from a little consulting and personal encouragement he'd likely render by phone to that quirky

Edward Showalter fellow. No need to return to the little circle-the-square town. And yet. . . .

Partonville was a small town not unlike the one he'd grown up in, not unlike many other small towns fighting to exist, some making it, some not. Nothing especially unique about it. And Colton had never been an intimate friend. Sure, they'd belonged to the same country club in Chicago when they were both upstarts trying to stake their claims in the business world. And yes, they'd sipped a few martinis in their day, shared a few leads, stayed in minimal contact. He'd always accepted Colton for what he was: a gifted, determined, shrewd and occasionally ruthless tycoon. But as far as he knew, Colton never swerved into the illegal; he was simply good at taking advantage of every opportunity. Carl admired the man's tenacity and success at building Hethrow into a flourishing city. He found him fascinating, which is why they'd stayed in touch. So, why was he *still* so disturbed about their phone conversation?

He sat down on the cement bench near his favorite of their three ponds. He'd worked with a landscape architect to achieve just the right soothing ambiance in and around this particular pond, the closest to the house. He was glad they'd settled on the extra lighting, which made the pond appear like a reflecting pool, especially with the full moon illuminating the surface.

He recalled one night about a year after they'd moved into this home when he and his wife sat on this very bench. An overpowering sense of satisfaction swept over him and he'd never forget sharing it with Glenda. After sitting side-by-side in silence for a long spell, Carl said, "We have everything we could ever want, don't we, honey." It was an affirmation rather than a question, and they both agreed it was so. "In the day of prosperity, be happy," she said, a contented wistfulness in her voice. "That's what the Good Book tells us in Ecclesiastes. I just read that this morning." When they'd retired that evening, they'd made wonderful and sweet love to celebrate all their happiness. So why *this* evening did he feel something was lacking when he knew very well it was not?

"You ever go through this, Dad?" he asked, looking up toward the heavens. Carl's father had been gone six years now. At fifty-nine, Carl still talked to his father whenever he especially missed him or was confused about something. Tonight he was both. Thoughts of the dairy farm on which he was raised, now a subdivision, sprang into his mind during his conversation with Colton this afternoon and simply would not rest. Although he hadn't been to Partonville for a few weeks, his recent enthusiastic phone call from Kathryn Durbin telling him how glad she was she'd followed his recommendations for the lower-level mall design still satisfied him. She wasn't one to gush, but she was *so* pleased with the marriage of his vision and the chocolate shop. Yes, his architecturally splendid buildings were a feather in his cap, but it was always the little things that made him feel the proudest, the most satisfied. To know he'd helped one woman striving to make a difference in a small farming town was comforting.

Then there was Colton.

Well, maybe he *had* only witnessed one side of the Development Diva. Could it be true she was only investing in order to further the appeal of a town she was preparing to sell out for the financial kill? A town the Craig brothers wanted to destroy for the Next Big Thing too?

"What do you think, Dad? My natural curiosity is killing me," he said with a chuckle. "Do you think I should poke around a little or just keep my nose out of it?"

Carl looked through the oak branches above him and thought of the giant treehouse his dad helped him build when he was only seven. They'd worked on the plans for a week, an exercise that ultimately cemented Carl's unyielding desire to build and build and build, which led him straight to his career as an architect. Carl loved building as much as his dad loved the open spaces. "Does it grieve you, Dad, to look down here and see all the subdivisions where the calves used to roam, or does watching the young families filling those houses give you satisfaction?" Carl imagined his dad would say both. He'd always been good at trying to walk in that other guy's shoes, at least for two miles since one mile didn't always give you enough perspective, he'd say. "I guess progress is ultimately going to have its way whether people are ready or not. But is the demise of our farmlands and the loss of knowing our neighbors really progress? Or might it be our ultimate undoing?"

He looked up to the man in the moon his father often pointed out to him when he was a child. He seemed to be smiling extra wide tonight. "Yes, it is rather funny that a guy who makes his living designing new buildings suddenly questions others' integ-

186

rity on the topic of progress."

Integrity. Bingo! It was as if he'd heard the familiar lilt of his father's voice utter those words straight into his heart. Even though he was shivering, he smiled and whispered, "Thanks, Dad. And you too," he said to the man in the moon. He closed his eyes and offered up prayers of thanksgiving to the God who gifted him with both of those wonderful faces.

Finally the combination of cold, damp night air and the cement bench chilled him to the bone. It was dumb to be out here without a jacket. Glenda would have his hide if she saw him. He hustled back to the house, turned off the exterior lights, grabbed the throw from the back of his wife's chair and sat in the dark another hour before retiring.

Glenda finally dozed off. She'd been standing at their bedroom window from the time she heard the patio door slide open until her husband was safely back inside. Since the trees were still bare, the underbrush scant and the moon full, she could make out his familiar form as he sat by the pond. Whatever was on his mind — had been on his mind all evening — she prayed God would handle it.

Back in Partonville, a sleeping Dorothy Jean Wetstra had no idea how God had used the man in the moon this evening to move hearts clear in Winnetka. God had all but made that moon wink in response to His daughter's earlier prayer to let Katie Mabel. Carol Durbin know that there are people who were *for* her. *For* her projects. "Help those voices rise up and be heard," she'd prayed while she and Katie sat at her kitchen table.

Jacob looked at the numbers on his night-glow clock. 3 a.m. *What am I doing awake? I'm here, tired, in my own comfortable bed after a productive day at the office. Well, mostly productive,* he thought. He'd spent a good portion of his time in his office fielding questions about the transition, his new clients, his housing situation — or lack thereof, which caused a bit of ribbing regarding living with his mother — and inquiries about her health, which most believed had caused this surprising change in his life. Try as he might to assure them his mother was fine, well, as fine as an eighty-eight-year-old could be, he could see in their faces they didn't really believe him. But that was okay. He accepted and honored their concerns for him. What other choice did he have?

When he'd turned off his office lights late this evening, he realized it was going to be easier than he thought to say good-bye to most of his clients and the years of hectic court schedules. Although most of his longer-standing corporate clients said they would miss him, he knew it wouldn't be long — if any time at all — before he was out of their minds. To be honest, they were more concerned about their legal issues and needing assurances that Brenda Stewart, his law partner who'd bought him out, and the new attorney she was bringing into the firm were apprised of all their legal matters, both the pending and the possible. There were those few clients, however, who felt more like friends to Jacob, including one whose wife suffered with Alzheimer's. During the course of safeguarding legal things surrounding her illness, the grieving husband had shared many intimate stories with Jacob, things he said his priest didn't even know. That was one of the things Jacob had learned about the law over the years: secrets. Secrets that needed to be legally safeguarded in order to protect the innocent, and sometimes the guilty.

The reality of how much Jacob would miss that same client, however, shored up his reasons for looking forward to doing business with Partonville residents. To give peace of mind to someone — to look out for the well-being of the underdog and underprivileged, for a change — felt like going back to the root of why he got into this profession to begin with.

He sighed and laced his fingers behind his head. He'd have his secretary send his favorite clients his mom's address, just in case they . . . well, just in case. One day Alzheimer's would claim that wife, although probably not until after a few more torturous years, and Jacob wanted to know about it. How could he not?

He turned on his side, banging and flipping his pillow to fluff it and collect a fresh coolness. One thing he wouldn't enjoy was Partonville's hotter, more humid summers. Even now his mom kept her house warmer than he liked, but he hadn't complained. After all, he was the guest, no matter how much she said no son of hers was a guest. He also hoped it wouldn't be long before he'd find his own place to live.

But he wasn't gone yet. Rita and Randy had invited him for dinner this Saturday night, his last weekend in Philadelphia. Randy, who was never any good at deception, had a funny look on his face when he told him not to come early or to be late. Jacob said he hoped they weren't planning a surprise going-away party or anything. "Nope, no surprise," Randy said, looking somewhat sheepish. "You know about it now." Jacob sighed again just thinking about it. He wasn't one for parties, but then it would give him a chance to loosen up a little, to "feel" the move in a festive way.

He rolled over and thumped the pillow again. Since it was after midnight when he'd slid into bed, he'd forgotten to close his light-blocking shades. The full moon seemed to be pouring its brightness all over his face. It reminded him of the night from his youth when he, Vinnie and Caroline Ann, his sister who died at thirty-nine, begged their parents to let them sleep down by the creek.

"What will you do if you wake up in the night and you're afraid?" his mom asked.

"Now, don't put that notion in their heads, Dorothy," his dad said. "We've raised us three brave children, right?" They stood in a line, urgently nodding their heads. Whatever assurance it might take to keep their mom from vetoing the idea, they were ready. "Besides, look at that full moon," he said, pointing to the bright ball of beauty. "It's bright enough tonight that it's almost like they'll be out there in the daylight." First he winked at his wife, then at each of them.

Dorothy smacked her lips and said, "Four — make that five," she said, looking toward the moon, "against one. I don't stand a chance keeping you tucked in your beds tonight, do I?" Heads nodded wildly. "Okay then, first let's go in and gather up everything you'll need. Dad, you go out to the barn and grab Wagon" — the well-worn Radio Flyer was never referred to by anything other than its official given name — "and one of your tarps and we'll all meet out by the silo."

It was just like his dad promised. The moon was bright enough to light their paths without a single flashlight. He lay in bed now barely breathing as he recalled the sound of Wagon's squeaky wheels chugging down the path behind them, he, the oldest, leading the way. Their dad wanted to oil those wheels before they set off, but they were too anxious to get going. "I'll oil them when we get back in the morning," Jacob said, knowing his dad would be proud of the way he stepped up to the plate to handle a chore.

"NOW YOU BOYS TAKE CARE OF YOUR SISTER!" Dorothy hollered after them when they were almost out of sight.

"WE WILL!" the brothers shouted over their shoulders in unison.

They set up camp right where they told their folks they would: near the fire pit, which wasn't far from the bend in the creek where the swimming hole lurked in the darkness. Their camp consisted of a tarp on the ground, three bedrolls made up of one blanket and sheet and a pillow, each bundle held together by a piece of twine, one brown paper bag stuffed with peanut butter and jelly sandwiches wrapped in waxed paper and a marshmallow each. They'd tried to talk their parents into letting them start a fire to roast the marshmallows, but that's when their dad drew the line. "Maybe in a couple years," he told them.

After they had everything in place and finished off their sandwiches, Jacob suggested they take a walk in the woods to go look for ghosts. Caroline Ann's wide eyes immediately let him know that was a dumb suggestion. Maybe, he thought, he and Vinnie should have left her home tonight so they could scare the pee-waden, as their Grandma Jane used to call it, out of each other. But the thought didn't last long after she grabbed his hand, pulled him toward her bedroll and asked him to tuck her in. She'd been the family's surprise child, not coming along until six years after Vinnie. She was sweet, stubborn, and as loved, beloved and protected by her brothers as she could be. *If only we could have protected her from breast cancer,* Jacob thought now, his eyes welling. But then he smiled remembering how she pointed to the sky and asked him to show her where the big dipper was again.

"The big dipper," he told her, holding her pudgy pointer finger in his hand and aiming it nearly straight up, "looks like it's pouring right on us tonight, Sis, see it?" She giggled, imagining water from the sky splashing onto them while they slept.

Jacob remembered how bright the stars were on the farm, which was far away from any city lights, and how many layers of them there seemed to be that night, how much laughing they did before they decided within ten minutes of getting under their covers that they needed to go back up to the house for more sandwiches and how they might as well pack things up in Wagon for the trip. Then how once they got inside they decided how much better it felt than out there with all the bugs — aside from the lightning bugs, which they'd spent ten minutes chasing before eating their sand-wiches and crawling into their bedrolls. Yes, once they were back in the kitchen, that was that for that campout, although there would be plenty more in the future, the three of them enjoying nights by the creek and the campfire until Jacob went off to college.

Jacob stared at the moon now, which seemed to be streaming vivid memories his way. He recalled his mom walking in the kitchen shortly after they'd arrived back at the house from their abandoned adventure. She was yawning, acting like she'd been asleep until she heard them rummaging in the cabinets. Truth was, she told him many years later that she'd secretly followed them down to the creek and stayed until they returned.

"Where were you going to sleep if we'd stayed?" he inquired.

"On the soft bed of earth the Lord pre-pared for me at the base of Woodsy. I already had my quilt wrapped up under my chin!" Woodsy was one of the three trees by the swimming hole she'd named as a child. Jacob knew that having Woodsy, Weeping Willow and Willoway safeguarded in the Crooked Creek Park land grant had made the farm's sale bearable to his mom, who was very glad to know they'd be enjoyed for at least a few more generations to come.

Not too many more weeks and the weather will be nice enough to sleep down by the creek this year, he mused. One of the last times he'd ventured down to the creek was when they'd all talked — well, dared was more like it — the over-dressed Katie Durbin into taking off her shoes and joining them for a wade.

I'm glad Josh enjoys crawdad hunting as much as Vinnie and I did, he thought as sleep began to overcome him, the light of the full moon beginning to glaze over. *I'll have to remember to ask Josh if he's camped down there yet. Maybe we should* all *give it a go.*

"Timing is everything, isn't it?" God said to the man in the moon, who smiled back at Him with glorious satisfaction.

14

Arthur Landers, who was firm about his stand on things, nonetheless felt less firm Saturday morning when he stopped by By George's filling station to buy gas. George Gustafson, who was washing Arthur's truck window while the tank filled with gasoline (FULL SERVICE ONLY at By George's), had been bending Arthur's ear the entire time about how obvious it was everyone should vote for Sam come the election. "Gladys makes people plumb nuts!" George declared. *WHAP!* As if to accentuate his point, George released the windshield wiper he'd been holding up, allowing it to smack onto the windshield with such force that it caused Arthur, still sitting behind the wheel with the window down, to lurch. "And that *Durbinville* woman has never *once* bought gasoline at my station, Arthur. Now what do you think about that?" he asked, hustling — well, as fast as George ever hustled, which wasn't very fast — back toward the hose to top off the tank.

What did Arthur think about that? He thought a lot of things, but one of them was how grateful Arthur had always been for George Gustafson. "By George," George, who handled only the simplest of car maintenance and repairs, would tell his customers, "I think it's time you take it on out to Arthur Landers for a look-see at what's going on here. I'm stumped-ti-dee-dumped and Arthur knows just how to figure these things out." Arthur felt indebted to George, who had, in actuality, helped feed them all of his working years. But the other thing he thought was that Sam Vitner was nothing short of a loose cannon, and that no matter how much Queen Lady fancy-pranced around acting like she owned the world, in the end, she got things done. And as for Katie Durbin, he'd put his money on her — he'd *trust* her — far before he'd trust Sammy Boy Vitner, who seemed to have a vendetta against her for no good reason.

"You listening, Arthur?"

"Yup." *Nope.*

"Well don't tell me you even have to THINK about what I'm saying!"

"Thinkin', George, is somethin' that makes my brain hurt."

George gave Arthur a double take, then wrote up his sales ticket and collected his money. When he handed Arthur his receipt he also handed him one of Sam's election buttons. "Here ya go. Don't know how you missed getting one at Harry's the day Sam announced his candidacy since I'm sure you were in the thick of the action, what with it being breakfast time and all. I sure wish I could have been there!"

Arthur just nodded his head. "It was somethin', alrighty. I done thought the fur was gonna take to flyin' before it was over. Still might, I reckon." But that's all he said. He took the button and stuffed it into one of the side pockets of his bib overalls.

"Put that thing on, Arthur, before you lose it or pull it out and try to play it, mistaking it for your Hohner." George chuckled at the mere image, but Arthur grimaced at the thought of accidentally running the pin through his lip.

Arthur patted his middle bib pocket where everyone knew he kept his Hohner harmonica, ready for a quick draw and a quick tune. "Not ta worry. I know jist where everything is."

What I ain't sure about is what, exactly, I'm gonna do 'bout it so as not ta git my breakfast ruint every mornin'!

Sharon Teller reviewed her list of stories: the ones she'd already filed, those in progress, a few to start and file before the day was over, and a sprinkling of possible sidebars in various states of composition. She was beginning to doubt she'd make today's band practice since she'd probably have a complete meltdown by the 2 p.m. start time anyway. That would really be disappointing since every first band practice of the new month — and it was March first, to be sure — band members with birthdays during that month brought snacks like cupcakes, brownies or cookies and sometimes even pie. She'd taken two bags of Hershey's Kisses in red wrappers last month, not only because it was her birthday February 16 but in honor of Valentine's Day too, since she had no sweetheart to give them to.

Sharon never worked on Saturday, but today both she and Harold came in at 7 a.m. to put in at least a few hours on tomorrow's Sunday edition, which was usually put to bed by now, as they say in the newspaper biz. But not only was the meeting to select the mall-naming winner scheduled in their

office for 10 a.m. — all of *that* exciting information (winners, runner-ups) needing to be typed up and laid out for print — but the election had them going nonstop. They'd been knee deep in deciphering pages of interview notes; chasing down Gladys numerous times in hopes she'd finally completed her platform before they went to press (since Sam handed his in and they wanted to be fair), which Gladys hadn't thought about building until Sam stepped forward with his and therefore put her behind the eight ball; and keeping their own biases at bay while they listened and composed. They'd also been casually polling people the last couple of days to get a feel for how serious the competition might actually be or become. Maybe, they thought when they decided to engage in the polling, they'd find out there were so few people for one or the other candidate that there wouldn't be any real contest after all. But alas, that wasn't the case. They were surprised at how much doubt a few blindly devoted people could cast toward other basically nice and decent residents of their small town.

For instance, Harold was stunned to find three people spewing the same word-for-word phrase about Gladys's choice "to stubbornly stand behind that square-defiling monstrosity Ms. Durbinville is creating in the old Taninger building." He knew somebody was spreading what would be called a good sound bite for TV, and he guessed it was either Cora or Sam himself. They must have printed up that mouthful and passed it out along with instructions to memorize it.

"Monstrosity?" Harold finally asked one old farmer who wiped his brow with his bandana after he spoke, as though the mere thought of the entire monstrosity made him sweat — even though it was only in the high sixties that day. "Why do you call the mini mall a monstrosity?"

"Why do I call it a monstrosity, you ask?" He repeated the question back to Harold as if he, a *newspaper reporter,* were daft to even have to ask such a dumb thing.

"Yes, that would be the question," Harold said patiently, his steno pad and pencil poised in his hands ready to take down the response.

The old farmer eyed the pad, then turned his eyes up to the sky, as though hoping to spot a skywriter spelling out the correct quotable answer. "Why, you ask. Well," he said, shifting his eyes over to the right, "because sometimes old and empty is better than new and abused." Harold's pencil

flew across his pad. He had a feeling that phrase would soon show up on yet another new campaign button, or possibly already had. In fact, he wished he'd opened a button business since he figured the Hethrow Button Business (yes, that was its official name) must be working 24/7 just to keep up with Partonville's recent demand on both sides of the election coin.

He and Sharon started a bulletin board in the office called SLOGANS AND SMEARS. They posted it on the inside of a cabinet door, to be discreet since they often added their own sarcastic tidbits. It consisted of phrases they saw on buttons and/or some hand-scrawled signs in the rear windows of cars and pickup trucks. Of course MAYOR+MCKERN=MOMENTUM appeared on buttons the day after Sam passed his buttons out. But they'd also seen the likes of SWAP YOUR VOTE FOR A *TOILET?*, VITNER FOR VINTAGE, NOT MAYOR and MAYOR+VITNER=VANISHING TOWN. All this in three days! Some people were wearing so many buttons, Sharon told Harold, that it looked like the new Partonville fashion trend was polka dots!

At 8:30 a.m. Harold told Sharon he was going to take a stroll around the block to make sure they hadn't missed reporting anything obvious. "Hold down the fort while I'm gone. I'll be back in time to wrap up our election news, or at least shelve it for awhile, so we can switch hats for the mall meeting."

"Yes, sir," she said, not even looking up, her fingers clacking away on her keyboard.

"And you know, it occurs to me we might run out of space to run that picture you took of the cracked sidewalk." Hey, a guy could hope, couldn't he?

"Mr. Crab," she said, looking him straight in the eye, "you know very well you taught me to deliver the news, and Paul's fall caused by cracked and heaving cement is certainly news. You also know you'd be disappointed in me — not to mention how disappointed I'd be in myself — if we withheld something just because our newspaper was involved." He nodded his head. She was exactly right. "But I *am* going to shrink the size of the photo so I can run it side-by-side with the one I took of the *new* stretch of sidewalk." She smiled at him. He smiled back, then out the door he went as her fingers began smoking her keyboard again.

A few minutes later she heard the door open. "Find anything?" she asked, her eyes glued to her computer screen.

"I certainly did," a deep silky voice replied.

Sharon didn't have to look up to know who it belonged to. She would recognize that voice anywhere. Colton Craig stood at the counter in front of her desk, his white teeth sparkling through his broad, tan face. "No more searching for me," he said, his hulking frame nearly looming over her. "It turns out I've already located one of *the* best things about this town." He extended his strong hand her way. "Miss Teller. Nice to see you again."

Sharon hoped he couldn't hear her heart beating. She hated the way his animal manliness undid her. Hated it! She swallowed and set her mind to business, recalling her last encounter with him. "Mr. Craig," she said, giving his huge warm hand a brief up-and-down shake, then withdrawing it as though she'd latched onto a hot coal. "The office isn't open today, but is there something I can help you with?"

He withheld his words a moment while he allowed his smile to broaden, causing Sharon to swallow again. Then he relaxed his face until it looked all business again. "Friday's *Daily Courier* ran a small article about Partonville's surprise contested election. Since I know you to be a fine reporter with a nose for truth, I was wondering what you thought about our coverage. Did our reporters get the story correct?" Sharon noticed his eyes wandering toward her computer screen which sat at an angle on her desk. She quickly slid her mouse across the mouse pad and minimized the window.

It distressed her that the *Courier* had beat them getting the contested election news to print, but nothing could be done about it since the *Courier* was Hethrow's daily and the *Press* only printed twice a week — Sam's first posters having gone up in windows on Wednesday night, the day the *Press* came out. "I'd say you got the broad-brush strokes correct," she said rather curtly, "which is that Sam Vitner is running against Acting Mayor Gladys McKern."

His smile broadened, both at the fact she'd closed her computer screen and that she was working so hard not to give him an inch. "I'm sure you didn't mean to say *you* as in *me,* since I build things, I don't write the *Courier*'s newspaper articles." He wore the look of a supremely handsome Cheshire cat as he wove his web of words around her, which she recalled he did with stealth maneuvering the last time she'd interviewed him about his intentions for Partonville.

I will not *be ensnared by you!* She stiffened her spine and wiped any evidence of pleasantries off her face. "Since you referred to 'our reporters,' I assumed you were speaking for your town in the collective use of the word 'our.' And so likewise I responded to *you*."

He chuckled. "Touché." He rested his forearm on the counter and leaned toward her. "Please forgive my inept attempts to communicate," he said, leaning in just a tad closer, close enough she could smell his earthy cologne. "How about we start over, okay? I'm not here to spar with you, Ms. Teller. I've simply come to the most professional and knowledgeable source available to collect accurate information."

Dregs! How mad could she get at a statement like that — a thought which immediately set off her internal BEWARE! alarm again.

"You can read our comprehensive coverage in tomorrow's paper, Mr. Craig, which will be nearly a double-sized edition. And now if you will excuse me, I'm working under a very tight deadline."

"Well I just wanted to . . ."

"I'm sorry, sir, but our office is closed and I must ask you to leave now," she said, resting her fingers back on her keyboard.

Somebody smack me!, a little voice whispered in her single-and-looking head.

"Never let it be said I held up progress.

Good day, Ms. Teller, and thank you for your time. I look forward to reading your every . . . single . . . word." Although he spoke in a near monotone, it still came out sultry. *How does he* do *that?* she wondered as she shivered when he walked out the door.

Colton left the *Press* feeling not the slightest of dings to his ego, even though it was the second time this week he'd virtually been dismissed by a Pardon-Me-Viller. Sharon's red cheeks and fidgety fingers told him all he needed to know. But moreover, he knew he truly would learn more by reading tomorrow's *Press* than talking to her further since he'd analyzed her quite thoroughly (and accurately, as it turned out) the last time they met. She was the type of woman who worked hard to hang on to her emotions, which meant one of the reasons she'd likely gone into journalism was to find a written way to sort and express them. He imagined in another ten years she might be an intriguing force to be reckoned with, but for now, she was still too much the novice to keep her outward expressions from giving her away. Yes, she would work hard to be fair and square and he would read more about both sides of the electoral coin than if he'd continued pressing her for information today. He'd learned in business that when you force an issue with a weaker player, you usually only got half of the story since the rest of it would be lost in emotional spewing.

As it turned out, he'd had much more fun verbally sparring with Challie Carter the other day, who was a surprisingly shrewd foe. When Colton first arrived at his farm and told him why he was *personally* dropping by, Challie let it be known he was "not one bit happy" that Sam had blabbed about Katie's offer. But on the other hand, he invited the kingpin land developer right into his kitchen saying: "But look what that big mouth brought me." What Colton didn't know was that Challie had blabbed to the one person he thought might lure Craig & Craig Developers right to his door again. But not even he had expected it would be Colton Craig himself.

Their visit was so interesting and lively, in fact, that it got too late to make it to the *Press*'s office before closing. Finding Sharon there today was a bonus since he expected the office would be closed. But he'd circled the square on his way to take a more careful look at some acreage and noticed the *Press*'s shades were up, the lights on and

Sharon at her desk. He couldn't stop himself from going in.

Now as Colton drove on toward the northeastern outskirts of Partonville, he couldn't help but lust after the extensive breadth of Challie's land holdings, even if they weren't contiguous to Hethrow. He'd looked up the plats of survey maps the day after their chat so he could get an overview of all the boundaries, how they might overlap, or not, with his both new and renewed intentions. The few other properties *not* owned by Challie seemed too far out of the line of a sensible plan for development, but today Colton was taking another thoughtful driving evaluation anyway. Even if this journey bore no new fruit, it was good to know Challie was open enough — or hopefully ticked off enough at Katie's offer — to actually engage in conversation about "other" possibilities.

Colton also learned, without asking, that Challie did, in fact, lease and farm the fields on Katie's Crooked Creek, something he'd also done for Dorothy since her husband died. The fact Challie brought it up let Colton know Challie was fishing for response, too, and perhaps willing to play down and dirty. Challie was a shrewd one all right, Colton thought. It was no wonder

Katie hadn't been able to sew him up yet, since neither had he. Challie also knew how to play his cards close to his vest, yet just far enough away to be within peeking distance, enough peeking distance to draw two seriously interested and bankrolled parties into his hand. No, Challie was no dummy. As he drove along fumbling with maps, stopping occasionally to make sure he was reading correctly, Colton recalled how their conversation had ended.

"Well, well, well," Challie said, flicking the toothpick he held in his mouth from one side to the other after they'd bantered like they were old friends, laughed and plied each other for hints of pertinent information for over an hour. He leaned back in his chair, balancing on its back legs. "*Two* big-money dogs come a-barking at my door."

"What if I told you *this* big dog would let you name your price per acre for *all* of your properties, Challie?"

Challie studied him for a moment, tipped back in his chair just far enough so Colton thought he might actually go over backwards. "I'd tell you that you think I'm dumber that I am, and that you're dumber than I expected for saying such a thing."

"Oh?"

"I know some pretty high numbers."

"Such as?"

"Such as . . . ," Challie said, clamping down on his toothpick before letting his chair lean forward a bit. Then he snickered. "You know, maybe you'd be thinking higher than I'd name and then I *would* be the dumb one." Colton laughed. He liked this Challie Carter's style and intuitive smarts since he had indeed seen that exact scenario play out more than once, although he knew how to make the seller believe they'd taken him. Challie sucked air through his back teeth. "So in light of what we both know to be the truth in your tactics, I say you name a number first and then I'll see how it compares to my line of thinking . . . and that of the *other* interested party. Maybe better yet," he said, allowing his chair legs to thunk to the floor, "I'll conduct my own auction for the land and see which one of you is the bigger dog after all."

Colton fought his reflex to raise an eyebrow, which would reveal how he felt about what would surely be a worst-case scenario. No, he needed to keep the ball in *his* court. He briefly thought about how he'd lost the Crooked Creek deal to Katie, the way Katie had obviously played to Dorothy's emotions with that park deal.

"What's the most important thing to you,

Challie? Money? Timeline? Feeling like you have a say in what will happen to your land once you sell it?"

"Once it's gone, it's gone. Plant it, bulldoze it, build on it, burn it, let it go to seed. Won't matter a lick to me since I'll likely be living high on the hog in Florida."

Now Colton raised both eyebrows with perfect timing. "Hm. I own a wonderful senior development in Florida, just off that inland coast you like to visit," which was a little tidbit Colton gleaned when Challie previously talked about his vacations. "I just might be able to swing you a handsome deal."

"Is that right?"

"That, Challie Carter, is a guarantee."

Challie eyeballed Colton a good long while, then he stood. "It's time for you to go, Mr. Craig."

Colton didn't move. He studied Challie's posture, every detail of the man's face, trying to get a read on what had transpired, what he might be thinking. Was he mad? Intrigued? The guy must play a lot of poker, he thought, because he revealed absolutely nothing other than how he could walk to the door to usher him out.

15

"I don't know where the time goes," Delbert said to Katie, his tone sincere and apologetic. "Marianne and I have been meaning to have you and Josh over for dinner since . . . well, since last fall when we learned about . . . us." He was referring to their discovery in October that they had the same father. Through an old set of letters Katie found after her Aunt Tess died, she worked the pieces of a mental puzzle until the truth was finally revealed, thanks to Dorothy's courage and faith in God to work the healing.

"And several times I've thought about having your family out to the farm," she said, sounding neither quite as sincere nor apologetic, since she was loaded for bear after having waited two days to tackle this mess with her son's driving. "I know your children would probably love to play in the barn." Delbert and Marianne had two children, a boy and a girl.

"Probably you, too, huh Uncle Delbert?" Josh, who was seated at the kitchen table with them, asked with a nervous laugh. Delbert nodded his head and gave Josh a sympathetic smile. No, the heavy sense of mission for today's meeting could not be overcome so easily. They were *both* in the hot seat with Katie, and they knew it.

"But then . . . yes, time does slip away," Katie added. What she didn't say was that when she *had* thought about picking up the phone to invite them over, or asking them after church a couple of different Sundays, she'd changed her mind. She just couldn't force something so personal. The whole situation still felt awkward to her and she didn't want to be put in the position to have to act like she *felt* something for a man — a half brother — she was still getting to know as a *person.* The whole notion of their relationship was still surreal at best, and troubling at worst. How could her mother have deceived her about her father her entire life, taking such a huge truth to the grave with her? How did you overcome the kind of hurt imparted by learning that the same man who raised a son every day of his life never got to know his daughter?

"Well, at least some of us are gathered

together here at this table," Delbert said, "although this doesn't seem like the ideal circumstances through which to foster our relationship, does it?" Katie's eyes filled with thunderclouds and she started to open her mouth, but Delbert jumped right in again. As uncomfortable as it was to feel so on the spot, he'd spent a good deal of time thinking and praying about this meeting. He'd concluded a bigger hand than his was at work here. It was time to trust that Voice and proceed with courage. "Let's just take this one step at a time, Katie. I know it might seem odd, but I believe the truth here is that there is a great blessing for *all* of us within this unfortunate circumstance."

When Josh had dropped Delbert off at the church after last Wednesday's "kidnapping," he pleaded with his uncle to please just keep the little incident between them, since, after all, he hadn't even been issued a ticket. Delbert took note of Josh's fearful face. As much as he wanted to oblige, he also knew in his heart of hearts it would not be the right thing to do — for either of them. They both had to pay the piper.

"Josh," he said, "I've been thinking about how to handle this since the moment Mac pulled us over. Believe you me, I'd rather

216

not have to talk to your mom about my part in it either! But the truth is, we both messed up and we're not the only ones who know it. An officer knows it, and more importantly, so does God. And to be honest, I always feel better about myself after I fess up, knowing that God forgives me, and hopefully so will your mom."

"But you have no *idea* how mad my mom's gonna be! Maybe God forgives, but my *mom?* She's got a man-eating-plant kind of memory." He knew this from watching his mom hold a bitter root about his dad's remarriage for all these years. "What's the point of getting her all upset and ruining the next decade of my life?" he asked, still trying to cover his butt.

"The point, Josh, is that we need to be the men we need to be. We'll do it together, okay? In fact, I'm going to call your mom before you even get home."

"But . . ."

"Listen to me now. I have no idea if she'll go along with this or not, since I don't even really feel like I have a right to ask her. But since I'm your uncle — since we are legitimately family — I'm going to ask her if she might be willing to remain calm about this issue until the three of us can meet."

"A, too late for calm. B, she'll probably

already have killed me by then."

Delbert chuckled. "I have no doubt your mom is a tough cookie, Josh, especially since the whole *town* knows she can wield a hacksaw." (Images of the Thanksgiving turkey flashed through his mind!) "But I sincerely doubt she will kill you. Maim you, maybe," he said playfully, "but not until you're dead. Besides, if we don't tell her, somebody else might, and then we'd have twice the trouble. Just give me a chance, okay? For the first time in my life, how about you allow me the wonderful privilege to walk in a real uncle's shoes." Without warning, tears sprang into Delbert's eyes. "Thank you, Lord," he whispered, as he closed his eyes. No matter the discomfort, this moment, this opportunity, was God's surprising answer to months of prayers that the door to their familial relationship would find a natural opening. When he opened his eyes, he felt like he was looking into a mirror. Suddenly his own boyish vulnerabilities were washing back on him through the face of his nephew, whose own tear-welled eyes pierced him with familiarity, especially since Josh had the same ears and chin cleft as he did, both inherited from Pastor Delbert Sr.

Josh, who so very much longed for the ongoing presence of a caring male in his life, who loved his flesh-and-blood father but who also felt like they barely knew each other, filled with a surge of hope so powerful that he nodded his head. "Okay," he said through a slight quiver in his voice. He deeply inhaled and exhaled with a whoosh. "Let's do the manly thing we gotta do." Delbert leaned across the truck's bench seat and the two of them gave each other an awkward hug and patted each other's shoulders. It was a moment neither of them would forget. It was the beginning of something new and wonderful for both of their families.

Delbert didn't think to ask Josh for his mom's cell phone number when he was dropped off, so when he arrived back at his office, Delbert called Katie and left a message on the machine at the farm. Josh arrived home shortly after Delbert left the message. When Josh first listened to it, a couple of thoughts crossed his mind, and the first was to erase it before his mom got home. But then Josh remembered Delbert had played the big "God knows" card, and after listening to the message several times, he decided his uncle did such a good job referring to vague facts involving "my idea" and "pulled over" and "imploring" Katie to please wait to discuss this "important issue" until "the three of us can talk," that he figured his odds of survival were better with the message than if, say, Sergeant McKenzie blew the whistle on him.

Miraculously (and probably only because she was so stressed out about everything else), his mother did consent to wait (sort of), telling Josh she hoped this wasn't the thing that finally pushed her over the edge, reminding him of all she had on her plate and how she didn't need *this* type of thing right now. It was obvious she worked so hard not to scream that her body broke into a hot flash after the message ended. She picked up the nearest thing, which was the phone book, and started waving it — its pages flapping back and forth in the breeze — while warning Josh in no uncertain terms that severe and swift punishment likely lurked at the end of this meeting and how he better not forget it. But nonetheless, whether it was the power of Delbert's phone-message pleas or the fact she was just too worn out by the election backlash, she hadn't brought it up again.

But now here they were at the kitchen table with Dragon Lady flame-throwing her fiery eyes right at the both of them. She was plenty stressed out from a number of things:

holding in two days' worth of pent-up frustration with Josh's antics while also having to allow him to keep driving to work; and they were under the gun for time (Katie took her wristwatch off and set it on the table in front of her) since she had to be at the *Press* at 10 a.m. for the final mall-naming selection, which was testing her very last nerve since she worried that the rest of the committee wouldn't pick the entry she so badly wanted to win!

His Uncle Delbert systematically started laying out the chain of events dating way back to December and the night of the town Christmas party here at the farm. He told her about how he and Jacob asked Josh to show them his new wheels. How the three of them sat in the truck and the "older men" had swapped a few car stories from their youths, asked a few questions about the big engine. He told Katie that at his bidding, he'd invited Josh to drop by church some day — kidnap him, so to speak, "no doubt language which would entice a boy's wild frame of mind from the get-go" — and take him for a ride. *Go Uncle Delbert!* He also included the funny part about how the windows had steamed up, causing the three men to quickly exit the car before people at the party started talking about them, which made his mother smile. *Good one!* Then he fast forwarded to the other day. He included every detail about how he'd egged Josh on (*YES, so TRUE!*) and how he should have known better. He praised the "mature manner in which Josh owned the incident himself" (*DAZZLE HER, DUDE!*) and emphasized that he believed Josh had learned a valuable lesson. Josh nodded with such agreement that Delbert had to swallow down a smile.

And then he quit talking and turned to Josh. It was his turn to defend himself.

"Now you go on, honey, get yourself out of this house," Dorothy said to Jessica as she bounced Sarah Sue on her lap. "Every woman needs a little time to herself, especially a pregnant woman who's been going nonstop here lately. Sarah Sue and her daddy and I will be just fine."

"There's lunch meat in the fridge and some fresh bananas on the counter. Sarah Sue loves bananas. You don't have to mash them, just give her a little chunk. And the mayonnaise and . . ."

"Jessica, I bet Dorothy knows how to rummage in the refrigerator with the best of them, don't you?" Paul was sitting up in the recliner, leg extended in front of him, a fresh bag of ice perched on the cast to help with the swelling. Although his bruised face looked slightly better, it was still a mess, but at least he was smiling more easily today.

"Oh, I know how to way better than *rummage,* don't I, Sarah Sue? I can downright *pilfer* like the *best* of pirates. And this '*Sooo* Big' girl," Dorothy said, raising Sarah Sue's hands in the air, "can help me with whatever any of us need, right?" Sarah Sue giggled. Dorothy took hold of one of Sarah Sue's hands and began waving it at Jessica. "Say 'Bye-bye' to Mommy! Gone with you now, so the pilfering can begin!" Jessica reluctantly waved to all three of them, Paul waving back at her like a baby too. She smiled halfheartedly and blew them a kiss. After they heard the engine start, then saw Jessica drive by the front window, her arm hanging out and waving to beat the band, they breathed a collective sigh of relief. It had taken them nearly twenty minutes to assure her they'd be just fine in her absence. She'd shown Dorothy what was in every-single baby dresser drawer, gathered up pacifiers, set out the baby wipes, written out the doctor's phone number in case Paul's headache returned. . . .

"I can't tell you how grateful I am you came to my wife's rescue, Dorothy." Paul pushed back in his recliner a little, looking and sounding as though he'd been rescued too. "She's been sleeping — well, probably *not* sleeping — right there on the couch since Wednesday night, watching me like a hawk, tiptoeing around and whispering on the phone when she thinks I might be sleeping or need to sleep, when *she's* the one who needs the rest! Getting out of here is the best thing for her."

"You heard me assure her I have nothing better to do with my life today — nor can I think of anything more *fun* to do with my life today — than to play with this beautiful baby and take care of the likes of such a handsome man as yourself, especially since my son isn't back in town yet. I am just delighted to be useful."

Sarah Sue stiffened her body, letting Dorothy know she wanted to get down on the floor where she eyed her toys. She was crawling now and attempting to pull herself up on things, which is what Jessica kept warning Dorothy about. "You have to watch her every second, she's so fast!" she'd said.

Dorothy laughed in response. "I guess you haven't seen my afterburner then, have you?"

Sarah Sue shot straight past her toys and headed for the kitchen. "Afterburner time,"

Paul teased. "Sic 'er, Dorothy!"

"I'd say," Dorothy said, launching herself off the couch, "your head is just fine!"

"If only my leg could heal as quickly," he replied to the empty room. The living quarters of their motel were so small it only took Sarah Sue a few seconds to disappear around the corner and into the kitchen. But in a flash, Dorothy had scooped her up, plopped her back down by her toys and put up the gate between the two rooms. "Lifesavers, these things, aren't they? And boy, they sure do make them easier to use than those darned things we had when our kids were young. Those accordion-like wooden folding gates needed to be mounted to the wall and I was always afraid the kids would pinch their fingers in them. Goodness, this big plastic barrier goes in place just like one, two, three. And look how nice and snug it fits!" Dorothy marveled as she pushed on it a few times to make sure it was indeed secure.

"Jessica got that at the Now and Again Resale shop, which I bet is where she heads today. She is such a wise shopper, which is a good thing considering our financial situation," he said, pointing to his leg, even though Dorothy knew they scraped pennies way before the accident.

"You're a lucky husband and papa, isn't he, Sarah Sue?"

Sarah Sue, who was trying, one at a time, to put every toy into her drooling mouth, smiled at Dorothy when she heard her name. "Doesn't that just melt your heart?" Paul asked. "She looks so much like her momma."

"Indeed." Dorothy none too gracefully got herself down on the floor with Sarah Sue in order to stack a few of her giant plastic building blocks for her. Now that she was down there, she hoped she could get up in time, should Sarah Sue decide to head down the hall toward the bathroom — which is exactly what she did. "You get back here, you little monkey!" she said while she scooted herself on her backside toward the end of the couch so she could get some arm leverage to hoist herself up, her cranky knees acting especially cranky. "I guess my afterburner could use a little oiling!"

"Don't worry," Paul said through a chuckle. "Jessica always closes the bathroom door and our bedroom door, and we don't keep anything in her bedroom that can harm her — well, at least not within her reach — so there's really no trouble she can get into heading that direction."

"Good thing. And good thing your wife

can't see me *now!*" Dorothy said, arms outstretched, hands on the couch, feet on the floor, knees straight. "This must be some sight for you," she said to Paul, her backside aiming right at him.

Paul was unable to stifle a laugh. "To be honest," he said through his chuckling, "it's quite inspiring since I have no doubt that's exactly what *I'd* look like right now in the same situation, or rather when I'm even able to *get* into that situation down on the floor again, which will hopefully just be another day or two."

"Whew!" Dorothy said after she'd fully uprighted herself. She brushed off her hands, then took off down the hall. It was exactly as Paul had said: all doors were closed (and she made a mental note to keep them that way) but Sarah Sue's. She was in there happily chewing on one of her cardboard books. Dorothy pulled the wooden rocking chair closer to where Sarah Sue sat, then bent over and collected the chunky bundle onto her lap. "How about we read us a story?" Sarah Sue leaned back against Dorothy in a clear sign her mommy and daddy, too, probably had spent lots of time doing just that.

It wasn't long before the little book was over for the fifth time and Sarah Sue was grunting so hard she looked like a turnip, her face was so red. "Guess it's time for Grandma Dorothy to get ready for another kind of 'after' burner, right?" Sarah Sue twisted around to look at Dorothy's face, then turned around again and grunted some more.

"Once upon a time," Dorothy said, deciding to just make up a story while Sarah Sue finished her business, "there was a little boy just your size, and he pooped his pants too." Dorothy smiled, rocked a few times so as not to disturb Sarah Sue's progress. She lightly ran her knobby finger along the feather-soft curls at the nape of Sarah Sue's neck, then rocked one more short rock. "But in the land of real life in which he lived, time passes very swiftly, and suddenly the boy is a man in his fifties," she paused, her voice cracking and tears welling to her eyes. "But thankfully, sweetie," Dorothy said, kissing the top of Sarah Sue's silky head as she heard and felt the explosion, "it isn't The End of my story with the little boy yet. We're going to have a new beginning in only five short days."

16

People with too much time on their hands spent their Saturday morning trying to make sure they hadn't missed a dollop of election gossip. The Tap, Partonville's local watering hole, hadn't seen this much action during the early weekend hours since the area senior citizens' baseball league wound down at the end of last year's season, the Partonville Wild Musketeers winning the league. Those not at The Tap gathered on street corners or raced between Harry's and La Feminique, even if they didn't have an appointment at the salon. After the third gossip-mongering pop-in showed up, in order to keep her little shop from overflowing, as well as to sort out the money from the mouthpieces, Maggie spontaneously seized the opportunity to start offering "today's unadvertised special, a quick 'do' freshener which includes a comb-out, re-tease and re-spray for only two-fifty," an overt sales tactic that caused some of them to turn on their heels and depart (*Good!* she thought) and others to sit themselves right down until she could squeeze them in. (*Even better.*) She wondered why it had taken her over fifty years in the beautifying business to come up with such a clever scheme.

But even among the Saturday morning regulars, La Feminique Hair Salon & Day Spa was a whirring blur of color, cuts and wagging tongues. Sadie Lawson sat in one of Maggie's two waiting chairs while Maggie finished Ellie's hair. Ellie was the receptionist for both Doc Streator, who was pulling back toward retirement, and Dr. Nielson, Doc's replacement. Maggie only had two more curling iron crimps to perform on Ellie's hair before whirring into her wild teasing dervish, as Dorothy called it any time she witnessed Maggie's full-body aerobic backcombing action.

After the death of Sadie's son Rick, Maggie suggested Sadie move her standing appointment to Saturdays. Maggie said it would give her an opportunity to visit with people she otherwise didn't see on a regular basis and today brought quite the bounty. What Maggie was really thinking was that Saturday's lineup tended to be a more upbeat group of ladies, so she always made sure she had Sadie's favorite treats set out — Fig Newtons, M&Ms and vanilla hazelnut coffee — in order to entice Sadie to arrive early for her appointment and stick around afterwards, just for the company. "Sometimes the simplest of changes in our routine is helpful," Maggie told her when she'd first made the suggestion. Like a blind sheep being led to greener pastures, Sadie followed her suggestion.

"You know, Sadie," Ellie said, catching her eye in the mirror, "it's so good to see you *here* every week now, too, rather than just in our medical setting." Sadie suffered with terrible rheumatoid arthritis and a few other serious ailments, so due to her numerous drugs, she needed regular monitoring. Because of this, Rick had cared for his mom up until the time of his sudden and fatal automobile accident. Sadie was badly banged up in the incident, too, since she was riding in the passenger seat. The worst part was being trapped in the upside-down car with him until they got them out, a memory at first suppressed, but which now haunted her. Yes, it was good for her to be around a few live wires. "Thank goodness," Ellie continued, "Dr. Nielson doesn't book Saturday appointments unless it's an emergency, which allows me to come here and play with Maggie every weekend," she said, reaching up and grabbing Maggie's wrist in a friendly gesture. "And my, my, *my,* you two, don't we have more interesting things to talk about *today* than pains and pills! It's been a regular revolving door in here, Maggie. Your door chimes have barely stopped ringing since I arrived! You just can't turn around without someone flinging an opinion this way or that, can you?"

It always startled Sadie how different — more alive — Ellie seemed away from the doctors' office, causing her to wonder how *she* was perceived by other people. She stared at herself in one of the mirrors. She looked thin and drawn, that old woman in the mirror looking back at her. But even though the light had not returned to her eyes since the death of her son, she felt grateful she was at least engaging in more conversations now than she did a month ago, thanks to the ongoing and kindhearted interest of people like Dorothy, Ellie and Maggie. No, a mother would never get over the loss of her child. But Dorothy, who knew firsthand, modeled a great hope to Sadie that she, too, could one day learn how to live with such a terrible grief.

One of the best things to do, Dorothy told

her, was to get involved with new adventures and new people, when she felt up to it. Dorothy certainly modeled that. She'd befriended Katie and Josh, the newcomers to the town, the minute they'd arrived. It would have been easy for Dorothy to resent them living out at her old place, hosting the Christmas party that used to be hers, but she didn't. She in fact cheered them on. But Sadie wasn't as mobile as Dorothy, nor was she as extroverted. Just the same, she thought, forcing herself to sit up a little straighter, it would feel good to get her hair done, and the buzz in the shop reminded her that there was life in the midst of grief — even though her instinct this morning was to crawl back into bed and *never* get up. "One day, one step at a time," Dorothy had said, and today's step was dragging the pieces of her shattered heart to the beauty shop.

"As you know, Ellie," Sadie said, forcing herself to think about something other than herself, "I don't get out that much, aside from to the doctor's and here. But I'll tell you, my phone's been ringing off the hook with election chatter, too, know what I mean?"

"I surely *do,*" Maggie said, pulling a strand of Ellie's hair straight out and pumping her arm into its backcombing rhythm, which in turn pumped her whole body. Backcombing was an age-old art she maintained today's young stylists had no *idea* how to properly perform. Thoughts of her disastrous encounter with Cora's mean spirit flew into her mind and she had to stop the procedure for a moment lest she got caught up and accidentally rip poor Ellie's hair out by the roots. "If I had a dollar for every low-down backhanded comment made to *me* in the last two days," she said, pausing to force herself to lower her booming voice while gently picking up the end of Ellie's strands and making herself smile until her *hands* felt the smile, "I'd be a wealthy woman!"

"How do you respond to opinions contrary to your own?" Ellie wanted to know. "Must be tricky in a business like this."

Hm. Maggie would have to be careful lest she alienate half of her clients, since people seemed to be evenly divided. "Well, sometimes I don't do a very good job," is all she said before she picked up the hairspray to begin reinforcing the backcombing, which would be followed by the fine art of The Perfect Smoothdown. Visions of Cora leaving with half a haircut caused her to giggle. "No, sometimes I don't do a very good job at *all* of keeping my opinions to myself. But by Friday morning I realized I needed to maintain a neutral zone — or a least a neutral mouth — if I wanted to stay in business, lest half my clients end up with a curling iron stuffed down their throats."

Sadie laughed, envisioning some of Partonville's finest walking around town looking like sword swallowers.

"Maggie!" Ellie exclaimed, wincing at the thought of a hot iron cauterizing her tonsils. "You're in rare form today!"

"Nah, I'm just being me. And you know me, I also love to be on the cutting edge of fashion, so I've just come up with another brilliant idea."

"Do tell," Ellie said.

"Since campaign buttons seem to be the latest fashion craze," she paused here a moment as if uttering the very word *fashion* elicited the utmost of respect, "I'm thinking of having my own buttons made up saying I VOTE FOR WRINKLE CREAMS! and DON'T EVEN THINK ABOUT ASKING! or . . ." she grabbed her rat-tail comb and began the smoothing process, "how about YOU KEEP YOUR OPINIONS TO YOURSELF AND I'LL KEEP MY CURLING IRON OUT OF YOUR MOUTH!" Another round of laughter.

"Well, *I* will certainly refrain from asking

you what you think," Ellie said, "lest I can't help but disagree with it and end up causing Dr. Nielson to come in for my own Saturday emergency appointment!" Sadie laughed *again,* which felt very good indeed.

After a final flourish of hairspray, Ellie was done. While she was squaring up her bill, Sadie hobbled over to the shampoo station. Maggie had already moved the chair away, knowing it was easier on Sadie's poor body to stand at the sink and bend over forward than to try to get her ravaged neck bent backward on the headrest. No sooner had Maggie turned on the faucet than Loretta Forester arrived. Loretta was often referred to around town as Swifty's wife and Swifty was known as Mr. Sell It Like It Is, the name of his auctioneering business. She helped him run their business by passing out numbers and posting all the paperwork while the auction was in progress. Loretta was not only a genuine hoot but she was the drummer for the Partonville Community Band.

"Well aren't *you* the early bird!" Maggie exclaimed over her shoulders as she adjusted the water temperature for Sadie's wash.

"We've got band practice at two today, so I thought I'd see if we might get me done a little early." Band practices were held out at

the Park District building where Loretta stored her drums since she was afraid Swifty, who didn't much care for the "bang-edy-bang-bang" ("Who *could* stand it?"), might slip her expensive drum set into one of his auctions when she wasn't looking.

"Let's see," Maggie said, craning her neck the other way to look at the oversized calendar she kept on the wall revealing month after glorious month of muscle men, something Acting Mayor Gladys McKern vehemently objected to when Maggie hung the new calendar every January, but also never failed to observe every turn of the page when she thought Maggie wasn't looking. "Well Hel-LO again Mr. *March!*" she said, causing even Sadie to lift her head for a moment to get a gander at the tall, dark and scantily clad warrior. "I see by his six-pack there — same as I saw, or let me say studied, when I flipped the calendar this morning — that it's March first. Birthday celebration band practice, right?"

"Yes ma'am. I've been saving up my Weight Watcher points just for the occasion."

Maggie gave Loretta a quick up-and-down glance. "How's that going for you?" Nothing seemed obvious, but she didn't want to sound insulting.

"Let's just say I figure I'm already using August's points," Loretta said, causing all three women to laugh. *Oh, GOOD!* Maggie thought. This was just the kind of ongoing lightheartedness she hoped would transpire when Sadie changed her standing appointment. She felt very proud that La Feminique Hair Salon & Day Spa could deliver on not only beautification, but also a balm for a grieving soul.

"Say," Maggie said, squeezing shampoo onto Sadie's hair, "have either of you heard any *important* news, like perhaps a leak about the mall-naming winner?"

Loretta marched right up next to Maggie. "No, but have YOU?" She all but screamed in her ear, already figuring how she might spend her gift certificate when her entry, "Partonville Pickens," won, or at the very least placed.

"May Belle said the committee was meeting at the *Press* at ten this morning," Maggie said, getting right to the shampoo since Sadie couldn't remain upside-down much longer, "but my eleven o'clock said the shades were drawn and the door was locked when she went by, and that there was a sign posted on the door saying YOU'LL SEE THE WINNERS IN **TOMORROW'S PAPER!**" — something they'd resorted to after people started knocking on the door about 10:30. "Good gravy! You'd think they were naming the next president rather than a mall, what with all the rules and regulations and secrecy they've put people through."

"Did you enter, Maggie?" Sadie asked through the small towel she held over her face to keep water from running into her eyes.

"Of course, darling! Didn't *everyone?*"

"I guess I just wasn't up to it," Sadie said. "Oh, I thought about it a couple times, but my creative juices are just dried up for now, I guess."

"And who could blame them?" Maggie said, guiding Sadie to stand up now that she'd finished rinsing. She deftly wrapped a towel around Sadie's head, then led Sadie to her chair and helped her get seated.

"So Mags, how many times did *you* enter since your creative juices are *always* over-flowing?" asked Loretta, who had reseated herself after learning nothing about a mall winner. She selected a tabloid magazine from Maggie's pile and casually flipped through it, stopping to study a picture of Brad Pitt, then stealing another glance at Mr. March, then back to Brad, deciding that if she had her pick, she'd go with Brad.

"Only four, but they're doozies. I imagine

you don't stand a chance with me in the running."

"You sharing any of them?" Loretta asked, continuing to flip the pages, acting like she didn't really care but hoping she would hate every one of Maggie's ideas, should she choose to divulge them, which she doubted.

"Not telling. I'm not talking politics and I'm not sharing my entries. But you can probably read all about at least one of them in tomorrow's paper!"

Almost everyone in Partonville was thinking the same thing — that is, unless they were too busy trying to figure out how to keep the mall from even opening.

17

Josh pulled into the Lamp Post just as Dorothy was walking out the side door into the parking lot. "What a wonderful surprise!" she said as she sped jauntily over to his truck to give him a hug. "I've been thinking about you lately. You working today?"

"Yes, ma'am. I'll be putting in eight hours," he said somberly, "today *and* tomorrow," *and the same again next weekend, and for no money. And so much for Shelby and me checking out the Fire Pit, since aside from school, my slave labor and dinner with Mom at Uncle Delbert's house Monday night, I'm also grounded for two weeks!*

He could not believe visions of the Fire Pit had popped into his mind yet again, and while he was talking to Dorothy! He'd be grounded for life if *she* could read his mind, not to mention he'd also be mortified. She thought he was such a nice young man; she'd said so on numerous occasions. Then

241

again, she wouldn't know what the Fire Pit was anyway. Little did he know *her* father had appeared there at 9 p.m. one rainy night and caught her and Henry (the man she would go on to marry) kissing, banged on the window of Henry's dad's Ford and told her she better get on home with him, which she did — never to return to the Fire Pit again for fear her dad would cause a worse scene the next time, which he would have.

"Eight hours!" Dorothy said, snapping Josh out of his private dialogue. It took him a moment to get his mind away from the Fire Pit so he could remember what they were talking about. *Oh, my slave labor.* "Goodness me," she said. "I'm kind of surprised there's that much work. I don't recall seeing much action around here today in terms of check-ins or check-outs."

"How long have you been here?"

She looked at her wristwatch. "Let's see, I'd say about four hours."

"You got a part-time cleaning job too?" he asked, which seemed a rather funny question to pose to an eighty-eight-year-old, although he didn't look much amused with himself for asking.

"Nope. I came over to relieve Jessica from her wife, nurse and mothering roles so she could get out and about and just be a woman for awhile." Josh found that a curious statement since when wasn't she a woman? "Of course I had an ulterior motive, which was to spend time snuggling with that wiggly love bundle of a Sarah Sue."

"How'd it go?"

"Wonderfully exhausting," she said, yawning while rubbing her back. "That baby's growing like a weed and moving like a race car. To tell you the truth, I think I'm going to get myself home and take a nap. I was bragging to Jessica and Paul about my afterburner, but I think chasing Sarah Sue around flamed it out." Josh chuckled. He couldn't imagine Dorothy ever running out of steam, although she did look rather tired, her posture not as erect as usual.

"Why'd you say you were working eight hours?"

Josh chewed on his bottom lip. Dorothy could tell he was ruminating about something. He opened his mouth, then closed it. Then ruminated some more. "Dorothy, did you ever have a car accident on a gravel road?"

Now it was her turn to ruminate. "Why do you ask?"

"Oh, I was just curious."

"Why, did *you?*" She looked concerned.

"Nope."

They stood there staring at each other for a moment. "So *did* you?" Josh asked, breaking the silence. "Did you ever have an accident because of the gravel?"

She pursed her lips, as though arguing with herself. "I cannot tell a lie. Yes."

"How many?"

"Who have you been talking to?"

"Sergeant McKenzie."

"Do I want to know why?"

" 'Do *I* want you to know why' is the better question, although Mom'll probably blab anyway."

"Do you want me to know? If she tries to blab, I can cover my ears."

"I'll tell you. But," he hesitated and smiled, both of them obviously enjoying this game of cat and mouse, "only if you're curious enough to first tell me if you ever had a rollover."

Dorothy pursed her lips. *Oh, Lordy!* she prayed as she looked around him toward his vehicle. "Oh, Josh! Please don't tell me you've rolled your new truck, or your mom's SUV!"

"Okay, I won't tell you."

"Did you hurt yourself?" Her voice up-shifted an octave. "Was anyone else in the car with you?"

"I said I wouldn't tell you I rolled any-

244

thing . . . because I didn't." He sprouted a devilish grin.

"Thank you, Jesus! And let me just take this opportunity to say that I hope you never do, and also to add that I guarantee you gravel can be very dangerous . . . if you don't know what you're doing."

He lifted his eyebrows, crossed his arms in front of him, smiled, leaned back against his truck and crossed one foot over the other. "How did you happen to learn *that?*"

Now it was her turn to smile. He obviously wasn't going to drop this. "Let's just say you can trust me when I tell you I learned firsthand and the hard way. As for you, take the sound advice of people who tell you that gravel riding can be dangerous."

"People, huh?"

"Yes," she said, puckering up her lips as if to convey "smartypants" without uttering a word. "People who might just be oldsters who have indeed experienced their share of mishaps while riding the gravel, including brief episodes of . . . upside-downness, shall we call it. So, Mr. Kinney, do what I say and not what I did and you'll live to tell about it! Got that?"

"Got it, although inquiring minds still long for details."

"Inquiring minds will just have to wait since you need to get to work and I need to take a nap. And sometimes, Joshmeister, inquiring minds are too nosey for their own good," she said, patting his cheek.

"Oh, ES! Our contest meeting was so much fun!" Nellie Ruth said in a rush of breathless words. She switched the phone receiver between one hand and the other while she shucked off her coat which she uncharacteristically tossed over a chair before collapsing onto the couch.

"Nellie Ruth, how could it not have been? *You* were there and you're more fun than two kitties in a sock!"

Two kitties in a sock? As if on cue, Morning sprinted across the living room up onto the couch, then came to a leaping halt in Nellie Ruth's lap where he instantly began to purr like a well-oiled motorboat engine. "I can't even imagine putting one kitty in a sock, let alone two," she said, running her hand down Morning's silky back. "You wouldn't like it in a sock, would you, sweetie pie?" she said in her baby-talk tone of voice.

"I don't imagine I would. Plus, it would have to be a whale of a sock to swallow the likes of me!" Edward Showalter smiled at his own funny self, then smiled again picturing Nellie Ruth cuddling one of her kitties, which is the only time she ever used that voice.

"Oh! I wasn't talking to *you!*"

He laughed. "I know. I was just funnin' ya."

She loved the sound of his laughter. It might seem clichéd, and there was a song by the same title she'd begun playing on her saxophone when nobody was around, but he surely made her feel like a natural woman, which, after what her father had put her through, was a gift straight from God.

And *Oh!* Not until that moment did she realize she'd come right home after the meeting, picked up the phone and dialed him without a single thought for proprieties or protocol. It felt so natural — yes, a wonderful word, she thought — to phone him, to hear his voice, to enjoy the sound of his laughter washing over her. Surely this was a sign. He'd been telling her all along that it was okay for a woman to call a man, and so it was — so suddenly and so naturally so. *Thank you, Lord.* Sometimes she struggled with the simplest things about their relationship. Only God could help her get over her past — and herself — and He was obviously fast at work, even when she least expected it.

As if Edward Showalter'd sensed Nellie Ruth's miraculous discovery, the two of them were silent for a moment, each feeling the power of their connection on so many levels. Their relationship had grown by leaps and bounds, a familiar wonderfulness settling over both of them. There were still clumsy moments, but all in all, they were, without question, a steady couple growing more in love every day. She wanted to share everything with him, including the smallest details about her day.

"I wish I could tell you which entry won!" she said, leaning back on the couch and drawing her legs up under her, making more room for Morning to curl up and settle in her lap, which he did.

"Don't you mean *who* won?"

"No. I do mean *which* since Harold and Sharon are still the only two who have access to the master list that matches entries with names. After swearing us to secrecy about the results, they asked us if we wanted to know the who of it, but Katie, May Belle and I all said no, we'd wait to find out in the paper tomorrow, just like everyone else. All I know is none of my entries even made the final twenty-five, but that's okay since the winner and runner-ups were all so much more creative anyway."

"Did Katie seem happy about the committee's decision?"

"She surely did! We all instantly agreed, too, which made it easy, and made her doubly happy since she said she had to get back to work on the mall, especially now that it had a name. It was the world's shortest meeting, for something so important. The fact we all thought the same one was best seemed like a good omen for. . . . OHMYGOSH! I almost SAID it!"

"Don't mind me. Just keep talking," he quipped, egging her on to let it slip.

"Hey, you! I promised! And wait a minute! I was so excited to call you before I head out again to band practice that it didn't occur to me you'd probably be working, which you're obviously not. Did you get this Saturday off?"

"Nope. No such luck. But it's amazing you caught me here. I just ran home during our break to pick up my lunch sack. I left it on the kitchen table this morning. The phone was ringing when I walked in."

"I'm so sorry for keeping you! Oh, I'm sorry, ES, I'll let you go now. I don't want to be the cause of trouble with Katie and I know she's back there already."

"Don't worry. I had to make me a new

lunch anyway, which I've been doing while we talked. Seems Kornflake likes braunschweiger on rye with raw onion, which means I won't be kissing *him* tonight!"

"You are so funny," she said chuckling, then realized she was blushing just having heard him say the word kiss.

"Funny, I *am,* my dear Nellie Ruth. And now I need to get my funny self to the cammy-van and head back to the . . . mini mall, since that's all *I* know to call it. At least until tomorrow after my papergirl arrives, which I surely hope she does before I head to church!"

Dear Mom and Joshmeister,

Tonight is a big night for me, and tomorrow, as I recall, is a big day in Partonville for Katie and the mall. But to tell you the truth, I'd rather be going to bed early there tonight than attend the party here. My friends are throwing me a "surprise" farewell party, although I already know about it — thank goodness — and to tell the truth, they love *any* excuse for a party and my leaving gave them one. But now that the majority of us are in our fifties, the fact we can still work out at the gym is probably enough reason to party. I understand better every day why you love to celebrate birthdays, Mom! "Still alive and kickin'!" Isn't that how you say it?

I have most of my household things packed for storage until I find a permanent residence there. The storage company comes on Monday, so at least I can sleep in my own bed until then — not that there's anything wrong with the bed you offer me, Mom. It's just that this is the one my back is most used to.

I'm staying at Randy and Rita's Monday night, then beginning my drive to Partonville on Tuesday. I'm taking my time, stopping to visit another friend on the way. Mom, I might even take some back roads, just in honor of your love for the ROAD TRIP! I know you said you didn't want to fly out here and keep me company on the way back, but it's not too late to change your mind.

As I prepare to move, you came to mind, Josh. I know you haven't heard from me much, but when I think about saying good-bye to my best friend Randy, I consider how hard it must have been for you to say good-bye to Alex when you left Chicago. It was easy to think only about how lucky you were to be moving out of the city and onto Crooked Creek. I know how I loved that place when I was growing up. But I didn't give much thought to the fact that maybe you liked the city, and that you were leaving good friends behind. Just wanted you to know I'm aware of that now.

Mom, I can already hear what you're thinking! "He's getting mellow in his old age." Maybe I am.

Time to leave for the party. I'll see you both soon.

Jacob

P.S. How's the truck running, Josh?

Jacob pushed the Send button. Funny how sitting down to write a quick chatty e-mail had raised some emotions. Although he'd have a quiet chance to say his real good-byes to Randy and Rita at their house Monday night, he decided it was time to give himself an attitude adjustment about the party this evening. His mom was right, as usual. "Life is uncertain," she used to say when he grumbled about one gathering or another. "Party while you can!"

Dear Outtamyway, (cc to Jacob)

Jacob says he's going to take some back roads on his way here. Has any oldster you might happen to know taught him about safe gravel riding?

Sincerely,
An inquiring mind

Josh was laughing when he pushed the Send button. Dorothy would *love* that one. He could hear her laughing already, a thought which helped his tired, brooding self. Well, at least he hadn't been grounded from the Internet. Time to send Shelby a note.

But first, he decided to forward Jacob's e-mail to his mom, without Jacob's P.S. about the truck. He wanted her to have to think about how hard it had been for him to move. Even though he loved it on the farm and he had made new friends, he still missed his best friend Alex. Thank goodness for e-mail! As soon as he was done sending Shelby a note, he was going to get Alex caught up on all the gory details leading to his grounding. He'd also let him know how fast the truck *could* do 0 to 60 — well, make that 0 to 85 — since he'd finally had a chance to find out on his way to school the morning he missed the bus. Good thing Sergeant McKenzie hadn't been on his tail then!

18

It turns out there's nothing like the announcement of a new mall name to pour fuel on an election hotbed — at least in Partonville. By 9 a.m. Monday, Lester K. Biggs, solely responsible for *everything* at his grill, had hand-scrawled a sign on a piece of butcher paper and posted it on his entry door. The sign read: MANAGEMENT RESERVES THE RIGHT TO BOOT ANYONE OUT OF THIS ESTABLISHMENT WHO USES FOUL OR LOUD LANGUAGE. MANAGEMENT ALSO RESERVES THE RIGHT TO DECIDE WHAT LOUD IS!!! He felt like adding, "And don't forget, I own several giant meat tenderizers and I know how to wield them," but he stifled himself.

Nobody could argue that the mall name wouldn't do them proud, the way it summed up the whole venture into one tidy package. But that was assuming there was going to *be* a mall on the square, which half of the people had decided they were against, even if they liked the new name. Those people were, of course, backing Sam Vitner for mayor, and this, of course, was the cause of the volume in Harry's Grill.

The one grace in the situation was that Sam Vitner had gone to work this morning rather than come to the grill, which is what he was supposed to do, *had* to do, according to Acting Mayor Gladys McKern, who was holding court at the U. "I don't know how he thinks he would find time to run a town when he's got his hands full taking care of his business."

"As opposed ta you, who spends yer time tryin' ta take care of *everybody's* business," Arthur said, followed by a loud slurpy sip of coffee. Challie Carter, who was not normally in the grill this time of day (he sometimes came in for a late supper, but almost never breakfast) tried not to chuckle out loud, but he couldn't hold it back, which inflamed Gladys, which caused Lester to give her an eyeball since he'd already warned her once about her volume.

Since Challie's little heart-to-heathen chat with Colton around his kitchen table (although it was difficult to decipher who was *really* the "bad guy"), he found himself hanging around — all ears — in town whenever possible. Aside from his wife and his poker group, he wasn't one to do much socializing, but he felt a need to evaluate the situation, maybe drop a subtle word for Sam if and when the opportunity arose. But since Katie was still the lease holder to one of his bigger pieces of crop land *and* in contention to buy him out, he'd have to be careful as to what, if anything, he said about her. And if he were honest with himself, he really wasn't one hundred percent sure whether or not he was for Sam or against him — which circled him back to Katie. Sam was nothing more than an accidental and convenient connection right now, so Challie just wanted to listen and draw a few conclusions lest his lip slip and he play a card that caused him to lose *all* opportunities.

"Well, Arthur," Gladys said, yanking on the bottom of her blazer as though it was the ripcord to her mouth, "you should be thankful I *do* care enough about everyone who lives in Partonville to support our betterment. With the Number Nine in question, we need jobs, we need commerce, and whether you want to believe it or not — and to be honest, I can't believe I'm even going to hear myself say this to *you* after you have just insulted me — we need each other!"

"What we need," Arthur said, laying the money for his breakfast on the counter, "is a place ta sit and digest our food where thay's peace and quiet." He twirled around on his stool, slowly stood upright, walked over to the collection jar that had PAUL JOY'S BROKEN LEG FUND printed on the paper wrapped around it, dropped in a dollar bill and opened the door to take his leave.

"Well I know just the place for you to sit and digest," Gladys said to his backside, although he never so much as slowed down. The door was about to close behind him, so in order to make sure he could hear her (and everyone noticed they occasionally had to repeat things to Arthur now and again anyway), she yelled, "ONE OF SAM'S OUTDOOR TOILETS!"

"That is IT for you today!" Lester yelped, snapping his dishcloth down on the counter precisely on the word "IT." Gladys reared back so fast she nearly slid off her stool. Lester didn't realize how loudly *his* voice had resonated throughout when he threw down the gauntlet causing a hush throughout the room. "I'll thank you," he said while gritting his back teeth, "to pay up and take your LOUD voice O-U-T of here for this morning." Gladys's gasp seemed to suck the air out of everyone as they held their breath preparing for *this* showdown.

"Lester K. Biggs, you know very well Arthur Landers cannot hear worth a twit and he was . . ."

"I mean it, Gladys," he said, back-flipping his thumb toward the door. "You are welcome back tomorrow, but nobody — *nobody* — is above the rules of this establishment, and you've had more than your fair share of warnings today."

Gladys blinked several times, then caught a glimpse of Harold down at the end of the U, his steno open in front of him. She pasted on a smile, picked up her napkin and patted her lips. She folded the napkin precisely back into its original shape and set it down on top of her plate. "Oh, but you are *not* dismissing me, Mr. Biggs. I was about to leave anyway," she said, her voice not much louder than a whisper, which everyone heard anyway since the airwaves crackled with attentiveness. Gladys tossed her money on the counter and for the first time in her life left a decent tip. In a dramatic gesture, she dropped — one dollar at a time to make sure nobody missed the true size of her caring heart — two dollars into the collection jar and walked, not stomped, out the door and down the sidewalk, head held high all the way back to her office. It took a couple of minutes for the buzz to begin again, no one daring to raise a voice above a murmur.

Challie asked Lester for one more coffee refill. He needed to sit for a spell in the back draft of Gladys's mastery under fire. He wondered if Sam would or could do as well under the same type of circumstances, or perhaps even defending himself against that viper of a Colton Craig. Challie stayed just long enough to overhear growing talk about the call for a mayoral debate and a possible picket line in front of the mall. With the election just four weeks away, this was all very interesting indeed.

In the meantime, mall renovation progressed at whiz-bang speed. As far as Katie could figure (and she had spent a good two hours last night figuring, even e-mailing Jacob one short perfunctory question since he was more familiar with the small-town dramatics of her situation than her Chicago attorney), no matter *who* won the election, to the best of her knowledge there wasn't a single legal way anyone could shut her down, which left nothing to do but move forward. Most of the ten stores (four on the first floor, five on the second and one on the lower level) were nearly framed to size and nine of them were rented. UPS had already delivered two boxes to the mall for Alotta Chocolotta this very morning, causing Edward Showalter to scratch his head as he tried to figure out what to do with them so they didn't get lost in the construction shuffle. Their arrival caused Katie to spend a good portion of her morning phoning everyone on her rental roster to remind them to reread their lease agreement: there would be absolutely *no* deliveries until April 1. None. Period. That would, she reminded them, still give them nearly two whole weeks to set up shop before the target grand-opening date, which had — and who would have believed it? — now escalated to April 12. Under the chaotic circumstances, the sooner she opened, the better. Sometimes people just needed to *see* a thing in action before they could get used to it — as they had with her when she first arrived.

Jessica was floating on cloud nine for twenty-four straight hours. Paul said the pain of breaking his leg was worth it just to see the happy light dancing in her eyes and to hear her joyful screech when she opened the *Press* Sunday morning and saw the headline: **PARTONVILLE PLEASANTRIES**

COMES TO TOWN — OR DOES IT? ELEC-TION RESULTS MIGHT TELL THE STORY, the subhead read, although never once did Jessica even entertain the idea that there would be no mall. And she didn't have to see the name of the winner; she knew it was none other than her very own last-minute entry. The best part was sharing the news with Paul. They'd verbally replayed yesterday's excitement many times, especially when she called Katie at nearly the crack of dawn and she and Paul held the phone receiver between them as they yammered, thanked Katie and celebrated.

"A hundred dollars!" Jessica said to Sarah Sue for the umpteenth time Sunday morning. Sarah Sue sat in her high chair munching on dry Cheerios and a few tidbits of scrambled eggs. She seemed to think her mother's exuberance was funny. "We won a hundred-dollar gift certificate to *Partonville Pleasantries!*" She twirled around like Cinderella, the growing child within her obviously happy about the news, too, since he or she (the Joys told the doctor they didn't want to know) took to doing a few of what felt like acrobatics. Sarah Sue giggled again, bits of scrambled egg sliding down the strings of drool escaping her mouth.

"Honey, just think," Paul said between bites of home fried potatoes with bits of mushrooms stirred into them from last night's dinner, mushrooms one of his favorite things to taste in any dish. "The hundred bucks is nice, but what I'm proudest of is that every time anyone circles the square and sets eyes on the mall banner, or plaque, or whatever Katie's going to hang out in front, they'll see another slice of your creativity. I am just so proud of you, so very proud, hon. Your grandmother must be beaming up there in heaven."

Jessica's eyes teared at the mention of her grandmother, which also gave her goose bumps. One of her grandmother's favorite things to say about Partonville was how pleasant it had been to live there all of her life. When the idea for Partonville Pleasantries first struck Jessica that fateful evening, it was as though her grandmother had whispered it into her ear. In fact, Jessica felt her grandmother's spirit swirl into the room right now, as though she was letting her know that she, too, still felt their connection, even from the great beyond. Before Paul, Jessica's grandmother was the closest person to her heart. Grandma took to Paul as if he, too, were her own.

"We both know how much she loved this

town," Paul said, finishing his last bite of breakfast. "Yup. No doubt her buttons are surely popping over you today!"

Jessica set Sarah Sue's spoon down and stood behind Paul's kitchen chair where he'd hobbled and perched himself to eat, his leg extended under the table like a burdensome cane. She put her arms around his neck and kissed the top of his head. "My hero," she said. What she wanted to do was to plop in his lap where he could cradle her while she rested her head against his shoulder, but that familiar luxury would have to wait until the pain in his leg dissolved.

He reached up and took hold of her arms, which she'd clasped against his chest. "Thank you, babe. Thank you for loving me, even when I'm a *fallen* hero." They remained like that until Sarah Sue fussed. It was time to get ready for church anyway. Paul hadn't intended on wrestling himself around to go to church this morning, but that was before the paper arrived. He didn't want to miss a second of what was sure to be his wife's shining moment in her first public appearance as The Winner.

Neither of them was disappointed. Although congregants seemed divided on whether to mall or not to mall, Jessica and Paul Joy were loved by everyone. Pastor

Delbert called both of them, plus Sarah Sue, of course, who was perched on Jessica's hip, up front with him during announcements, just so people could applaud Jessica's winning entry and Paul's heroic endeavor. Then he offered a prayer of thanksgiving for "this bright and promising couple — and their wee one and the one in the hopper." The special blessing helped set the tone for his sermon which was on the peace of the Lord, which, he said, is "*surely* and *sorely* needed in the streets of our little community today."

Too bad Pastor didn't include the sidewalks and the grill along with his prayers for our peaceful streets, Dorothy thought Monday afternoon when she stopped by Harry's for one of Lester's good old hamburgers and fries. Calls for debates and picket lines? What on earth were they coming to?

"Lord," Dorothy said aloud as she walked home after her late lunch, "I know You know everything, but it just doesn't seem like You're acting like it right now. I'm trying to keep wearing my hat of trust here, but I'm beginning to think You might just need a hand with this one. Or . . ." she drifted off, walking until she'd stepped over three consecutive cracks so as not to break her mother's back . . . She picked up her train of thought again. "Maybe this whole mountain of mayhem is part of why You're sending Jacob Henry back home. Then again, if it is, picket lines, mayoral debates and crabby people aren't going to feel like much of a Welcome Wagon, are they?" She carefully observed a few more cracks until she decided she needed to watch where she was going lest she run head-on into someone. When she looked up, May Belle and Earl were right in front of her.

"I hope you're praying," May Belle said with a generous smile. "I told Earl that's what you must be doing, walking along staring at the ground like that. We could hear you muttering clear down the way."

"Indeed I was. I just came from Harry's and I'll tell you *what,* people are acting plumb nuts. I was just having a few words with the Big Guy, wondering if He might need a little help with this situation."

"Such as?"

"Such as you and me and Earl march ourselves straight to the grill and start banging a few heads together, see if we can't knock some sense into folks."

"You were talking to God about *that,* about banging heads together?" May Belle looked puzzled while Earl looked shocked.

"Well, not exactly."

"I'm glad to hear that," said May Belle. "Besides, I'm not in the mood for knocking heads together today and neither is Earl. Right, Earl?" Earl, a gentle giant of a man, was never in the mood for violence, so he vehemently shook his head. "We're far too happy being happy for Jessica Joy! She looked like a glowworm in church yesterday, and have you ever seen anyone look prouder of a spouse than Paul?"

"Thank You, Lord," Dorothy said, looking up, "for Your perfect timing. Once again I am reminded that Your perfect timing isn't always ours. If You didn't send my friends out the door exactly when You did, it's likely I'd still be grumbling. *Amen!*" she said, shifting her eyes toward Earl, "and that is enough of that. Right, Earl?" He nodded. "So where are you two off to?" although she didn't have to ask since May Belle was pushing her folding metal grocery cart in front of her, a system she'd switched to (rather than pulling it) when her back started bothering her several months ago.

"Your Store. Wilbur's got whole fryers on sale this week. Want to join us this evening for fried chicken, mashed potatoes and whatever veggie looks good in the produce section?" She looked at her wristwatch and took note it was already 1:30. "Then again, maybe you're not going to be hungry by five if you just finished lunch."

"Are you kidding me? I can already taste your crunchy white chicken gravy. Count me in, you two. See you then. I gotta get me home and make a few phone calls. Want me to bring anything?"

"Just Sheba. We haven't seen her lately and we've got a nice little pile of scraps waiting."

"You're on. And Earl, we need to talk about my yard. I think it's time we figure what all needs to be done, now that the snow's done flying. It's nearly time to mow."

Earl beamed. Nothing made him happier than to help his Dearest Dorothy.

19

Katie's discomfort was obvious to everyone but Stephanie, the Carols' seven-year-old daughter. Katie wished she could be more at ease in her own skin tonight, but not only was this the first real social gathering with her half-brother, it was also the first time she had shared a meal with *any* pastor, let alone in a rectory. The whole church thing on its own was still somewhat new and odd to her without these additional complications. What if in the privacy of their own home Delbert and his wife prayed in tongues or some strange thing, or asked *her* to pray out loud? She felt oddly ill equipped, or peculiar, or . . . on guard. Because of this, she started to bow her head twice after dinner was on the table and everyone was seated thinking Delbert was launching into grace when he wasn't. When the prayer did come, it wasn't, as she had feared, some kind of soulful plea for God to make them all feel like family. Instead they sang a happy child-like prayer (obviously their routine) asking God to bless the food, their family and the world — Stephanie's and nine-year-old Scott's voices the loudest. Katie was glad for the blessing's simplicity and felt stupid to have fretted over nothing. She was also impressed by the beautiful table Marianne set, complete with linen tablecloth and napkins, place cards (reminiscent of her few dinners at May Belle's), Waterford crystal and stunning red glass candleholders.

Although they'd chatted in the living room a few minutes before Marianne called them to the table, she really didn't have a chance to look around the way she wanted for fear she'd appear nosey — which to be honest, she was feeling. What kind of home did her father's son live in? The house had also been his father's — *their* father's — since it was the rectory. (Delbert Junior followed in his father's footsteps filling the pastoral duties at United Methodist.)

Had things been different . . . this might have been my *childhood home.* She suddenly found herself longing for evidence of her father's fingerprints on the world, a place to rest her hand atop where his might have landed — a touchstone to *him,* the father she'd never known. Of course it was decades since his death, and a home usually ended up looking and feeling more like the woman who lived in it than the man, but still, Marianne came to this house of her husband's youth, so some things would surely remain the same, like the stunning dark woodwork that encased the tall doorways. *My father would have probably touched that very wood many times . . .*

It must be odd, she thought, working to distract herself from unfamiliar longings, *to move into your husband's home.* She couldn't even imagine moving into Bruce's home when they were first married. Oh, the place had been nice enough — his parents were nice enough — but a woman needed to put her mark on a home, make it *her* nest. Katie's taste was decidedly contemporary and Bruce's folks liked French provincial. Making her contemporary taste work at the farm was enough of a stretch. Thank goodness they hadn't moved into Bruce's house, since after their divorce that might have made things even more complicated, were that humanly possible. Learning about the other, younger woman was cross enough to bear without *her* having to be the one to move out. She hadn't trusted a man since.

"So, Josh, how goes the job?" Delbert asked, ending a rather long silence.

Josh chuckled. A pop-off about slave labor perched on the tip of his tongue, but he knew better. He was way too excited about this evening to mess up. "Pretty good and pretty exhausting. Earl came over to work with me yesterday afternoon though, and that was cool."

"What have you been working on, besides cleaning rooms?" Marianne asked.

"We didn't do much actual total room cleaning this weekend, but we sure did our share of spot-cleaning carpets. And we moved the washing machines out to clean behind them. Man, Earl is as strong as a horse. And . . . let's see, what else . . . oh, and I learned how to prepare flower beds for spring planting," he said somewhat more sarcastically than he meant to, causing his mother to raise an eyebrow.

"I planted a flower seed today," Stephanie said. "Our teacher brought seeds and we each got our own pot. But it's a secret what it's for," she said, looking at her mom and grinning.

Katie couldn't help but notice a small grouping of framed photographs over Marianne's shoulder. They were arranged on a red velvet scarf draped across the top of a piano. She wondered who played. Not Delbert. He wasn't the piano-playing type. She didn't have a musical bone in her body either, other than expertly loading her SUV's six-changer CD. Aside from her workout DVDs, she usually preferred listening to NPR's news anyway, so one of the first things she noticed when they'd arrived was the classical music playing quietly in the background. Marianne probably played the piano.

"The children both take lessons," Delbert said, as though he'd read her mind. Katie smiled, acknowledging the fact she'd been busted. "And this might sound corny, but *I* enjoy playing ragtime and old music from the twenties and thirties."

"Corny. You can say that again, Dad," Scott said, torquing up his face and smiling at Josh, who he was clearly enamored of and obviously trying to impress.

"Talk about corny," Josh said, "my dad doesn't listen to anything but jazz. Do you know what jazz is?" Scott nodded while Stephanie shook her head. "Let's just say it's not nearly as cool as ragtime, which is beyond cool and majorly *radical* if you ask me."

"Radical." Marianne said the word as if she'd never heard it before. "I have to admit to you, Delbert, that over the years I have thought about you in many ways but radical has never been one of them."

Delbert chuckled, as did Josh. Katie thought just being a pastor was radical, but she withheld comment.

"How about you play us a radical ragtime tune or two after dinner, Uncle Delbert? If that would be okay," Josh said, turning his eyes toward Marianne, who insisted he address her by her first name rather than Mrs. Carol, which she said made her feel like she should be Delbert's mother. Katie insisted Josh use proper names with adults but she could tell this was a special issue with Marianne so she let it slide.

Marianne looked at her wristwatch. "If everyone is done eating I'll serve up dessert," she said, rising from her seat. Suddenly noticing Katie's plate was still half full she sat back down and added, "But don't let me hurry you, Katie."

"Mom never finishes a meal unless it's some kind of salad," Josh blurted, wishing he hadn't since Katie shot him a look.

"Oh! It never occurred to me you might be a vegetarian, Katie! I should have asked," Marianne said, her eyes scanning the table noting the rolled pork roast and the bacon in the green beans.

"No, I'm not a vegetarian," Katie said, dragging her eyes away from Josh. "I'm just not a big eater. Everything was wonderful!"

"Wish I could say the same," she said, holding her hands to her waistline before removing Katie's plate. "I'll get these dishes to the kitchen and serve up the cake roll. I asked the kids what they wanted and cake roll it was." Katie smiled. She hadn't seen a cake roll — didn't even know they still existed — since her mother, who loved them, died. She always had one in the freezer. She recalled her mom letting the ice cream melt a little, then mashing it with her fork until it looked like mush. Must be another of those Partonville things, she thought. "The children need to get to bed pretty soon, but I think we'll have time for one tune, if you think you can limit yourself, Delbert." A plate in each hand, she raised her eyebrows at her husband, who looked either a little sheepish or guilty, Katie couldn't tell exactly which, but he nodded agreement. "Let's just say the pastor at First United Methodist Church has an evil twin who comes out when he sits down at that piano. Not even an earthquake could knock him off that stool, I fear."

"Evil twin?" Katie asked, before Josh had a chance to get the words out of his mouth. She looked quite amused and pleasantly surprised by the notion. Ah, something she could finally relate to!

"May I please be excused?" Scott asked. "I want to go play Nintendo in your bedroom." Delbert and Marianne had fretted over whether or not to get him a Nintendo, finally deciding they would hook it up on the television in their bedroom, only to be played when the whole family was gathered together on the bed, or for a special occasion, which apparently Scott decided this was.

"Before dessert?" Josh quipped. "What kind of kid bails on dessert?"

"Okay, I'll stay for dessert, but I've heard Dad play the piano plenty of times before. It's not that great. Trust me," he said. "You'll see."

Katie was blown away. The man played ragtime like a professional. Such abandon! He reared his head back, closed his eyes, rocked forward, nose almost to the keys as he fingered a few rowdy licks. Yes, rowdy, she thought. That was the perfect word. Watching him play the piano was like witnessing Clark Kent come out from behind the pulpit and change into a Piano Man costume just so his fingers could soar across the keyboard. He worked the foot pedals so hard Katie thought they'd surely crack off.

Josh was up on his feet clapping and tapping his foot. . . . It was nothing short of magnificent.

Oh, how Katie longed to drop a few of her barriers, just let loose a little, throw her head back and. . . . What? Now there, she mused, was something to think about.

When Katie went to bed that evening, she felt more alive and relaxed than she had in a long while. Delbert played two more tunes before Marianne tactfully reminded him that people had school and work tomorrow. Not once had anyone brought up "family" or "relational" issues; they'd simply enjoyed each other's company. Katie would never again listen to him preach without picturing the wild man *inside* the poised preacher at the pulpit. She'd now received a hint as to why Delbert and Josh got in trouble in the truck. The redeeming part was that Delbert was a real champion during their meeting at the farm when he came to discuss the issue. He was utterly level-headed and genuinely cared about Josh's well-being. Josh listened to Delbert. Building a relationship between her son and a man who cared about her son, one who would serve as a good role model, made her pleased with the evening.

She rolled onto her stomach and cradled one of her many lush down pillows in her arms. *Ragtime!* Who wouldn't want to know more about a man like that? Did he get his musical talent from their father? she wondered. She'd have to ask. And if so, where was her portion?

Jacob looked in his rearview mirror. It felt funny to be driving his Saab for more than a few hours at a time. City living had its advantages. On the other hand, it would feel good not to be breathing someone's exhaust or listening to honking horns every time he buckled up. Today he'd traveled far enough on the interstate so that traffic had thinned out a bit, for which he was thankful. If anything made him nuts on the road it was tailgaters.

His mom told him to call her when he stopped for the night. Although he'd be staying with friends tomorrow night, this night he was on his own. Nobody expected him at any certain time so he could drive as long as he wanted and find a hotel somewhere when he got tired. He told her he wouldn't call if he stopped after 11 p.m. and that he'd give her a buzz when he was back on the road in the morning. Her response: "You call me when you stop for the night, Jacob Henry. I don't care what time it is."

Moms.

He wondered how old a child had to be before a mom stopped worrying. He recalled how tense and worried Katie had been last Christmas until Josh made it back from his first solo long-distance road trip. He remembered his mother's exact bedside prayer when his sister was dying at the age of thirty-nine. "Lord, hold my baby girl in the palms of Your hands." She said she never felt so helpless in her life. "My babies." At fifty-six, being referred to as a baby felt like both a hard nut to swallow and a rich thing to hear.

Funny how now that he was moving back his mom's propensity to worry about him seemed greater, or maybe he was just more aware of it. When he was halfway across the country, she had no idea what he was up to, how late or early he was coming or going. But now that he would soon be living under her roof, her worry radar was activated and spinning like a top.

But then, she was the main reason he was doing what he was doing. The older he got, the higher *his* propensity for worry about *her,* so he guessed they were even. Why had her voice sounded so weak their last phone call? he'd sometimes think. Had she been crying? Would she tell him if she were sick, or keep it to herself so as not to worry him? "Are you sleeping and eating well, Mom?" "Are you taking your heart medication, Mom?"

Moms and their sons.

20

Katie sat at her kitchen table rearranging three-by-five note cards while trying to convince herself she was ready for this evening's long-ago scheduled community meeting regarding Partonville Pleasantries, which now shared double billing with a mayoral debate. Could it *get* any worse? Gladys, Sam and the townsfolk agreed that the two issues were inseparable, so why not combine the events. When chatting with Dorothy or Jessica, Katie referred to the day she first learned about the double billing as The Flood since her body's response was a tidal wave of hot flashes she claimed produced enough sweat to drown her. Thank goodness she'd been in the privacy of her own bedroom talking on the phone with Jessica, who read her the news straight out of the *Press*.

She peeled through her cards again memorizing every step of her agenda. First she would present an update on the mall's progress and her vision for how it fit into the town's long-term planning. Then she'd talk briefly about the specific shops within the mall. *Then* she'd deliver the grand surprise olive branch: she would offer a "Partonvillers Only" invitation to a Partonville Pleasantries open house the Friday evening *before* the official grand opening, which was now only four-and-a-half weeks away, during which — and she would announce this with *great* gusto — she would conduct an on-the-spot drawing for a fifty-dollar gift certificate to any shop in the mall.

She stopped reading and wrote out a new three-by-five note card. "Make sure you ask Swifty to make it <u>clear</u> I will <u>not</u> be opening the floor for questions until <u>after</u> I announce the preview open house and drawing." Several Partonvillers were inherent buttinskis and the fevered climate in town had rallied them to new heights of bad behavior. She figured this tactic was at least worth a shot. Perhaps a spoonful of gift certificate could help the particulars go down, but she could already hear Dorothy saying, "HA!"

This preview for townsfolk was Dorothy's idea. Something to further help residents claim the mall as their own. Dorothy came up with the notion last Saturday night when she and Jacob came for dinner out at the farm. Katie called it Jacob's official welcome-to-Pardon-Me-Ville dinner, which she hosted in exchange for some legal advice about wording on a few things for the meeting. "Fair enough," he'd said in response to the invitation. They also met again last night around Dorothy's kitchen table just to make sure Katie had covered all the bases. ("Like *that's* humanly possible with Pardon-Me-Villers," Dorothy quipped.) It was also the meeting at which Katie asked Jacob to serve as the lawyer for Partonville Pleasantries, to which he agreed. "My first new corporate client," he said with a hint of sarcasm and a tad more enthusiasm than he was feeling, leaving Katie hoping she'd read his response correctly and that it was just his dry sense of humor.

Only after his formal acceptance did she present the caveat.

"Good. Now that you're on board as my lawyer, you can step up to the microphone in your official capacity during the meeting, should the need arise." Although he raised his eyebrows — his professional entry into Partonville suddenly feeling nothing short of a baptism by fire ants — he consented.

Katie flipped through her note cards one last time before tucking them into the front folder in her portable file case that still traveled with her every trip she made between the farm and the mall. She decided to bring the whole thing with her this evening, just in case. She hated how wired she felt, how . . . alone. She snapped the lid closed, scooted the case to the edge of the table and strode to the bottom of the stairway.

"You coming?" she hollered up to Josh, hoping he could hear her above his stereo.

"You say something?" he yelled back after turning down the volume.

"YES! Are you *coming?*"

"You *want* me to?" He sat dumbfounded at his desk, staring at his bedroom door as though she were standing there. This was the first time she'd mentioned this, although he sure knew about the brouhaha. *You'd have to be dead not to know about it,* Shelby quipped at school today. He quite agreed. Nobody around town talked about anything else these days. But he was grounded. Besides, he was sick of the whole thing anyway.

"WELL?" she yelled.

Part of him wanted to just stay away from all of it. The mall was her life lately and he hated that. However, the other part of him said to himself, *What are you, NUTS? You're grounded and you're going to turn down a chance to get out of this house?* "Just a sec! Let me comb my hair!"

"I'm leaving right now," she said emphatically, spinning on her heels, passing by the kitchen table and scooping up her file box.

Josh hopped in the SUV just as Katie put it in reverse. They drove in silence until she turned onto the blacktop. He noticed she sat ramrod straight while her index fingers tap-danced on the steering wheel. "You nervous about this meeting?" he asked.

She thought a minute. "Nervous isn't the right word. On guard, maybe. I'm not sure what to expect, really. Sometimes people in this town act like savages."

After a moment of silence he begrudgingly — and that was obvious by his tone — spoke. "Dorothy said you'll do fine and so will Gladys. She's also glad Jacob's going to be there in case you need his help."

"When did she say all that?"

"E-mail. Is Uncle Delbert gonna be there?"

"I don't know."

"Have you even talked to him since our dinner . . . seven, eight . . . no, *nine* days ago?" Now his tone was accusatory.

"No. And do *not* push me on this, Joshua Matthew Kinney. I've got enough on my mind right now."

He sighed and slumped down in his seat wishing he'd stayed home since nothing, not even her own brother, mattered to her but her precious mall.

When they pulled into the parking lot for the Park District building, Katie was stunned to see that even though she'd come a half hour early, the lot was nearly full. She'd hoped to check out the podium and set up her notes in private. No such luck. After finding a spot near the back of the lot — her eyes scanning the cars hoping to spot Jacob's Saab — she parked the SUV. Josh opened his door to get out before she even turned off the engine.

"Josh! Wait a minute," she said, grabbing him by the arm.

He turned his scowling face toward her. "What?" he snapped.

She pursed her lips, then relaxed them. Then her eyes welled. "I'm glad you're here with me, Josh. Truly. Thank you for coming."

He nodded his head, swallowed. He was as stunned as if she'd just sat down at the piano and played ragtime.

Jacob and Dorothy pulled up in front of May Belle's to find May Belle standing on the porch waiting for them, her age-old tweed coat buttoned tight up under her neck, a large brown paper grocery bag in each hand. Jacob hopped out, relieved her of her packages and helped her into the back seat of his car.

"I thought the doughnut shop donated coffee and doughnuts for the meeting," Dorothy said, turning around as far as her stiff old neck would allow, which wasn't very far.

"I baked a few dozen cookies anyway, just in case the meeting runs late and the dough-nuts run out. Anything to help prevent the natives from getting *more* restless," she said with a nervous chuckle.

"Not a bad idea. Not a bad idea at all," Dorothy noted. "I'm glad I don't have to do anything but sit there tonight. I don't envy *anyone* involved in this mall."

"Oh, *thanks!*" Jacob said.

Dorothy smiled, leaned over and patted him on the arm. "Don't worry, son, the Big Guy's ultimately in control, even if it might not feel like it this evening."

"I've been reminding myself of that all day too, Dorothy," May Belle said. "The tension in this town is prickly. But even though God *is* bigger than all of us, I'll have the cookies in the car if we need them. Never hurts to help Him out every now and again, right?"

May Belle smiled, recalling Dorothy's last mention of helping God out by knocking heads together.

"Right." Dorothy would never disagree with *that.*

"And if we don't need your secret ammunition, I bet Mom can figure a few personal ways to help relieve you of it. She's got an extra mouth to feed right now, you know," he said, catching May Belle's eye in his rearview mirror and beaming her a smile.

"I sure do!" Dorothy chirped.

She sounded so content with him under her roof, Jacob thought, which was another reason he needed to find his own digs before she got too used to his presence. Plus, a man needed his space and he was tired of feeling cramped. He just hoped that after tonight's meeting he didn't need to find himself a cave.

"Now, Nellie Ruth," Edward Showalter said while reaching across the front seat to take her hand, "I'm sure we won't be the last ones to get there. You can't help it if you had to work late, and neither could I." Then he erupted in off-key song. "Ya load sixteen tons, and what do you get? Another day older and . . . *Tar*-dy," he added in the tone of a ding-dong doorbell. Nellie Ruth, a consummate musician who played the saxophone like a professional and possessed the gift of perfect pitch, chuckled and squeezed his hand.

"Tell me true, ES, how are you holding up, *really,* with all of these long hours? I know you say okay, but do you mean it, *really?*"

"I'm a tough old goat, Nellie Ruth. Tougher than you might think," he said.

She thought about how he always opened her van door or gathered Kornflake's silky ears in his hands, gently rubbing them between his fingers, and recalled his tender prayers. "Tough as nails," she said, flashing him a coy smile. "But still, here we are on our way to listen to what might turn out to be a debate about your very job, and after all the dedication you've shown! Are your long hours and all the personal conflicts with your coworkers, who are also your friends — not to mention all the danger you endure every day — *worth* defending?"

"Danger?"

"Scaffolding, ladders, live electrical wires . . . ," things she simply could not stop fretting about, no matter how much she prayed.

Edward Showalter sucked his lips inside

his mouth. *A debate about my very job?* By golly, she was right! He'd never once in the midst of all this mall bashing and mayoral haranguing had time to consider his job might be in jeopardy. Why would he? His boss lady was smart, rich and determined, and he was a laborer worthy of his hire. Sure, he was putting in a lot of hours, and there were occasional ruffled feathers with the work crew, and tensions about the mall, *and* a mayoral race in the works. But a debate about his *job?*

Sure enough, if the mall was somehow defeated, so, too, he would be. He would no longer be a man with a managerial title and job security, a man who could one day care for a wife. He would be nothing more than an unemployed — or at the very best not consistently employed — recovering alcoholic. What was that to offer anyone, least of all a lady like Nellie Ruth? He weaved his way through the maze of cars in silence, his Adam's apple bobbing up and down in an attempt to keep his dry throat from slamming shut.

"Would you please read this for me, Glenda honey?" Glenda looked up from her knitting. Her husband stood before her holding a short stack of papers. He handed her the double-spaced pages hot off his printer.

"Is this what you've been working on the last few nights?" she asked, setting her knitting aside and receiving the offering.

"It is. But I've been working on it in my head for longer than that. Now it's time to stop working on it and submit it."

"I'm proud of you, Carl."

"How do you know? You don't even know *what* it is and you haven't read it yet."

"First of all, I'm always proud of you. But second, when you take a stand for something, I've never known you to be wrong. Once you finally shared what was bothering you, I knew you'd have to do something. You're a chip off the old block, as your dad — a wonderful old block — used to say." She shuffled through the pages, surprised at the length.

"Too long?"

Sometimes maybe they knew each other too well, she thought. "First let's give it a read, then I'll give you my honest opinion."

"Since the first day I met you, I've never expected anything less," he said, bending down to plant a kiss on the top of her sparkling gray-haired head.

The last gentleman to arrive in the Park District building stood in the shadows of the rear door through which he entered. He'd held his foot in back of him to keep the door from slamming shut so as not to draw unwanted attention. He stayed put for a number of reasons, not the least of which was to make sure he could be the first one out. Katie Durbin was just being introduced. He leaned against the wall, withdrew a tape recorder from his interior sport jacket pocket, turned it on and held it out in front of him. *So that's the dame under Colton's skin.*

Harold Crab sat directly in front of the podium watching Katie shuffle through her note cards. He was close enough to notice the moisture on her upper lip and the faint beads of sweat trickling onto her brow. Even though it was cool outdoors, the packed room felt stuffy — but not *that* stuffy. She must be more nervous than she was letting on, although his reporter's sixth sense had already detected a slight air of anxiety swirling around her when she arrived. Herb Morgan had grabbed her by the elbow the moment she entered the building and escorted her to her reserved seat in the front row next to Gladys, who was uncharacteristically quiet. Dazed was more like it. But then she hadn't been at Harry's the last few mornings either. Maybe she wasn't feeling well. Katie seemed perturbed about the seating arrangement, although Harold wasn't sure why until he saw Josh shrug his shoulders and begin looking around for a single seat somewhere else, the front row already full. At least that's what Harold thought Josh was doing. In reality he was using the opportunity to search for Shelby.

But now there Katie stood at the podium after Swifty Forester's introduction (Swifty was solicited to emcee the evening due to his loudly seasoned auctioneer's voice and impartial presence) stating her name as if under oath and as though every single person in the room *aside* from Swifty didn't already know who she was and hadn't arrived for the sole purpose of either cheering her on or verbally gunning her down.

Harold had been the second person to arrive this evening. The first was the janitor. It was hard to keep from laughing out loud as Harold observed the first half of the arrivals either head to the right or left of the middle aisle, as though they were on the bride's or groom's side of a feuding family. He'd written as much in his notes. And who among them seemed to vie for those front-row seats? Of course Cora Davis was third to arrive and she parked herself in the front row on the left. Gladys was the fourth in the door and she roosted herself right next to him since the podium was slightly to the right of the center aisle and her positioning quickly took the form of those "for" everything in question on her personal agenda. Sharon, right on Gladys's heels, pulled a chair out of one of the rows and parked herself up at the front facing the crowd, almost directly sideways from Katie so she could correctly attribute audience comments while still getting a good view of the speakers' facial expressions. She also wanted to send a clear signal that she was neutral, striving to equally report both sides of the story — although in her heart of hearts, she knew she'd vote for anything that might sink that smug Colton Craig.

When Dorothy, Jacob and May Belle showed up, they took seats near the middle on the right since that's as close to the front as they could get. Harold took note that Katie seemed to be watching for them and was relieved when she saw them enter. In fact, she didn't fully settle into her seat until after she gave them a relieved nod. Of course Herb Morgan was on the right, too, but even though he was relatively early, he had to settle for a seat at the beginning of the second quadrant.

Once the front half of the seats was filled and the heavyweights were no longer visible, the "sides" weren't as obvious, so people parked anywhere, then stood wherever they could.

Now, Katie stood before the deathly silent crowd sweating hot-flash bullets while "setting the record straight," telling them it was time to "shine our town lights," "revitalize, display our talents, sell our goods," "come together with purpose and viable plans," and "put a new face on our quaint town." And if there was one thing she wanted to assure them of, she was, whether they believed it or not, "no longer The City Slicker but a country dweller with a heart for the entire of Pardon-Me-Ville." Why else, she asked them — *implored* them to consider — would she invest her personal money in Partonville or Partonvillers by keeping a separate file for qualified locals seeking employment positions in the mall *and* by showcasing their local wares. Had they forgotten she helped Dorothy secure land to establish Crooked Creek Park, which would break ground in the beginning of May? Did she not "evidence" her "genuine pleasure" when she hosted the annual Christmas party out at the farm? And then the clincher: would any of them honestly believe she would be, *could* be, a Happy Hooker if she was not truly a Partonviller?

At the mention of the Hookers, Dorothy spontaneously popped up and began to applaud. Harold wondered if Katie and Dorothy had staged this maneuver. (Which they had not, really, although Dorothy did encourage Katie to at least mention the Hookers.) Raising her clapping hands high over her head, Dorothy shouted, "Hurray for the HOOKERS!" thereby inciting every other Happy Hooker in the room — Nellie Ruth McGregor, Jessica Joy, Gladys McKern, Maggie Malone, Jessie Landers and May Belle Justice — to do the same.

Dorothy had been waiting for the right moment to rally her personal battle cry for Katie without it seeming too obvious. When she heard Katie mention the Happy Hookers she barely had time to think *If not now, when?* before she was on her feet. It was the perfect opportunity. Since everyone in town knew about, and celebrated, the Happy Hookers, people on both sides of the aisle joined in the applause, finding it a momentary respite from the otherwise strained atmosphere. Dorothy was deliriously happy with the response, especially when she saw Katie break out in her first smile of the evening, raise *her* hands above her head and begin to clap. It was good for everyone to be reminded that Katie Durbin had been *invited* into the decades-old, time-honored and sacred club. Whether you were for Katie Durbin or not, you cheered for the Happy Hookers. That's just the way it was. (Unless you were Sam Vitner, who forced himself to rest his hands in his lap during this shameless electioneering taking place before the debate even began.) Frieda Hornsby cheered so loudly and so long that Fred grabbed her by the arm and yanked her back down in her seat lest people think she'd jumped ship and swapped sides.

The man holding the tape recorder at the back of the room almost dropped it. He was unfamiliar with any of the ins and outs of Partonville, and in particular the happy *hookers?* In his state of shock all he could think was *What in the world is going* ON *in this town!*

21

Carl sat in his chair, book in front of him, trying to read Glenda's face while she turned the pages. She held a pencil in her hand and occasionally wrote something in the margins. In some cases he thought she made nothing more than a check mark, although the look on her face didn't reveal if it was because something was good or bad. Other times she seemed to either jot a few words or draw a line, maybe both. When she finished the last page she took off her glasses, closed her eyes and pinched the bridge of her nose. She tidied the pages, took a deep breath and for the first time met his eyes, which she felt burning on her the whole time she read, even though he pretended to read a book.

"Well?"

"It's beautiful, Carl," she said, a lump catching in her voice. "Moving. This article," she said, patting the top of the stack, "is perhaps as strong as any building you've ever designed. It makes me wonder if a romance writer lurks inside your lovable, geometric, architectural self." She smiled. "I can almost feel your heart beating — your father's heart beating — within the rhythm of the words."

"That's mighty high praise, Glenda," he said, his voice quiet.

"I also have to be frank here. There were a couple places I don't believe you communicated exactly what you were trying to say. And it is too long, at least for your intentions. I've marked a few paragraphs where you can trim it without losing any of the meaning or impact. But I think you'll still need to shorten it, even after that."

"Thank you, honey," he said, standing and straightening his tall lanky body, stretching first one arm over his head, then the other. He retrieved the papers and headed back down the hall to his office where he remained until nearly 11. Even though an unnamed sense of urgency drove him, he wanted to get it right. He'd allow his mind a rest for the night, give it another read-through in the morning, let Glenda have one final shot at it, then get it to the post office.

■ ■ ■ ■

Even before applause for the Happy Hookers began to wane, Katie noticed a hand shoot up in the front row. Fred Hornsby. He was glowering. Katie nodded, said she would answer all his questions — everyone's questions — but quickly reminded him of the ground rules.

"It's time," she said, leaning slightly toward the audience and strengthening her voice, "to give you the specifics about the shops and put the rumors to rest." A chuckle rose from the middle of the pack, which set off a brief wave of laughter throughout the room that momentarily silenced her. It hadn't occurred to her that was a funny statement. "Well, I'll at least put them to rest to the best of my ability and for this fleeting moment in time.

"You know, I was going to present Partonville Pleasantries stores from the top floor down to the lower level, give you a mental walk-through. But instead I think I'll save that pleasure for your own eyes during our private premiere in a few weeks. Tonight I'm going to present them to you in the order — at least in part — of their immediate importance to the community."

Dorothy, who was taking mental notes on the points where she thought Katie was the strongest (because Katie asked her to), had to keep from cheering out loud again.

"There are two stores I believe will not only help set Partonville apart but that will best showcase our unique talents, as well as complement the warmth of our community and the long-standing established businesses already on the square. The first is the Tea Cozy, owned and operated by Partonville's own Theresa Brewton, who many of you know from Saint Augustine's Church and her involvement with the community Thanksgiving dinner held at United Methodist. Theresa has a background in food service. When she caught wind of my desire for a tea room, she told me she's always wanted to open her own venture and what better place to do so than right in her own backyard. Theresa, would you please stand so we can acknowledge you?" Theresa popped up, lifted her hand and gave a wave to a polite ripple of applause.

"Theresa tells me," Katie said after Theresa sat down and the applause died out, "that she will be serving a variety of teas, a select group of specially ground coffees, plus daily featured finger sandwiches and desserts, some of the desserts made by our own May Belle Justice." Katie nodded May Belle's way but she didn't ask her to rise, knowing her well enough to understand May Belle never invited public attention. Instead Dorothy stood and pointed down at the top of May Belle's head, starting a quick round of applause.

May Belle put her hand over her mouth, wishing the gesture could make her disappear. "That's enough, Dorothy," she said behind her hand. "Please sit down, dear."

Katie scanned her cards and continued. "I'm sure I don't even need to tell you about Calico Corner Creations, our consignment shop, which is one of the stores the mall is most delighted to host. We have so many gifted and creative people in town and now they'll have a place to showcase their wares year-round. After observing how quickly items moved at the craft booths during our Pumpkin Festival last fall, I have no doubt Calico Corner — and it is literally a corner store — will be among the highest trafficked stores since new and original items will arrive daily giving shoppers a reason to return again and again. From what manager Arlene Riford tells me, shelves are sure to be full on opening day since she's already been cataloguing consignment items for two months and storing them in her basement, which she claims, and this is a direct quote, 'is full to the rafters.' Arlene, please stand up and take *your* bow."

Katie glanced at Gladys. She wished she'd had more time to talk to her this week, do a bit more strategizing and coordinating on presentation points. Gladys had scooted in and out of church so quickly on Sunday Katie didn't have time to nab her, and oddly, Gladys hadn't returned her call yesterday, or the one from the day be-fore. And now tonight, although Gladys looked at Katie, it appeared she didn't really see her. Gladys's eyes were sort of glazed over. *I trusted you to be ready for this debate. Surely that wasn't a mistake. Come on, Gladys! Pull yourself together!* Katie tapped her stack of cards on the podium while drawing her attention back to the task at hand.

Although she looked at Katie, Gladys hadn't really heard a word she'd said. Her heart was beating so fast that she felt dizzy and actually thought she might become ill a time or two.

Since shortly after the morning Lester sent her packing, she felt as though pieces of herself had been falling away. She'd been blindsided by Sam's bid for mayor, his tenacious pursuit to outdo her every slogan and his unrelenting replay of every mayoral mistake she'd ever made — including that ill-fated time she tried to change the direction of traffic on the square causing the worst traffic jam in Partonville's history. Even the *Daily Courier,* Hethrow's syndicated newspaper, picked up on the calamity — both then and now. "ROUND-AND-ROUND SHE'LL TAKE US" appeared on one of Sam's campaign buttons seemingly within moments of him dredging the incident up again, and the *Courier* ran a picture of the button along with a brief recap of the incident. Then she'd been kicked out of the grill. The *mayor,* kicked out of the *grill,* which Cora immediately spread around town in a souped-up version. She felt her confidence eroding by the second. As for tonight, the more security, eloquence and professionalism Katie projected, the less Gladys felt qualified to follow her. Who *could* follow that act? And here Gladys was supposed to be Katie's equal, her partner in the revitalization projects.

Before she arrived for the debate this evening, Gladys had sat for a long while with her favorite picture of Jake, her deceased truck-driving husband, in her lap. He was standing next to his truck cab, one foot up on the running board, his forearms resting on his elevated thigh. They'd only been married three years then and at her encouragement he'd just taken a big financial risk and purchased his own shiny blue rig rather than drive for someone else. He was so swashbucklingly handsome, so grateful to her for pushing him to step out on his own. What had *happened* to her the last few weeks? Where was her fight? Where was *he* when she needed *him?*

She clutched the picture to herself and swore she could feel the vibration of his laughter rippling against her chest. *You? Run out of* fight? *NEVER!,* she heard him say. She imagined not a single person in town would believe it possible either. After all, she was "Gladys the Gladiator!" Since she was a child Gladys understood that she had a strong personality, one that could be off-putting, which is why kids had taken to calling her that terrible nickname. But since she'd become mayor she'd finally learned to claim her gladiator status. Serving as acting mayor of Partonville was the first time in her life she'd been afforded a mission in which to channel her God-given attributes in order to make a *real* difference.

And now, now here she sat in the front row of a packed room waiting her turn to take a stand for herself, for the whole of Partonville, and it was all she could do to breathe.

22

"I'm sure," Katie said, looking directly at Sam Vitner, "you've all heard *plenty* about the antique store setting up shop in Partonville Pleasantries." She paused to allow for an expected ripple of laughter. Although a couple people did chuckle, she was surprised by the weakness of their response since Sam had single-handedly started his campaign against her by talking about how she was going into direct competition with him. But she thought she'd nipped his rising anarchy in the bud at the Christmas party when she not only solicited his help with pricing (so as not to damage either of them), but even suggested they occasionally swap merchandise and therefore help to freshen and advertise both of their businesses. Yes, all seemed smoothed over — won over. What a surprise to learn his rumblings never disappeared, but instead festered into a full-blown attack and bid for mayor! But tonight, now that his hardhead-edness had left her no choice but to move forward without his expected help, it was her turn to rally the troops. "Manager Wade O'Shea," she said, nodding toward him, "would you please stand and unveil the antique store's name for us?"

Wade, a large, stocky, brown-eyed, freckle-faced man in his fifties who'd lost his job in one of the mine layoffs, stood, removed his weathered and ever-present fedora hat and encouraged his wife, Margaret-Mary, to stand beside him. "New to You!" he said proudly. "I can't take all the credit, though, since my wife here is obviously the clever one while I'm just the go-fer," which he pronounced as two words. "But we make a whale of a tag-team operation," he said, giving her a wink. "And we want to thank all of you," he continued, first turning his head 180 degrees in one direction, then the other, "who might have shopped at Margaret-Mary's booth over in the antique mall in Hethrow. That's what gave us the confidence the two of us could expand on her idea and start our own place together, right here in our own town. And don't forget, we'll be accepting . . . what do you call those, sweetheart?" — he looked her way and she whispered something to him — "consignments, too, so start cleaning out those attics! If you need help with that, let me know since that's what coal mining best trained me to do is to pick and dig for the right stuff!" He waited for chuckles to come and go after a fellow miner let out a big *AMEN!* "I'm also available for any handyman jobs too."

"This isn't the time or the place for our entire life story, Wade," Margaret-Mary said, taking hold of her husband's hand, encouraging him to sit down with her, causing another brief burst of laughter in the room.

Katie glanced at Gladys again while she rifled her cards waiting for the room to quiet down. She was stunned to notice Gladys looked like she was fighting back tears. *What on earth?* But no time to think about that now. "Another unique store I believe will draw customers from near and far is A Tisket A Basket, a supplier of made-to-order custom gift baskets, baskets filled with unique goodies from the store including an array of 'Welcome to Pardon-Me-Ville' souvenirs like coffee mugs and refrigerator magnets — and don't forget to pick yourself one for half price the night of our private grand opening — but also with items customers can buy from throughout the mall, which will build an even greater internal synergy." (Edward Showalter leaned over to Nellie Ruth and asked her what in the world synergy was, since it sounded like something a preacher ought to be preaching *against.*) "Jenna Olsen, a previous manager of Now and Again Resale in Yorktown, implemented a natural segue for her career with this choice. Our own Jessica Joy, who has her hands otherwise full right now, recommended I contact Jenna. Although Jessica won't be working in the store, along with producing babies and her wonderful crafts in Calico Corner" — chuckles around — "she'll also use her God-given gifts to occasionally consult with Jenna. It was a welcome basket that Jessica made up for the architect for Pleasantville Pleasantries that gave me the idea for a gift-basket shop, and as luck would have it, we found the perfect match! Jenna, Jessica, please take a bow."

After a brief rundown of Baths, Boudoir and Babies gift wear, the Stitch-in' Time yarn shop, Helping Hands massage therapy, and The Word Exchange, a used-book store, and an energized tidbit about Alotta Chocolatta anchoring the lower level (she didn't linger on this because they'd been written about more than once), Katie finally got to the last store on her list. "Garden Goodies will sell everything from lawn decorations to hummingbird feeders, a small assortment of wild-bird foods and an amazing array of kites for kids and adults. They will also feature seasonal and holiday items. Store owners Matt and Melissa Dertinger will be new to Partonville, moving here the day after tomorrow from my old neighborhood in Chicago. I've kept them apprised of Partonvillers' enthusiasm to put themselves back on the map.

"They've hired a manager to operate their well-established suburban location and this new expansion project offered the opportunity they've been looking for to move their children to a safe and quieter environment. They like everything I've told them so far. They're sorry they couldn't be here for tonight's meeting, but between packing and ordering merchandise for their Partonville Pleasantries spot, they're more than busy. The Dertingers' two grammar-school children will be a welcome addition to our community, as will they. Their move to town — their faith in the success of our mall — has affirmed my vision for growth for us, as I hope it does for you.

"I want to thank you for your time, and patience," Katie said, smiling and nodding at Fred Hornsby, who, since she'd declined to answer his question, avoided eye contact and exhibited an urgent need to find something in his pocket. "As you've heard, the opening of Partonville Pleasantries is a community effort. Shops are not only owned, operated, staffed and in many cases stocked with inventory by Partonvillers, but the mall will also help serve us as consumers.

"And now, I'd like to take a few moments to answer any questions. I know we're all anxious to get to the debate, though," she said, looking at Gladys who was as white as a sheet.

Before she was even done with her sentence, several hands shot up at the same time as a surprisingly hearty applause broke out. Shelby, clapping with gusto, leaned over to Josh, who'd sat remarkably still during his mother's entire presentation. She had to holler over the mounting applause to be heard. "YOUR MOM IS SOOOOO SMART! YOU MUST BE SOOOOO PROUD OF HER! WHAT A GREAT THING SHE'S DOING FOR ALL OF US! SO MUCH WORK! *I* AM SO PROUD TO KNOW HER, TO BE DATING HER *SON!*" She planted a quick peck on his cheek. "EVEN IF YOU *ARE* GROUNDED!" she added, unfortunately just as the applause was dying down so nearly everyone in the room heard her.

"Yes, Sam," Katie said, nodding her head at him. How could she not start with Sam?

"Please tell us, Ms. Durbin," he said while rising, "who actually *owns* the mall, the coffee shop and the resale shop. Not the antique store that *will* be competing with me," he said with emphasis to let her know he'd heard her every absurd word, "but that place with the crafts?"

"I'm assuming you're referring to Calico Corner Creations and the *Tea* Cozy, right? The technical answer to your question is of course me." Sam, who had not taken his seat, folded his arms across his chest, nodded and continued nodding while he turned to face the audience. "Which also means," Katie continued, "that one hundred percent of the money invested in the purchase of the long-ago vacated and deteriorating building, the extensive rehabbing and remodeling project — from the asbestos removal to the wiring and new heating system to the exterior facelift and the addition of skylights in the roof to enhance the entire ambiance of the building — have come from my business funds.

"I am the sole owner of Calico Corner

Creations. Just as any other shop in the mall, I pay rent. Arlene Riford is on my payroll as manager and I have given her complete control over any and all decisions. Of course profits from every single item sold in the store go to the consignees and the store makes a small commission, which goes into the business itself, not my pocket.

"The Tea Cozy is currently held in a joint ownership between Theresa Brewton and myself and every six months Theresa has an option to buy me out, a day which we're both looking forward to. Theresa gave me permission to divulge that piece of information at this meeting if need be. Thank you, Theresa." ("GREAT ONE re Theresa!" Dorothy wrote on her notepad. She added a star to both ends of the statement.)

"Of course the financial specifics of my arrangement with Theresa are private, but if you'd like to see any broad-brush documentation regarding sales tax documents, licensing, building permits . . . I'd be happy to give your attorney contact information for the corporation. In fact, let me go ahead and make that easy for you or anyone else who might be interested. Jacob Wetstra, would you please stand and give us a nod?" ("SUPERB re my SON!" Dorothy scribbled in her biggest handwriting yet, just before she broke out in applause.) Jacob, who was blindsided by the mention of his name and was instantly none too happy that Katie had clearly used him to manipulate the audience toward her favor, worked the kink out of his back and did as he was told, giving a quick 360-degree nod before quickly sitting down. "Thank you, Attorney Wetstra.

"While I have the opportunity, let me also clarify any questions you might have, Sam, concerning ownership of New to You. While Wade and Margaret-Mary O'Shea are leasing space from the mall, they are sole owners of that business. If you will recall, during the Hookers' Christmas party I talked to you about an occasional exchange of merchandise. If you're still interested, the O'Sheas are excited about that opportunity too. They'll be getting in touch with you soon, Sam. I'm glad you brought all of this up. Thank you! Do you have any other questions? If not, we'll move on."

Sam, who stood and faced the crowd again, said, "I just want to make it clear to everyone here tonight *who,* exactly, is making money on our square, and also make it perfectly clear when I point out that you've undoubtedly already been paid rent before any of the rest of . . ." and he stopped to draw air quotes . . . " 'us' . . . have had a chance to find out if we'll make a cent."

"I was hoping I'd already made myself clear here, Mr. Vitner, and now I'm hoping I speak for more than myself when I say *many* of us plan to make money on *our* square in *our* town. But most importantly," she paused to cast her eyes around, allowing herself to connect with as many people as possible in a short amount of time, "we plan to do it together."

Any worries Nellie Ruth harbored about her beau's boss were forgotten when Edward Showalter jumped up and started a standing ovation. "Didn't she do *fine!*" he said to Nellie Ruth, as he grabbed her around the waist and snuggled her close up beside him.

Although Maggie Malone was still a tad miffed Katie didn't frequent her shop, and worried that Hands On might try to steal some of her spa business by selling its own line of aromatherapy products, she suddenly felt akin to a woman who was unafraid to so boldly take a risk and fight for it. *A sister entrepreneur! WOMAN POWER!* she thought as she joined in the applause. Plus, she was already wondering what kind of hair Melissa Dertinger had on her head and how soon she could get her hands in it.

Lester K. Biggs had never let on to a soul

that he worried about competition from a silly tea room. One night after he'd locked up, he took a good look around his business establishment. It was as if time and routine had blinded him. He couldn't remember when, if ever, he'd last redecorated the place, when he'd stopped noticing, really, the small tears in the vinyl stool covers, the yellowed plastic covering the hand-scrawled and photocopied menus. How long *had* the Wednesday special been liver and onions? But at the end of his surveying, even after asking himself all of these questions, he'd come up with one conclusion: what was the point of fixing the place up when the usuals came all the time anyway? Who really cared?

But tonight, after listening to Katie Durbin speak so proudly about the future, perhaps it was time he did. Yes, he had the familiar U-shaped counter filled with his usuals who nestled around his work area surrounding him like the family he never had, but the Tea Cozy would offer curiosity, new paint, fresh choices in eats. And if the mall *did* attract as many new visitors as Katie seemed to think it would, how many of the non–Tea Cozy types who circled the square would even bother to stop to check out his burgers when the place looked so rundown? It was time, he concluded at this very moment in his clapping, to give Harry's Grill a good sprucing up. Might even be time to at long last rename it *Lester's* or *The Biggs Place.*

Challie Carter chewed on his toothpick, deftly using his tongue to switch it from one side of his mouth to the other as he stood with his hands buried deep in his pockets. Although he'd always considered Colton Craig the king of development, it was clear he didn't have a thing over Ms. Durbin. He wondered if he shouldn't give the gutsy broad a call, see if they had something more to discuss.

Pastor Delbert Carol Jr. and his entire family looked like their buttons might just pop. To think they'd recently entertained the likes of Katie Durbin, his half-sister, no less, in their very own dining room! What a sibling duo, Marianne thought: a brother who saves souls and a sister who saves the town!

The guy back in the shadows, who had acted in college theater productions, wondered if he hadn't just witnessed the greatest performance of the decade. He could smell greed a mile away, but there it stood fewer than one hundred feet in front of him wearing high heels at the end of those shapely legs.

George Gustafson knew one thing: that

silver-tongued woman continued to drive right on by his gas station to spend her money, right out of the town she claimed was *theirs.* She hadn't uttered a single word this evening to change the truth of that.

"Hows bouts we take us a ten-minute break here ta grab some of those there dough-nuts!" Arthur yelped before Swifty could take the microphone to begin the debate. Smatterings of "I second that motion" filled the room and before anyone could officially recess the meeting, a mad dash was on for the refreshment table.

"People," Swifty said after tapping the microphone with his finger several times, "we will begin again in exactly ten minutes, so get your doughnuts, hit the bathroom if you must, then get back in your seats so you don't miss a word of the debate. Our election is exactly three weeks away and this evening is the best chance each candidate will have to set the record straight and dialogue with each other in front of all of us."

Nobody was listening since it seemed everyone who wasn't racing for a doughnut gathered around Katie to congratulate her. You'd have thought *she* just won the elec-tion. Before she even had a chance to grab a sorely needed cup of coffee, someone flipped the lights on and off a few-times and people scurried back to their seats. Swifty first introduced Sam, who bounded up to the front of the room and took his place behind the podium on the left, which had been moved into place during the break. Sam clasped his hands over his head, pumped his arms and hopped up and down as though he were a prizefighter taking his corner, attempting to rev his supporters back up after Katie's knock-down applause before the break. Then Swifty introduced "Our very own Acting Mayor Gladys Mc-Kern!"

Who was nowhere to be found.

23

In the privacy of her dark house, Acting Mayor Gladys McKern removed her ever-present bronze mayoral name tag, carefully placed it on her dresser, then collapsed face down on her bed and wept. It was clear that after Katie's sterling performance, Partonville Pleasantries was here to stay. But after *her* own spineless breakdown — and what else could she call it but that? — it also seemed inevitable that a new mayor would be performing the ribbon-cutting ceremony which was to take place less than two weeks after the election. There was no point dragging out the misery until then, especially since it would be too cruel to lose her life's mission on election day, April Fool's Day, which suddenly seemed prophetic.

What was she to do with the rest of her life now?

Sam made a snide comment or two about

the "Acting Mayor acting like a disappearing act." He laughed but barely anyone else did. Whether people were for or against Gladys, most were unnerved by her disappearance since knowing Gladys, they were pretty sure only illness or foul play could keep her away from standing in front of an audience. The meeting was dismissed early, thereby causing a race on the remaining doughnuts.

In order to beat the crowd, Harold scooted out the back door and went straight to his office to write up a recap of Katie's presentation while his notes were still fresh. Sharon set out following Sergeant McKenzie, a man of the law in search of a missing person. Sharon, right on his heels, was a reporter chasing her first possible abduction case since what else could possibly explain Gladys's disappearance? Caleb, Gladys's son, told them both he couldn't imagine his mother voluntarily just skipping out on such an important event nor had he noticed her leave, and he'd been sitting right behind her.

Mac began his search in the parking lot, stopping each vehicle at the exit to make sure Gladys hadn't arrived with them as a passenger. Before the debate was declared defunct he'd already checked for her car (not there) and phoned her home (no answer). When some folks volunteered to form their own search parties, Mac told them to go on home saying that if he needed help, he'd have the churches simultaneously ring their bells, which was the town's un-official alert system for just about anything including tornadoes. (Arthur used to tease everyone saying that if he ever won the lot-tery, "them bells'll be pealin' fer hours cuz I'll ring 'em till we're all plumb deaf!")

On the way to their car, Dorothy invited May Belle to come on over to her house for awhile, what with all those cookies still safely wrapped in her bags and it being so early due to the unexpected and abrupt halt to the evening.

"That would be nice," Jacob said. "We'll give Earl a call when we get home and have him join us."

In the glow of the parking lot lights, May Belle checked her wristwatch. Not quite 8. "He's likely still up, but first you'll have to get him to answer the phone, which isn't likely. If you don't mind swinging by our house, Jacob, I'll run in and see if I can't talk him into it. Whether he's interested or not, though, *I'll* take you up on that since this is one of the rare events I didn't have to stay late to clean up and pack up, thanks to the doughnut shop. It's not that I ever mind cleanup detail, but it's nice to just eat somebody else's goodies for a change and head out."

"Personally, I skipped the doughnuts," Jacob said, first opening the car door for his mom, then for May Belle. "When I saw all those dozens of doughnuts on the table, I figured you wouldn't need to serve your baked goods. I better get your sweets for free while I can, before I have to buy them from the Tea Cozy," he said with a grin.

Jacob reminded May Belle to buckle up just as Mac approached their car to make sure Gladys wasn't inside.

"Oh, sorry, Jacob," Mac said. "I already checked with you. I still need to get used to your car." He motioned them out of the lot.

"How's the house hunt going?" May Belle asked from the back seat, leaning slightly forward to make sure she heard his reply.

"It's not."

"You mean you've quit looking and decided to just stay with your old mom?" Dorothy said playfully, although she certainly wouldn't complain if he did.

"No. Herb's still keeping an eye out for me, but he hasn't found anything yet that matches my criteria. Although I didn't get to see the interior, the house that Matt and Melissa Dertinger bought . . . they're the owners of the new Garden Goodies, right? . . . might have been perfect since it had an extra bedroom for home office space, not too much yard and yet good privacy, but since Katie has the inside track with Herb, by the time I saw the listing it was sold. Plus, there was a house about the right size off the south side of the square, which would have made a convenient walk to work, but Katie snapped it up too. Herb said she was banking it for another of her off-square speculation opportunities." Jacob sounded somewhat miffed.

"Before you stop by May Belle's, would you take a quick drive by Gladys's home? I want to see if her lights are on. I can't stop worrying about her. I remember that time way back when she was suddenly struck with bacterial pneumonia and we almost lost her."

"Sure, Mom, but first tell me where she lives."

"Turn right up there in about three blocks, then I'll maneuver you through the side streets." In order to pass by her house they first had to get in a long procession of cars. Seemed everyone had the same idea. But Gladys's home was dark and her car wasn't out front, where she usually parked it in nice weather, so people slowly drove right on by.

"I can't believe Gladys wigged out!" The minute Josh and his mom got to the parking lot, closed the doors to the SUV and were safely out of earshot of anyone, Katie's game face was gone and her fury unleashed. "How *dare* she fall apart now!"

"Mom, simmer down. How do you know she didn't get sick or something?"

"Because I saw her sitting right there in front of me. I watched the whole meltdown. I just didn't realize what I was looking at, or that she would get cold enough feet to sneak out!" When the SUV hit the pavement Katie's anger got the best of her and she gunned the vehicle a little faster than she realized, causing the tires to squeal. Mac, who was standing near the road, put his hands on his hips and shook his head. What was *up* with that family and their driving? Between the terrible examples set by Josh's mom and his uncle, the kid didn't stand a chance.

Sharon, driving her little Ford Escort, followed Mac in his squad car as he slowly drove the darkened road out of the park. He stopped every once in awhile and flashed his spotlight around the fields and into the ditches. Sharon held her breath with each scan, hoping above all hope he wouldn't find anything. Once he reached the black-top, he headed straight toward Gladys's house since he'd already phoned the hospital and been assured that Gladys was not there. Sharon pulled in Gladys's driveway right behind Mac, who told her if she didn't back off he would give her a citation for tailgating. "And move your car out from behind the squad car, Sharon. You cannot block an officer of the law!"

Gladys's house was pitch black and by the time Mac and Sharon arrived, everyone in the snaking line of gawkers had made their way home. If the church bells didn't chime tonight, whatever happened to Gladys, they knew they'd learn about it through the grapevine tomorrow. After Sharon moved her car onto the street, Mac, who'd had time to consider things, repositioned his squad car until his headlights shone right on the house, then he got out and ordered Sharon to get back and *stay* back and let him do his job.

He first went to the carport behind her house, where he discovered Gladys's car. He felt the hood. Still slightly warm, so she must have come straight home. Perhaps she *had* taken ill. As he walked on around to the front door he swooped his flashlight back and forth to make sure she wasn't lying in the yard, a thought that made Sharon shudder. He tried the front doorknob. Locked. Then he began knocking and calling her name. Just after he loudly announced he was going to bust in, Gladys came to her door without uttering a sound and yanked it ever so slightly open, which startled Mac, although he tried not to show it. Gladys, her blazer hitched up on her bosom, eyes red and swollen, mascara streaking her face, stood squinting into the blinding bright of Mac's car headlights.

"Mayor McKern!" Mac put his hand on her door to push it open but she firmly blocked him. It was then she noticed a few people beginning to gather on her sidewalk. Speaking in muffled sobs through the cracked door, she said, "I herewith concede the election." Sharon, who had snuck across the lawn when she saw the door open, could not believe the words she found herself quoting on her steno.

"Mayor McKern," Mac said, a quiet and steady gentleness in his voice, "we haven't *held* the election yet. Are you okay, Gladys?"

"I herewith . . . concede."

"Can you hear me, Mayor McKern?"

327

"Why, yes, you are standing right here," she said, her voice strengthening somewhat as she swiped at the tears on her cheeks, causing Mac to reach for his handkerchief, wondering why he hadn't done so before.

Mac turned, saw the people on the sidewalk, noted Sharon writing and motioned her up to his side. In a loud voice, he then ordered everyone to go on home, which they didn't do, but at least they did back up. "For goodness sakes, Sharon!" he said through his teeth so only she could hear him. "Stop writing! Can't you see Gladys isn't . . ." Although he didn't finish his sentence, it was clear to all three of them he was thinking "in her right mind?"

"But I'm just . . ." Sharon started to argue, but Mac cut her right off.

"Disobeying an officer of the law is what you're doing, Sharon Teller, if you don't put that pen down and right this *minute,* young lady."

Sharon reluctantly stopped writing while she argued with herself. *Young lady?* How dare he talk to her that way! She was an educated and trained journalist on duty to report the whole truth of the news. But she also knew she was a citizen in a small town that cared deeply for its own. She turned to look at the growing crowd, Cora Davis now right at the forefront of them. This was *news* and Sharon needed to report the facts before Cora spread her own version.

"I have to report to Harold," she said to Mac, her voice defensive, "and I have a duty to the citizens of Partonville to report the news as it happens."

"Tell Harold and anyone else you'd care to tell that Gladys was suddenly taken ill. Sharon Teller, you've known Gladys Mc-Kern, *Mayor* McKern, since you were a little girl," he said, speaking as though Gladys wasn't standing right there while at the same time trying to remind *her* of her post, "and you know very well Gladys here isn't herself. Quote *me*, okay? And I say she's taken ill. If there is more to this story tomorrow, you'll be the first person I'll call. Well, the second. Right now I'm phoning Caleb," he said, reaching for his cell phone after Gladys closed and locked the door.

24

Before there was even a knock, Colton Craig opened his front door. "Got it?"

"Here ya go," the man responded when handing over the digital recorder.

"Anything I need to know that's not on the tape?"

"It might be longer than you think; it might be shorter than you're expecting. You might not recognize the main player."

"How so?"

"It seems Kathryn Durbin is known as Katie Durbin by everyone but you."

"I know."

"She's good and she's convincing."

"I know. Tell me something I don't know."

"The tape ends without a debate."

"The debate didn't happen?"

"Right."

"Why?"

"The current mayor was a no-show."

"She didn't show up at all?"

"She was there at the beginning but she disappeared during the break between Durbin's talk and the debate."

"You didn't *follow* her, find out where she went or why she left?"

"You paid me to tape, not trail." With that, he turned and left.

"Right," Colton muttered as he closed the door. McKern probably didn't matter anyway. As far as he could tell, she didn't wield any real power. The only reason he was curious about how it would go between her and Vitner was to get a feel for the climate of leadership in Partonville *aside* from Durbin, find out if Sam was gaining any influence. Then again, whether anyone in Partonville was aware of it or not, from what he knew of Kathryn Durbin, she was already their leader and they better hang on to their wallets.

Dorothy's phone rang at 6:30 a.m. She nabbed it on the third jingle in hopes it hadn't awakened Jacob. "Dorothy, it's Caleb. I'm sorry to wake you," he said, sounding like he'd been up all night, which he had. "I didn't know who else to call, Dorothy. People are such busybodies and you're the one person I know I can trust."

"Caleb! What is it, honey?"

"Mom is in a state of . . . I don't know what you'd call it, but. . . . She needs your help. *I* need your help. Could you please come over? I'll come get you, if you'd rather not walk or Jacob isn't up or able to bring you. I just don't know what else to do, short of phoning a psychiatrist, and we don't have one of them here in Partonville!"

"When did you want me to come by?"

"Now, if you can."

"I'm so glad you called, Caleb," she said, thinking what an unsuspecting hotline God ran through the cosmos in light of her morning's prayers. "I'll get myself there. Sounds like you better stay with your mom. Is your wife there with you, honey?"

"No. She was, but Mom wouldn't talk to her either. Thanks, Dorothy. Good-bye."

"WAIT! Caleb, are you still there?

"Yes."

"Do you think she needs a doctor or maybe Pastor Delbert instead of me?"

"Let's start with you, okay? We'll take it from there."

"Gladys," Dorothy said in a quiet voice as she gently knocked on Gladys's bedroom door. Caleb, who'd let Dorothy in, told her he was heading back to his home to give them some privacy. "Maybe Mom will talk to a woman — an unrelated woman. I need to take a shower and go to work for an hour or so, then I'll be back — unless you need me before then." He'd handed her a piece of paper with his work number scribbled on it and took off. "Gladys, it's me, Dorothy." Silence. "Gladys, is it okay if I come in?" she asked in a stronger voice followed by a louder rap on the door. Silence. "Gladys," she said firmly, putting her hand to the doorknob. *Lord, help me know what to do, what to say and when to do and say it!* "Gladys, I'm coming in, dear." *I'm counting on You, God. Here goes!* She took a deep breath and inched the door open. Since the shades were drawn tightly shut, she could barely see the made-up, yet rumpled and empty bed. At first she wondered if Gladys had somehow snuck out. But after Dorothy's eyes adjusted to the dimness, she noticed Gladys sitting in the corner on a small straight-back chair next to her dresser. Aside from her shoes, which were neatly placed together on the floor in front of her, Gladys was a fully clothed, wrinkled and motley mess.

"I'll be right back, Gladys. I'm going to put us on a nice pot of coffee." Dorothy whirled on her heels, made her way to Gladys's kitchen and rifled around until she found what she needed to brew a pot of strong rich coffee since Caleb had drained whatever was left in the coffee pot on the counter. She noticed a small bag of familiar doughnuts and figured Caleb must have snagged himself a batch last night. She cut one chocolate and one powdered-sugar in half and set them on a plate, then stood watching and waiting for the drip coffee to produce enough for two cups. Gladys kept an old metal Coca-Cola serving tray on her kitchen counter, so Dorothy used it to arrange a couple of napkins, the mugs and doughnuts, then carried the tray to Gladys's room where she placed it on top of the dresser, taking note of Gladys's bronze mayoral name tag. *No wonder Caleb phoned me! Gladys is certainly* not *herself!*

She placed one of the mugs on a napkin and held it in front of Gladys. "Here. Have a sip." Gladys stared at the coffee as though she'd never seen it before. "Gladys? Gladys." Dorothy picked up Gladys's right hand and placed the mug in it, which Gladys thankfully then secured for herself. She stared at it for a moment, then turned her eyes up to Dorothy wearing the most sorrowful, defeated look on her face.

"I'm through."

"Through with what, Gladys?"

"Through with my mayoral duties," she said, casting her eyes to the empty spot on her blazer where her name tag used to reside, covering the sacred spot with her left hand. "I conceded my loss last night to Sergeant McKenzie."

"You can't concede, Gladys. The election doesn't even take place for more than two weeks."

"It doesn't matter. I can't win anyway. Even if I thought I could. After last night, I don't deserve to win."

"Take a sip or two of coffee, Gladys." Gladys mindlessly did what she was told, then made a sour face. "That's *terrible* coffee."

Dorothy startled Gladys by smiling and giving her hands a solid clap. "GOOD!" she yipped. *Oh, THANK YOU, Jesus!* Gladys's complaint gave Dorothy the hope, direction and ammunition she needed to help Gladys find her way back to herself, she was sure of it. If Gladys could still complain under *these* circumstances, then she was certainly still Gladys!

"Good?" Gladys asked, clearly annoyed at Dorothy's ridiculous statement. "I said your coffee was *terrible.* There is nothing good about terrible coffee."

"Gladys Rose Standish McKern," Dorothy said, standing up in front of her and placing her hands on her hips, "I have known you for your entire life and you are not a quitter. No ma'am, Gladys McKern does not concede. The Gladys McKern I know is a woman with strong opinions about everything — whether it's about good or bad coffee, or what's right or wrong for a town — and you have never been afraid to speak those opinions." Even though the mug was halfway to Gladys's lips again, Dorothy removed it from her hands and set it on the tray. "Now you march yourself into the shower and change into fresh clothes. You are *through* with this pity party and I mean right this minute. The people of Partonville *need* you!"

"But. . . ."

"No buts about it, Gladys. *Now!* Get yourself up off that chair and into the shower. You have an election to win and like it or not, you've just acquired yourself a campaign manager."

"I don't need a . . ."

"MARCH!" Gladys stood up and yanked her blazer down, which had, as always, ridden up on her ample bosom. Dorothy had to stifle herself from yelling *Hallelujah!* The well-known blazer yank-down maneuver had always been Gladys's signal that she was preparing to do business or battle, or just give someone a good what's-for. "THAT'S the ticket!" Dorothy said, breaking out in a big smile. "You get in the shower and I'm going to phone Maggie to let her know we need us an emergency visit. After you're cleaned up, you put that name tag back on your blazer where it belongs, you hear me? This town *needs* you, Gladys. They *need* the likes of somebody who understands that progress is good. They *need* somebody to let them know that Sam Vitner is just a misguided windbaggin' bunch of sour old grapes. He does *not* care about the people of this town the way you do, Gladys, and it's time you make that clear. Now move it!"

Gladys only knew one thing — which played right into Dorothy's scheme: *nobody* was going to stand there and tell *her* what to do! So she made up her own mind it was time for a shower, and she made up her own mind to eat a half of a powdered-sugar doughnut. She ordered Dorothy to phone Maggie to make her an emergency hairdo appointment. "And when you're done with that," she added as she slipped off her blazer and reached for the side zipper on her wool skirt, "phone the Hethrow Button Business and tell them I want five hundred three-inch buttons made — no, make that *four*-inch buttons — and N-O-W. And quit being so bossy!"

"That's the spirit, Gladys! What should the buttons say? Should we go with MOVING FORWARD IN TIME like your last year's clever Centennial Plus Thirty slogan?"

"No, Dorothy. No, *no,* NO! They should *not* say that."

"Are you sticking with your MAYOR + McKERN = MOMENTUM then?" *Even though the jokes have been endless?*

"Absolutely not, Dorothy. I'm going with something new. Something bold. Something powerful!"

"Well, what then?"

Gladys looked up toward the ceiling, as though she could picture her plan. "I want white buttons with gold print in the biggest font they can use to allow my *new* slogan to fit on it." She stopped talking to give Dorothy a serious eyeball, the familiar look she burned into anyone to express her dissatisfaction with whatever.

"What *is* that, Gladys? Not even a campaign manager is a mind reader."

"When you get a pencil and paper so you can write it down, Dorothy Jean Wetstra, I'll tell you. I don't want you to order me five hundred incorrect six-inch buttons."

"I thought you said to order them four inches," Dorothy said, turning toward the kitchen where she'd previously noticed a writing tablet and a few pens near Gladys's phone.

"I DID," Gladys hollered down the hall. "BUT THE BIGGER THE BETTER. AND WHILE YOU'E ORDERING, TELL THEM I WANT ONE HUNDRED BUMPER STICKERS AND . . . TWO HUNDRED BALLPOINT PENS MADE UP WITH THE SAME THING ON THEM. AND ASK THEM," she bellowed now since Dorothy was in the other room writing as fast as she could to keep up with Gladys's rapid-fire instructions, "IF THEY PRINT BALLOONS TOO."

Dorothy appeared back in the bedroom, tablet in hand. "Are you sure they print *anything* other than bu. . . ."

"*No,* Dorothy! I am *not* sure. But it is your job as my campaign manager to find out! And while you're at it, see if you can hire me a skywriter." With that Gladys disappeared down the hall and into the bathroom, leaving a frazzled Dorothy in her back draft.

As happy as it made Dorothy to know that

the Real Gladys was back, she also wondered what on earth she'd gotten herself into. Since the St. Patrick's Day band concert was only two days away, Raymond Ringwald, the director and trumpet player, had called for an extra practice this week before Saturday's concert and it took place this evening. Unless Gladys had a mental relapse, which Dorothy highly doubted since she heard her singing "I Will Survive" at the top of her lungs in the shower, Gladys would surely spread the word about her new campaign manager by then. At least, thank goodness, Gladys wasn't in the band.

But Sam was.

"Oh, Lordy-*Lordy!*" Dorothy said as she went to the kitchen to look for the phone book. "Buttons and balloons and skywriters? Oh, *my!*" Then she chuckled and repeated the mouthful again, this time performing the yellow-brick-road shuffle with her fingers as they began walking through the Yellow Pages in search of the proper tools to wage a campaign to beat all campaigns.

At eighty-eight, Dorothy wondered if she'd just found herself a new career or set herself up to do herself in.

"Thank goodness the mall phones are

340

finally up and running properly!" Katie told Josh when he had been getting ready to leave for school. But when she answered her first call of the day all she heard was a click. "Darn it!" she said as she looked at the caller I.D. to see who she'd missed. "Hornsbys Shoe E." *Hm. Tom must finally be ready to ask his question — or not. Or maybe the phones* aren't *working.* She highlighted the number and returned the call to check. To her surprise, Frieda answered.

"Hello, Frieda."

"Who is this?"

"Katie Durbin. Did you just call me?"

"No. Well, yes. I mean I decided not to . . . I'm sorry for the interruption. I shouldn't have bothered you."

"Frieda, you're not bothering me." Katie heard a door close in the shoe store. "What can I do for you?" The memory of Frieda's surprise visit to the mall a few weeks ago popped into Katie's mind. Acting on her instructions, Edward Showalter turned everyone away that day, but Katie now remembered her curiosity when he told her Frieda had stopped by. Until this moment she'd forgotten all about it.

"I, um, I really can't say right now," she said, sounding like she was putting her hand half over the mouthpiece. "We don't carry that size. Understand?" she whispered. "I'll check into it and call you back another time." Click.

Katie removed the cordless phone from her ear and stared at it a moment before pressing the OFF button. Something odd was going on with Frieda Hornsby, but what?

25

Nellie Ruth was beside herself. With St. Patrick's Day just around the corner, Your Store was busier than ever. While she struggled to keep heads of cabbage and bags of red potatoes shelved, Wilbur was forced to place an emergency ("*That's* gonna cost me!") order for more packaged corned beef since he sold out of the fresh stuff only one day into the sale. Band practice was this evening and between last night's town meeting and heart-pounding ride home, putting in extra work hours, playing with (and cleaning up after) the kitties and spending time with ES whenever she could, Nellie Ruth had barely found time to start planning for the Hookers' arrival next week *or* to put her saxophone's mouthpiece to her lips, let alone finish memorizing the music for her "Danny Boy" solo. She was so distracted she caught herself displaying turnips where the onions were supposed to go, and then in a subconscious attempt to steal a moment of practice, she mindlessly fingered a stalk of celery as though pressing the keys on a saxophone.

"Kinda looks ta me like ya's playin' our song, Nellie Ruth!" Arthur loudly proclaimed when he caught her. He whipped his ever-present Hohner harmonica out of his top center coveralls pocket, leaned in toward her and began playing "Love Me Tender."

"Arthur!" she said, quickly depositing the celery where it belonged and glancing around her. "*Stop* that!"

"I know ya already gottya a beau," he teased, grinning like a goon. "I was jist gittin' *me* a little practice in before tonight." Arthur stowed his harmonica back in its handy pocket house, picked up a head of lettuce, tossed it between his hands and proceeded to laugh himself all the way to the cash register. *Doesn't that man have anything better to do?* Of course his wife had asked him that very thing today when he was feet-up in his La-Z-Boy with the television blaring, which is when she sent him to the store for lettuce.

After Nellie Ruth quit blushing, she began to wonder if *anyone* had practiced their music. After all, Sam, the violin player, was busy campaigning for mayor. If she could believe Gladys's mid-morning announcement in the frozen food section (and what a miraculous recovery from whatever had struck *her* ill last night!), Dorothy, who played first clarinet, was now a campaign manager. Sharon, who played flute and sang vocals, was running from one end of town to the other like a chicken with her head cut off in an attempt to keep up with the ever-changing news. Arthur was impossible, and who knew about the others. Poor Raymond. She feared they might sound more like a pickup band without a plan rather than a practiced group of musicians striving to infuse a little Irish spirit into the community. Then again, the whole town was so crazed and loud and yammering that maybe nobody'd notice if they sounded terrible. Perhaps that was their only hope.

Nellie Ruth heard Wilbur calling for help at the check-out. As she made her way to the front of the store, she pondered last night's ride home with ES. Just thinking about it made her heart race a mile a nanosecond again. He'd been so excited and encouraged by the evening's events. Yes, he expressed concern for the then-missing Gladys, but the overriding factor for him was that after Katie's dynamic speech, he said he was sure of one thing: Partonville Pleasantries — and therefore his job — were here to stay. "Security, Nellie Ruth! That's what I heard me tonight. A fella needs job security if he's to amount to any kind of a family man, and by golly, job security's what I've got me now!"

"Hello, Nellie Ruth," Jessica said while Nellie Ruth flipped her lane sign from CLOSED to OPEN.

"Oh!" Nellie Ruth said.

"I'm sorry! We didn't mean to startle you, did we, Sarah Sue?"

"Good to see you, Jessica and Ms. Cutsie tootsie-wootsie," Nellie Ruth said, giving Sarah Sue's cheek a gentle pinch. "Isn't it great news about Gladys?"

After Gladys had arrived at the grill, all she said was, "Just a touch of the flu. Bad timing. But I'm up and running full speed ahead now. Keep your eyes open for my new campaign slogan!"

Family man. What did he mean by that? Was he implying . . .

"Excuse me, Nellie Ruth," Jessica said, as she removed Sarah Sue from the grocery cart seat to prevent her from leaning over and grabbing the packages of gum so neatly lined up in the display, "but if I saw correctly," she said, pointing to the customer

346

viewing screen, "my frozen peas didn't ring up."

Nellie Ruth realized she'd started skimming things across the scanner without even considering the position of the bar codes. She checked the printout and moaned. "You're right, Jessica! I'm so sorry. Thank you for your honesty! Why, you could have gotten away with half a cart of free groceries while I daydreamed!"

"Must have been a good daydream. You were blushing," Jessica said with a warm smile. "We all have our turns, don't we, Sarah Sue?" she asked her wriggling baby whose hands were still reaching for the gum. "Some days lately I wonder if my mind is *ever* here with my body!"

"It's no wonder," Nellie Ruth said as she slid the items back across the scanner, "between chasing Sarah Sue, a new one on the way, Paul off of work, running the Lamp Post, doing crafts and helping out at the new gift basket store, which I just learned about last night — and good for you," (scan, scan) "*and* didn't I hear," she paused and checked the register tape to make sure the items were indeed ringing up, "that you're helping Katie with mall banners and the like too? How do you *do* it?"

Jessica teared up and her mouth froze

open. Nellie Ruth looked up and noticed her face. "Oh, Jessica! I am so sorry! I didn't mean to. . . ." She reached into her sweater pocket, pulled out a tissue and handed it to Jessica. "You've got enough on your plate without me overwhelming you. In fact," Nellie Ruth said, her own throat beginning to tighten, "I should know better since I'm overwhelmed enough myself right now."

Nellie Ruth noticed three people standing in line behind Jessica so she forced herself to focus her attention, finish ringing up the items and total Jessica out. Jessica plopped Sarah Sue back in the cart, fastened her seat belt and pushed her far enough forward to move her little fingers out of reaching range, then she wrote her check.

"No need to apologize, Nellie Ruth," she said, writing as quickly as possible. "It's just my hormones. I'll see you Saturday night at the concert, unless we get any late check-ins. As much as I want to see the concert, I'm hoping for a flurry of surprise business this weekend. But I'll for *sure* see you next week at your house for bunco. I can't *wait* to see your new decorating!"

"Hey, how's Paul's leg doing?" Nellie Ruth asked, already ringing up the next person's groceries.

"Dr. Nielson said he can go back to work

part-time if he continues to use his crutches and doesn't put his full weight on it. Not too handy when you're a coal miner. But Paul's boss said he'll see if he can find him *something* to do. We could really use the money so we're hopeful," she said over her shoulder. Sarah Sue started whining. "I gotta run!" she added on her way out the door.

It was a band practice to be remembered, or forgotten as quickly as possible, depending on your point of view. It became clear before people even sat down with their instruments that Sam was wearing his campaign hat. He was intrusive, disruptive and in their faces, saying the mall wasn't what it appeared to be and neither was Katie Durbin.

When Sam arrived home after the "debate," he felt good since, according to him, Gladys's disappearance proved she was not up to his challenge. "She obviously turned tail," he told his wife, who neither agreed nor disagreed with him. But in the morning, after several people stopped by Swappin' Sam's to ask him how he was feeling after his "whoopin'," as Arthur put it, he had to re-think things. It seemed Katie Durbin had single-handedly crushed much of the election momentum in his favor. An early morning call from Colton Craig didn't help his frame of mind either. Colton asked him how he planned to challenge "Kathryn's compelling rally" last night, which, Colton said, he'd heard about this morning. Plus Colton asked him, in a tone of voice none too kindly, why he hadn't taken better advantage of his opportunity to deliver a thoughtful speech on the future of Partonville and touch on Katie's land-buying attempts to lock them in, rather than just delivering a few rude comments about the current mayor and calling it quits. It was a tongue-lashing Sam neither expected nor, in his opinion, deserved. It briefly caused Sam to wonder how Colton knew all of this; he hadn't seen him in the building last night. Did the man have spies watching him or something?

By the time Sam arrived at band practice, he was determined to make up for lost ground. Whether members wanted one or not he handed everyone a VOTE FOR VITNER button and rambled on about how slick-tongued "that Durbin woman" was. He all but pulled Sharon's flute out of her mouth and handed her a pen so she could quote him. Gertrude Hands, the keyboard player for the band and organist at United

Methodist, drowned out one of his rants by playing a C-chord and holding it at nearly full volume until he stopped talking. Of course she claimed she was just warming up, but they all knew better. Since when had she ever warmed up her electronic keyboard? Loretta Forester threatened to bean him with her drumsticks if he didn't pipe down. But when Sam called Dorothy — and right to her face — a "turncoat" for becoming Gladys's campaign manager, Wilbur had had it. *Nobody* had the right to attack Dorothy! He'd heard enough of Sam Vitner and he banged his cymbals together so hard it made everyone's head hurt. Wilbur told Sam if he didn't hush, he'd bang his head between them.

"If ya think yer winnin' votes by pickin' on our Dearest Dorothy," Arthur said, "well ya ain't!" Several in the room clapped at Arthur's statement and Raymond told them that was enough, that it was time to get down to practicing. In the brief moment of silence between his comment and the first downbeat, Dorothy stood and bowed her head.

"Lord God," she said, "we are *all* your children and you want what is best for *all* of us. We play music because it's *fun*. We perform because it blesses people — and

351

oh, Lord, make it so! Despite our differences in this room, help us come together and practice as one band. One band playing music together that sounds like music. Amen."

"Thank you, Dorothy," Raymond said. Then he quietly blew a G on his trumpet to find his pitch. With his right hand he lifted his trumpet in the air, his left hand simultaneously rising with it. He waved the trumpet in a cloverleaf to set the 4/4 time, then he gave the downbeat with his left hand and began to sing, a capella, at the top of his lungs, "Oooooooooooooooooooooooooh, my name is MacNamara, I'm the leader of the band." Then he drew his trumpet to his lips and played the melody while the rest of the band chimed in.

Raymond wasn't known for his singing. But every time the band opened their St. Patrick's Day concert with this song, it drew a standing ovation since everyone loved and treasured the Partonville Community Band.

Lord, Dorothy prayed while she played, *help us be better by tomorrow night!*

Alex,
    How are things in Chicago? I have no control over my life here in Pardon-Me-Ville. My mom is a jailer, which means I

still haven't checked out the Fire Pit. (Not that I've even asked Shelby if she wants to go yet. PLUS, she accidentally let everyone in town know I was grounded!) Gasoline is so expensive I can't afford to take the truck many places anyway. School sucks. The weather's still too cold for crawdads and it's been way too long since you've been here.

Your pathetic friend,
Joshmeister

Joshmeister,

You're pathetic but not as pathetic as I am. I don't know what to say other than whether you get to the Fire Pit or not, at least you *have* a girlfriend to take. Yesterday Jennifer told me she — no "*we* need to take a break from each other." Why don't girls just say go take a flying leap rather than making up dumb stuff like that. Gheesh!

Your bachelor friend,
Alex

P.S. Keep your eyes open since if I ever DO get to come visit again (Mom's holding my grades over my head), I think a blind date is in order. A double date to the Fire Pit sounds good to me!

Dear Bachelor Number One,

Man, I'm sorry about Jennifer. I know you dug her. But my eyes are already open for brunettes, your preference, as I recall. You work on the grades and I'll work on the possibilities.

Joshmeister

Dear Outtamyway,

Jennifer broke up with Alex. I'm busy being grounded, going to school and working. Mom tells me you're a campaign manager now! Can't wait to hear *that* story!

Ain't life grand? (Well, at least for one of us.)

Joshmeister

Dear Joshmeister,

Glad to find your e-mail bright and early this morning! It's been too long since we've chatted.

Yes, I'm a campaign manager, which caused quite the stir at band practice last night, during which we sounded terrible. (I'll tell you all about it another time.) If your mom lets you come to the concert Saturday night (or maybe you're done with your grounding by then? — and wait, Saturday night is TOMORROW night!

Where is time going?!) you might want to stuff some cotton balls in your ears. I think I will!

Sleep tight and stay positive. Your mom loves you and you've got the hottest wheels in town. Even my old Tank (can you still remember what my '76 Lincoln Continental looked like before she blew herself up?) would have been jealous!

See you when I can,

Outtmyway, AKA Campaign Manager Extraordinaire (read going plumb nuts!)

Jacob climbed the squeaky wooden stairwell steps to his office. He was glad it was Friday. For a guy who had moved from the big city to a small town and a law practice not even one-tenth the size of what he was used to, he felt extraordinarily battle worn, especially since he'd only been in town a little over a week. *Is that true?* He counted it up, and yes, it was true. *Funny, feels more like a year. I wonder what it'll feel like in an* actual *year? A lifetime? I hope not!*

About five steps from the top landing he heard Helen's keyboard clacking away. Try as he might to talk her into an ergonomic keyboard, she told him to save his money for other things. "You've already spent enough on the new door and coffee machine!" she said. (She was as careful with money as his old firm was lavish.) Besides, she thought she was too old to learn to work on a "curvy looking thing like *that!*"

Sometimes the whole town smacked of Hicksville and it made him feel small each time that thought crossed his mind. He'd been born and educated here. He'd learned family values and hard work ethics from his salt-of-the-earth parents and the good citizens of this town. But he'd been away for so many decades. He wondered if Katie still — or ever — battled these types of feelings, or had he, pure and simple, become an arrogant snob?

Katie, he thought after he said good morning to Helen, hung up his jacket, laid his briefcase on his desk, rifled through the mail Helen set there and went to his office window overlooking the square and therefore the Taninger building. *Partonville Pleasantries,* he thought, correcting himself. The building lights were on throughout, but then the work crew arrived every morning at 7 a.m. Before the interior had been subdivided and framed in, he'd been able to see her sitting at her makeshift desk or notice her SUV parked out front on the square. But now she parked in the rear of the building and her office was on the second floor back in a corner.

Katie. That was some stunt she pulled the other night.

Or was he being ridiculous? May Belle and his mom thought it was *nice* of her to give his business a plug, and maybe it was. Why did the gesture strike him as so self-serving? Of course his whole housing issue complicated matters. But after all, wasn't she helping the community by adding new business residents and securing real estate for future commercial development? Wasn't he glad to add the mall to his growing client roster?

Maybe *he* hadn't been aggressive enough in his house search by letting Herb know he was anxious to get out on his own. Maybe he should find a different Realtor, one with broader reach and no conflict of interest with Katie.

"You'll find the perfect house in God's perfect timing," his mom said to him after Earl and May Belle had left the other evening. He was probably just crabby because he wasn't getting enough exercise. Yes, that was it. He'd spend time tomorrow in the Yellow Pages looking for health clubs in Hethrow, then he'd take a ride and explore a few of them, get himself signed up, get some sweat time in. Then Monday he would stop by Herb's and make his intentions clear: he needed a house. And he'd let Katie know that too. After all, she wasn't a mind reader. Isn't that what countless women had told him over the years — told *every* man throughout the ages? "I am not a mind reader. You need to *tell* me what you're thinking."

Yes, he needed to tell her what he was thinking, which he realized, even though he was trying to fight it, and even though it was easier to be perturbed than attracted, and even though it would open the potential for a whole barrel of complications if not outright trouble (professional relationship, Josh, gossips) and even though his mother saw it coming before he did (which *really* got his goat), was this: Would you like to have dinner with me tonight?

"I'll be back shortly," he told Helen as he slung on his coat and headed down the stairs.

26

Challie Carter worked his toothpick from one side of his mouth to the other with such deft speed it was all Katie could do to concentrate on the numbers spilling from his lips. They were sitting across from each other in her office, door closed. Challie had phoned her a day earlier and asked if they could meet again. Katie said he'd need to come to her office — she was just testing the waters, hoping for a new kind of home-turf advantage — and was surprised when he consented. *He must* really *want to talk to me!*

As it turned out, the man was indeed there to do business, but he drove a hard bargain, one she wasn't sure she could match. He hadn't settled with Colton yet, but whether or not *she* could come to terms with Challie remained to be seen. At least they were talking business again, which was progress. However, the longer they talked, the more she realized he had her over a barrel: it would either be his way (although he hadn't named a do-or-die price) or she'd lose her whole investment in securing Partonville's borders, so to speak, from the Craig brothers.

She pulled her mind off his wagging toothpick to take note of his posture, his arm position, his knees. His body was completely relaxed. He was enjoying this! "Tell me, Mr. Carter, aside from trying to bilk me out of more money," she said, leaning back and smiling but making her point, "what is it you think I can bring to the table that Colton Craig can't?"

"What makes you think there's anything? As far as I can tell, you're both in it for the same reason, which is makin' yourselves rich. Two peas in a pod."

"But you're back, and I believe you're aware you could probably name your price with either of us. In fact, I'd be willing to bet Colton Craig would and could perhaps up *any* price I name since his development firm has already raised Hethrow out of the cornfields."

"And you? Wouldn't you best him just to ace him out? Seems to me there's some bad blood there and — too bad, so sad — I'm the lucky one with the chance to take advantage of it."

She steeled herself, put her elbows on her desk, laced her fingers and leaned toward him. She and Challie shared a brief but amicable working relationship. He leased her land, something he'd been doing when Dorothy still owned Crooked Creek and a deal she'd kept intact when she bought the place. When she purchased Challie's pickup truck for Josh, they settled on a "fair-and-square" handshake, he'd called it.

"Challie . . . you don't mind if I call you Challie, do you, since you've seen my money before and we're getting so personal here?" He shook his head and chomped down on his toothpick stopping it dead in its tracks. "Challie, this conversation is not about bad blood or bilking or besting. It is strictly business on the up and up. I like you, Challie Carter. We've accumulated a business history on a couple matters, now, and I like your hard-nosed style. But that's beside the point too. We don't *have* to like each other. We just have to come to terms if we're to do business together on *this* deal. We *each* have to end up feeling like we've made a fair-and-square deal . . . or there will be no deal, at least not with me."

Pure and simple, they both knew it was the showdown moment. They stared at each other. From Katie's standpoint, there was nothing left to do now but to make her best offer, no looking back. She announced her final offer — "This deal is only good for the next two minutes" — nothing about her body moved but her lips.

Challie's toothpick remained frozen in place and the air seemed to crackle with anticipation. He blinked, looked from one of her eyes to the other, then removed the toothpick from his mouth. "For a woman who wants something as badly as you do, Ms. Durbin, you drive an inflexible bargain, which is why . . ."

Knock-knock. Katie threw her hands up in front of her to signal Challie to hold his thought. "Who is it?" she asked, assuming it was Edward Showalter coming to report on something.

The door opened and in walked a smiling Jacob, catching Katie Durbin and Challie Carter looking as uncomfortable and un-happy to see him as if they'd just been caught with their fists in the money jar. "I'm sorry to interrupt you," he said, backing out of the room and slowly starting to close the door behind him, giving Katie time to stop him, which she didn't.

Jacob spent the rest of Friday morning

wondering who he was more frustrated with: Katie for brushing him off or himself for barging into a closed-door meeting without waiting for a "Come in." He knew better than to do that in the world of business. But then, what were those two up to? Maybe she wasn't a woman to be trusted after all. It was time to get to work. He walked over and pulled the window shade down. Enough of Partonville *Pleasantries,* he thought.

His phone rang at 11:30. He'd never heard such a lilt in Katie's voice. She wanted to know if he was available, and if so, she'd like to take him to lunch, not only to apologize for her earlier behavior, but to celebrate a grand victory. Reluctantly he said yes.

Katie told Edward Showalter she was taking the rest of the day off and that he should hold down the fort. She figured she and Jacob would grab a bite of lunch at a nice restaurant in Hethrow, after which she'd ask him if he would officially please step in to handle all the land agreements as she exercised the option clauses.

Jacob told Helen he'd be back in an hour or two, but he didn't return.

"Here's to the advantage of being your own boss," Katie said, raising her celebratory glass of midday sherry.

"Here's to my largest client," Jacob said, raising his empty beer glass, "not only the owner and manager of Partonville Pleasantries, but the town's largest landholder in the area and . . . mother to a great kid." They gently clinked glasses.

Katie took her last sip of sherry, and leaned back in her chair and swallowed. "Thank you," she said, a sudden and gentle quietness in her voice. "Thank you for saying that about Josh. The two of us definitely have our moments, but you know, he *is* a great kid, and it's clear he enjoys your company too. I think he was as excited as anyone when you said you were moving here to Partonville."

Enjoys my company too? "What about you?"

"What about me, what?"

"Were you happy to hear I was moving back?"

"Everyone was," she said, feeling a hot flash bubbling up.

Jacob took note of her sudden flushed

cheeks and smiled. "Thanks for inviting me to celebrate with you. I have to confess something, though. I came to your office this morning to invite you to dinner tonight — but how about next weekend instead?"

"I must tell you, Jacob Wetstra, that I am dumbfounded."

"Is that good?" he asked with a twinkle in his eye.

"It just *is*," she replied, not knowing what else to say.

"Should I accept that as a yes then?"

Her face turned serious and she momentarily tucked her lips together. "We're business partners. Your mom is a dear friend of mine and you live with her. Partonville is a small, gossiping town. There's Josh to think about . . . ," she said, her voice trailing off.

"Good! Then what time should I pick you up?"

"Jacob, I'm serious!"

"Believe me, you haven't mentioned anything I haven't already thought about. But let's don't make more of this than it is."

She picked up her napkin and dabbed at her lips. Forty-eight, she thought, was too old for this, this . . . fluttery feeling in her stomach. *The man, okay, the handsome man, only invited you to dinner. It's not like your social calendar is booked up!* "Yes," she said.

"Yes, we're on for next weekend then?"

"Yes, barring any Partonville Pleasantries disasters."

"Great. We'll set a time later. Now," he said, switching to his strictly business tone of voice, "let's talk about the paperwork for your land acquisitions." He retrieved a small notebook and pen from his pocket, acting as though his casual change of topic hadn't just left them both with emotional whiplash.

The date was never mentioned again. For the rest of the afternoon and early evening they talked business. They discussed the legal issues surrounding the completion of *all* her acquisitions, including informing people who were waiting to find out about the exercise of her options. Jacob was surprised to find the Landerses on her list and asked if his mom knew about it. "Nobody aside from the participants knows," she said, "and even they don't know who all is involved, either. Confidentiality was key. Confidentiality is still key," she said, giving him a look.

"Of course."

"Nonetheless, Challie confided to me on Friday that Colton Craig somehow found out about my bid for his properties, but he didn't tell me how or who made the breach.

I guess it doesn't really matter now."

Katie asked for the check. Jacob didn't try to intervene. He'd dated enough savvy women to know that when they did the inviting, not to mention the driving, you didn't insult them by treating them like . . . women, he thought, smiling to himself.

"What's that smile for?" Katie asked as she closed the leather folder containing the signed credit card receipt.

"Nothing. Thanks. And since I didn't offer to pay," he said, letting her in on his joke anyway, "I have a favor to ask. Would you mind briefly stopping at a health club I spotted on the way here?"

"Not The Build Back?"

"Yes!"

"I've wanted to check that out for myself but I've never found the time."

Although Katie liked the atmosphere and looks of the place, if Jacob joined, she sure wasn't going to. Even though she needed to whip herself back into shape and burn off some of her nervous energy, there was no way she'd have Jacob watch her doing it! She'd wait until after he made his choice before making her commitment. There were other gyms. However, when Jacob removed his sports jacket and tie and unbuttoned his top two buttons in order to try out one of

The Build Back's new weight machines, she couldn't help but notice his biceps bulging against his shirt — at which point she couldn't be sure if menopause was the cause of her momentary spike in temperature or not.

27

While a few folks were still arriving, the band members, including Sam Vitner, took their seats. It was then that Acting Mayor Gladys McKern made a grander than grand entrance. It was all Sam could do not to stand up and protest, but he feared he might be clubbed to death by saxophones, tambourines and possibly an entire drum set.

Gladys, holding up the concert by a few minutes to finish her grand promenade, first circled the entire perimeter of the room before making her way, front to rear, down the center aisle, occasionally blowing what looked to be an old ram's horn, one she'd purchased for a song from Swappin' Sam's just today, which made Sam want to kick his own self in the head! She stopped every few feet to hand out fistfuls of her new buttons ("Just pass them down!") while loudly proclaiming her new slogan, then blowing the horn yet again. "Gladys the Gladiator,

Gladiating FOR THE PEOPLE!"
Booowaaaaaaaaaaaaaaaaaaaaaaaaaaa!

"Talk about momentum," Lester leaned over and quipped to Harold. "I'd say Gladys is back, and by golly if *that* doesn't sound like a good campaign button, huh?" The two of them laughed out loud. Even though Gladys occasionally drove just about everyone nuts, the thought of her *not* being mayor had become oddly unnerving.

Although the band's playing wasn't the best, a good time was had by all and everyone picked up their free engraved GLADYS THE GLADIATOR, GLADIATING FOR THE PEOPLE pens and pencils on the way out. (Dorothy informed Gladys that a skywriter wasn't in her campaign budget. "What campaign budget?" Gladys wanted to know.)

Katie, who clapped longer and louder than anyone else at the concert, was still riding an emotional high from her land deal with Challie Carter and lunch with Jacob. When she and Challie had regrouped after Jacob's untimely interruption, Challie had said he liked doing business with somebody gutsy enough to lay down fair-and-square limits, then live or die by them. If that alone wasn't enough reason to celebrate, Gladys phoned Katie to say she better get to the concert early Saturday and hang on to her hat because "I'm launching a very bold campaign strategy, one you're sure to like!" Katie was so caught up in these victories she even granted Josh a one-night early dismissal from his grounding so he could take Shelby to the concert. "I have a feeling Gladys is going to put on a show *nobody* should miss." Wasn't *that* the truth!

Josh, riding high on his freedom, mustered the courage on the way home from the concert to ask Shelby if she'd ever heard of the Fire Pit. "Who hasn't?" she said.

"And?" he asked hopefully, his cheeks reddening.

"And?" she responded, her own cheeks now flaming.

"And, I was hoping we could maybe check it out tonight."

She stared at him as he drove. He felt her eyes boring into him, imagined their lusty longing, in fact had to let up on the accelerator realizing he was suddenly driving over the speed limit. He smiled and glanced over at her, saw her sweet face, wrinkled brow . . . reared-back palm just before it landed with fury on his cheek.

"So much for the Fire Pit," he told Alex in an e-mail that night.

■ ■ ■ ■

Thank You, Lord. Thank you, Carl Jimson.
Dorothy sat in her prayer chair, Sheba
nestled on her lap between Dorothy's Bible
and the newspaper folded open to the
opinion page, which these days never lacked
for political attitude, judgment and general
tongue lashings. A mean spirit pervaded the
town, and she'd almost quit reading the section, deciding no good could come of it.

But this Sunday morning the entire space
was taken up by a man from outside their
community. She needed to get ready for
church soon, but clearly a Sunday morning
blessing had already been delivered and she
wanted to give it just one more read.

Thank You
Good citizens of Partonville, I was
raised by hard-working parents on a
dairy farm in a small scenic town in
central Wisconsin, a town not unlike
Partonville in size and character — a
town that no longer exists in the way I
remember it from my childhood. Gone
are the fields, the mom-and-pop stores,
the remnants of big barns, neighbors

who've known each other since their youth. Gone are the intimate gathering spots like your Harry's Grill and the homespun respite offered by the Lamp Post motel. Rolling vistas are now camouflaged by townhouses, shopping centers and towering office buildings. Modest farm homes have been demolished to make way for spacious tudor dwellings.

Am I implying that my old hometown is worse off, that today's citizens aren't decent or that "progress" is wicked? Of course not! As an architect trying to make a living in change, certainly not! People everywhere are striving to find their way. I am simply saying that although something new has grown and flourished on my family's farmland, bringing with it opportunity and excitement, something dear and precious was also lost.

Partonville's gift is that its mere presence reminds us that some things — the most important elements of life — should *not* change. Who we are matters. What we decide to do, or not to do, makes an impact. What we stand for — especially when we choose to stand alongside each other — can, one person, one block, one town at a time, surely and ultimately impact all of humankind. Since my encounters with Partonville, I have considered anew many important things, such as who *are* my neighbors? How might I get to know them better, learn to care about *their* well-being? How might *we* stand together to discover — or rediscover — what is dear to *us,* to lift it to the light, polish off the dust left behind by racing past each other, and together knit something strong, lasting and meaningful, as you are doing with the revitalization of your town square?

Thank you, Partonville, for reminding me where I came from, who I am because of it and what means the most to me. May God bestow his grace upon your endeavors to stand strong in a changing world. As for the rest of us, whether we live in the heart of New York City, the suburbs of Cincinnati or on the coast of Oregon, may we live with a sense of small-town purpose such as I witnessed in Partonville.

> Sincerely, respectfully
> and with gratefulness,
> Carl Jimson

Dorothy petted Sheba's head. What, she wondered, would Carl think of Partonville if he stopped by today and walked into the midst of their squabbling selves? She prayed God would anoint Carl's words to help breathe gratefulness and a sense of oneness back into her beloved townspeople. *Come on, Big Guy! That's simply not too much to ask!*

Edward Showalter read the editorial to Kornflake. The first time he read it to himself, but this go-around he wanted to hear the words out loud. Kornflake, striking a pose much like the old RCA dog, cocked his head from one side to the other while his master spoke.

"Now listen to this part, Kornflake, and see if you don't start thinking what I'm thinking. 'How might *we* stand together to discover — or rediscover — what is dear to us, to lift it to the light, knit something strong, lasting and meaningful?' Now I ask you," he said, lowering the paper enough to make eye contact, "doesn't that just beg for a marriage proposal? And if not now, when? We're sure not getting any younger!"

28

Turns out Sunday was The Day of The Editorial That Changed The Election for good. After Colton heard about Katie's land lock (because Challie called and told him their pending deal was off the table), he no longer answered Sam Vitner's phone calls. "After all," Sam said into the receiver, "you agreed to back me. I figured that added up to more than button funding, especially after I told you about Challie Carter!" But his pleas fell on deaf ears. The momentum had shifted. By Monday, it was clear that pretty much the only ones for sure remaining in his corner were George Gustafson and Tom Hornsby, and even Tom seemed to be waffling since his wife made it public she'd never agreed with her husband's choice for mayor — which is what she'd been trying to tell Katie.

Also by Monday, Carl Jimson's editorial had most people all but hugging in the streets. Of course nothing would last forever, but for now, citizens were proud of their town and grateful for each other. Dorothy, Sadie Lawson, Harold, Paul Joy, Katie and Pastor Delbert each made calls to Carl Jimson, who thanked them for their feedback and promised them he would try to make it down for the private grand opening of Partonville Pleasantries, which he was begged to attend. He told Paul he'd be there only if the Lamp Post had a room available, which Paul guaranteed him it would, "as our treat."

Gladys, back at Harry's usual morning lineup for the first time since her ousting, was so puffed up on her own Gladiator Glee (and *that* button was ordered, against the advice of her campaign manager) she would have been airborne if the weight of her Gladiator buttons wasn't holding her down. By Tuesday afternoon, the day Partonville Pleasantries' new sign went up over the front door of the old Taninger building causing quite the stir, Sam Vitner officially withdrew from the race saying he realized he didn't have time to run a business and a town. Due to the fact the town was still wallowing in the afterglow of their newfound love fest, nobody rubbed his failure in his face, for which he was grateful.

By Wednesday, the Hookers could barely wait to come together just to roll the dice at bunco.

Morning and Midnight were scampering from here to there faster than Nellie Ruth could keep up with shooing them from there to here. Her face was flushed, her heart raced and the clock indicated her doorbell would likely be ringing in five minutes. What was a perfectionist to *do* with unruly critters?

She'd phoned all the Happy Hookers to make sure nobody was allergic to cats, although over the years many of them had had pets. Well, other than from Gladys, of course, bless her Gladiating heart (Nellie Ruth prayed for everyone) who said she had no *official* allergies to cats. Nellie Ruth was torn as to what to do with the kitties: leave them out so everyone could meet them and trust they'd behave? Leave them out so everyone could meet them, then hope she could corral them before bunco began? Just put them away now (as if that was humanly possible!), sequestering them to her bedroom, which seemed cruel and unusual punishment.

"Can I trust you two?" she said to Midnight who switched her tail, licked her armpit and looked at a paw as if to say, "You are so boring I'd rather do *anything* than listen to you."

Nellie Ruth decided to give her manic fretting about the cats a rest and get back to her manic fretting about her readiness for the Hookers. She took a look about. Dice at both tables, score pads ready, bowls of bridge mix set on the corners. . . . "OH! Cocktail napkins!" She went to the kitchen, ripped open a new package of spring floral cocktail napkins purchased just for the occasion and placed them precisely at each setting, then tossed the packaging and perused the kitchen. Prizes wrapped and waiting on the counter. Coffee perking, tea pot and tea bags readied. Chocolate cake passable but not to her standards. She should have stuck with the *simple* white frosting and skipped trying to create the pink flowerettes she saw in a magazine, which ended up looking more like frosting puddles than pedals. "Oh, well," ES told her earlier on the phone. "You did your best, sweetheart. Everything you've ever served me has been wonderful. The Hookers won't remember the flowers, they'll remember the flavor."

Sweetheart. She tingled again at the memory of his charming term of endearment. She fussed with the coffee tray on the table again, switching the positions of the creamer and sugar bowl.

Ding-dong.

The bell startled Morning, who leaped off the counter and ran down the hall — leaving cake crumbs and frosting footprints in his blazing wake. How could this *be?* She'd only turned her back for a moment!

"NO!" Nellie Ruth wailed, not sure whether to answer the door or bolt it.

She stood horrified, staring at the terrible mess. But she couldn't let any of the Hookers stand outside on her raised porch on such a cool, windy evening, could she? What if it was Dorothy or May Belle out there? She put her hand on the doorknob, then turned and took one more look at her smashed cake (had Morning leapt into it or simply batted it to pieces?) and the trail of chocolate crumbs and bits of frosting smears that disappeared into her bedroom hall.

The bell rang a second time. She had to open the door. When she saw Dorothy and May Belle, who walked over together, Gladys, Jessie, Maggie and Katie, who all happened to arrive at the same time, huddled together, her bottom lip quivered. She squeaked out "Come in" and then burst out crying. By the time they all made it through the door, they discovered what her tears were about. Nellie Ruth was as neat and tidy as a pinhead. It was surprising she hadn't fainted dead away.

Maggie was the first to break the ice by exploding with laughter. "Oh, *honey!* What a clever and thematic design scheme!" she said, bowing, lowering her hand and pointing to the messy path as though she were one of Bob Barker's beauties showcasing a gorgeous watch. "Did you learn this technique in Martha Stewart's latest article on pawprint patterns? You shouldn't have gone to all this trouble just for *us!*"

"Yes," Dorothy chimed in, picking right up on Maggie's brilliant tactic while throwing her arm around Nellie Ruth and drawing her close up to her side, "and how clever of you, honey, to come up with the perfect brown, white and pink compliment to your new Splendid Pink paint!" Maggie laughed so hard her new blue mascara began to run.

May Belle walked around the messy pawprints to rip two paper towels from the dispenser. Katie did the same. Jessie gathered coats while Dorothy continued to hold the now crying *and* laughing Nellie Ruth. Gladys, who decided there was no point in telling Nellie Ruth what she was *really* thinking about this mess, feigned a "Here kitty-kitty" battle cry and Gladiated herself down the hall. "Who else but a Gladiator," she said over her shoulder, "to seize the heinous runaway!" Maggie nearly peed her pants and said so. Everyone was just howling!

Ding-dong!

Nellie Ruth recuperated enough to stagger to the door and open it. "Jessica! Come on in! Welcome to Nellie Ruth's house of. . . . bwaaaaaa-ha-ha-ha-ha-ha!" Nellie Ruth doubled over with laughter. She simply could not speak. Maggie, appearing as if blue veins ran down her face and under her chin, came over and said, "She's trying to say welcome to our . . . bwaaaaaa-ha-ha-ha-ha-ha! Oh, NO!" she said, looking startled. "Your bathroom's down the hall, right Nellie Ruth?"

Gladys appeared looking slightly askew but holding up frosty-pawed Morning by the scruff of his neck. "Victory is mine!"

It was another several minutes before anyone could explain to Jessica what on earth was going on. Throughout the entire evening's play, rounds of laughter broke out as one or another of them reviewed the whole incident. The ladies ate every bit of bridge mix and polished off a bag of Oreo Cookies Nellie Ruth had stashed in her cabinet. Gladys went on to win first place and most buncos. The woman was on an unstoppable roll.

The only person who smiled more than Gladys that evening was Dorothy. Every time she looked at Katie she just beamed. Jacob told her about their upcoming date only because he knew she'd somehow sniff it out anyway. Dorothy didn't mention it to Katie, but it was obvious to Katie she knew.

Dearest Dorothy,
What do you think about my mom and your son (that sounds SO weird) going on a date (Egads! My MOM on a DATE!) tomorrow night? Although mom didn't call it that. She said they were just going "out." HA!

Joshmeister

Dear Joshmeister,
I think it sounds grand. Do you think we should wait up for them? HA!

Outtamyway

Dearest Dorothy,
Don't freak me out. She *better* be home before midnight or I'll have to ask you to ground your son!

Joshmeister

■ ■ ■ ■

Dear Joshmeister,
    You worry too much. ;>) But do you re-
alize if they ever got married that would
make you my grandson?"
    Outtamyway, whose imagination is run-
ning wild and WAY ahead of itself.

Dear Wild One,
    YIKES! It's not that I wouldn't like to be
your grandson, but this is just a first DATE.
And if I EVER hear my mom or your son
mention ANYTHING about the FIRE PIT,
I'm TAKING ACTION!
    Joshmeister, who you bet your BIPPY is
worried! No wonder me and Shelby make
mom nervous!

Katie felt like a spinning top. The mall
opening was exactly three weeks away. Her
phone rang off the hook. She was writing
all the time: press releases, so many checks
to so many people it occasionally made her
dizzy, a feature article for *BackRoads Illinois*
that included detailed information about
the town as well as the mall, thank-you
notes, work orders and reminders for Edward Showalter, who was suddenly a com-

plete airhead. What a time for that! But at least her harried schedule kept her from fretting about her date with Jacob tonight. He phoned to tell her he'd made reservations to dine at The Driscoll, if that was okay with her, which it certainly was, and purchased tickets for a play at the junior college. Josh teased her mercilessly when he noticed she had two outfits laid out on her bed. He also e-mailed Jacob about his mom's midnight curfew. Although he was joking, then again, maybe he wasn't.

As it turns out, he needn't have worried. Aside from the drive to Hethrow, which suddenly felt awkward now that they were on a date, once they settled into dinner — and my, didn't he look charming in *that* suit! — they both seemed to relax. They had plenty to talk about so conversation came easy. The play was wonderful, funny and poignant, which gave them fresh things to discuss on the way home. Although he asked her if she'd like to go for a nightcap, she declined. "Thanks, but I've had a long week with more long weeks to come. Plus, I've got a teen son at home who's watching my every move. I need to set a good example."

"Well, at least this first time," he said, his voice sounding unusually low and manly, which made her heart skip a beat. When he drove up the lane, Katie suddenly felt like a teenager again, thinking about a goodnight kiss. She recalled how he'd caught her off guard under the mistletoe during the Christmas party and how she'd told him, as she quickly scooted away, that she thought mistletoe was hokey. As much as she didn't want him to try to kiss her tonight, at the same time she wondered if he *was* a good kisser and was embarrassed to find herself thinking such a thing, especially when she noticed her son watching out the kitchen window as they pulled up to the house.

Once again, she needn't have worried. He walked around and opened her car door, same as he'd done all night. When she stood up she caught a whiff of his cologne again. Mm. He walked her to the door, asked if he could come in and say hello to Josh, who appeared uncomfortable, then told them both goodnight. After Jacob departed, Josh stared as his mom.

"What?"

"Did you have a good time?"

"Yes. It was nice."

"Are you going out again?"

"I don't know."

"Do you want to?"

"I haven't thought about it."

"Did he kiss you?"

"Joshua! That is a rather rude and personal question."

"He DID!"

"No, he did not — even though it's really none of your business. If you're done with your inquisition, I'm going to bed. I'm working tomorrow, as is the whole crew. You're working at Jessica's tomorrow, too, aren't you?"

"Yes. More slave labor."

She smiled at him. "You know, I'm proud of you."

He reared his head back, as though he'd been slapped. "For *what?*"

"For caring. For not doing nearly as much whining during your grounding as I thought you might. For doing such a good job at Jessica's. She brags on you, you know." She kissed him on the cheek and went up the stairs.

If Jacob asked his mom out again, Josh hoped she said yes. He was obviously good for her attitude.

29

Tuesday. April Fool's Day. Non-election day in Partonville. Rain. Spring in full bloom. A crazed work day for Edward Showalter since Partonville Pleasantries would open in a week and a half, and tenants were moving in.

Up the stairs, down the stairs. Walkie-talkie squawking all the time. We need you here. We need you there. Edward Showalter! Where ARE you? He'd been run ragged and yet, all he could think about was getting himself over to Nellie Ruth's because to-night was the night. He would explode — literally, his head would blow off his neck and hit the atrium skylights — if he didn't just get it over with. He'd so wanted to talk to his best friend Johnny Mathis about this first, ask about protocol and finesse. But what if Nellie Ruth. . . . No, he simply would not allow himself to consider that possibility.

He arrived home at 7:30 and whipped through a shower. His hands were shaking so badly he couldn't keep control of the soap and had to pick it up off the tub floor at least three times. He put on the set of clean clothes he'd actually chosen yesterday, a first in his life. He told Kornflake to wish him good luck, hopped in the cammy-van, cranked over the engine, then popped right back out again leaving the van running while he ran back into the house to get the all-important package he'd left on his dresser.

With every step he took up to Nellie Ruth's door, his legs felt heavier until he wondered if he might not make it and have to use his cell phone to call for help. He was running late, but nothing could be done about that now. His work schedule was what it was, but more importantly, Nellie Ruth McGregor was who *she* was: the woman he wanted to marry. One more step. One more step.

Nellie Ruth saw his van pull up, then heard him on the stairs. She waited for his familiar *knock, knock-knock-knock, knock* but it didn't come. She finally opened the door to find him standing there with his head bowed, looking as if he were praying, which he was.

"ES! Come in!" she said, opening the door and greeting him with a warm kiss on the cheek. She laughed. "Your entrance feels like a reversal of the Hookers meeting!" He looked puzzled. "I didn't want them to come in when they arrived and they had to ring the doorbell twice. But I couldn't wait for you to walk through that door and you didn't even knock!" She chuckled but he still looked puzzled. "Never mind. I'm being silly. I'm glad you're here. Let me take your coat."

"*No!* I mean, I think I'll keep it on," he said, fingering the ring box in his jacket pocket. "Let's sit down on your couch, okay?" Nellie Ruth thought his behavior odd, but she obliged.

After they were seated she asked him if he'd like anything to eat or drink. Although he'd been plenty hungry when he got off work, his stomach was so topsy-turvy right now he didn't think he could keep anything down. "No. I'm fine. Just stay here. Next to me. On the couch."

"I'd love to," she said, moving closer, resting her head on his shoulder. "But are you okay? You sure you don't want me to take your coat? You seem . . . well, I bet you're just tuckered out, aren't you," she said, patting his knee.

His knee. He hoped when he got down on it he could get back up again. *Tarnation, Edward Showalter! You're having the dumbest thoughts! I hope your mouth works smarter than your brain when you go to ask her!*

"Would you like to watch television?"

"No. I'd like to talk," he said, unzippering his jacket.

"Good. Me too," she said, nestling her head further into his chest until she heard his wildly beating heart. "ES! Your heart is racing a mile a minute! Do you feel okay?" She put her hand to his forehead.

"Nellie Ruth," he said, suddenly dislodging her from her cuddled position and standing up in front of her so fast it unnerved her, "let me tell you how I feel. I feel like a man who is hopelessly in love with the beautiful woman in front of him. I feel like we're the luckiest people in the world to have found each other at this time of our lives. I thank God I am sober and saved and that I have job security," he said, getting down on one knee, causing her mouth to fall open and her heart to leap into her throat.

"Nellie Ruth, we're not young and we're not getting any younger, but I don't want to spend another minute of my life without you by my side." He reached into his pocket and withdrew the black velvet ring box. She watched with disbelief as it quivered before her in his trembling left hand. "Nellie Ruth McGregor," he said, taking her right hand in his, "I love you. I know this is an awfully fast courtship, but will you become my lawfully wedded wife, to have and to hold until death do us part? Please?"

"Oh, ES," she said in barely a whisper. "I can't believe this. I just don't know . . . what to think, what to say." His face looked tortured, but she was having trouble collecting her thoughts to save him — to save both of them — from the terrible silence. "You are the sweetest, dearest, most wonderful thing that's ever happened to me," she said as she raised their locked hands to her face and kissed his thumb. Tears spilled over her lashes and dripped onto their fingers. "Oh, ES!" She let go of his hand and reached out for his tense face, drew it toward her, unabashedly kissed his nose, his closed eyes, each cheek, tasted the saltiness of his tears on her tongue. She took his hand in hers again, leaned her forehead against his and rested it there. Together they sniffled until he began to kiss her face, their tears melting together.

He kissed her lips five delicate times whispering "Please" between each union.

"Please, Nellie Ruth. I know I don't deserve such a saintly woman as yourself, what with my boozin' and carousing past. But God has given me a second chance and I want to spend the rest of my life proving my worth to you. *Please.*"

When he referred to her as a saintly woman, Nellie Ruth was overcome with an onslaught of fearful thoughts. Fear that since her father had abused her as a child . . . what if she *couldn't* be the wife this beloved man deserved? But God had brought her through that, claimed her as *His* own. *No! I won't allow fear to ruin the rest of my life, this opportunity!*

They were each survivors of life's hard circumstances, she thought. Two people deeply in love with God and each other. He'd never done anything to cause her distrust. He was a genteel, hard-working, caring human being. How could she say no?

"Yes," she first whispered. "Yes, Edward Showalter! I say *yes!*" She all but threw herself on him to give him a hug. Since he was down on one knee, over he toppled, Nellie Ruth going right over with him. The ring box fell out of his hand and skittered toward the coffee table which Midnight was hiding beneath. When the two of them saw the kitty staring at the box, they broke out laughing until they grabbed each other and desperately engaged in a deep, long, passionate kiss. "ES," she said, pulling herself away, even though she didn't want to, "I think we better get up off this floor right *now!*" Although she was blushing, she no longer felt worried about her ability to respond to this man who was to become her husband — and *soon,* she hoped!

"I believe you are exactly right," he said, helping them both to their feet after grabbing the ring box. "Now sit yourself down here on this couch so I can give you an engagement present. Guess what it is?" he said, a breathless mischief and excitement in his voice.

"Another kitten." She eyed the box with merry eyes. "A teensy, tiny one."

"No." He held the box in front of her and slowly opened the lid to reveal a delicate gold band with the most beautiful round sparkling diamond she'd ever seen.

"Oh, ES! It's . . . *perfect!*" She sobbed. Just sobbed.

He took it out of the box and just like in the movies, placed it on her left hand ring finger. It slipped over her knuckle like silk on silk. "I know it's a small diamond, Nellie Ruth, but I also know you, and I figured you wouldn't want some big showy thing."

"You figured exactly right," she said, staring at the ring through her tears, flickering it in front of their faces, giving him a kiss, sobbing and repeating the cycle again and again. "I just cannot *believe* it. After all these years, me, sixty-three-year-old Nellie Ruth McGregor, getting *married.* God is so unbelievably good." Again she cried as he once again cradled her in his arms, his own tears dampening the top of her head. For a long while they didn't speak, remaining locked in their silent prayers.

"Would you like to call anyone?" he asked.

"Did Johnny and Mary know you were going to ask me?"

"Nobody knew but God, although I know the two of them will just bust a gut of happiness when they hear!"

"I'd like for us to tell them together. How about we give them a call right now? Do you think it's too late?"

ES looked at his watch. 8:30. "Johnny would never forgive me if I thought it was too late to tell him about *this!*"

"One more kiss," she said, "and then we'll dial."

30

Chaos reigned the night before the community sneak-preview grand opening. Twice this week, Sheldon Prescott, owner of Alotta Chocolatta, burned batches of fudge while "breaking in" his new commercial-grade equipment (he'd previously only cooked on the stovetop in his kitchen, a little fact he hadn't quite mentioned to Katie) and due to the atrium, the entire mall still smelled bad all day Wednesday. So much for the enticing, make-you-want-to-stay-and-shop-a-little-longer fragrance of the coco bean! Between exhaust fans, the new furnace's fan, fumigating fans Smackman "borrowed" from someone somewhere and a break in the weather that allowed store owners to open their windows, the "atmospheric scent," as the exuberant Edward Showalter referred to it, was almost gone.

Although most store move-ins were synchronized so as not to tie up the elevator all day by any one store owner, it seemed everyone suddenly needed last-minute boxes moved in, up and over there. Horns blew in the shipping dock as delivery vans blocked pickup trucks. Coupled with the excitement of watching dreams come to life, tempers flared (so much for love your neighbor) as tired store owners trained sales clerks, rearranged displays and made hysterical phone calls asking "Where is it?" and ranting "You promised me it would be here by now!" Although Katie would have loved to have held a pre-*pre* grand opening just for mall owners and employees to become familiar with each other's wares and services, it was clear they'd all be working down to the wire just to get their own businesses in shape on time.

When the boxes of mall directories arrived a week ago, Katie had put Josh and Earl to work applying labels for the residential mailing that had just gone out. It was the perfect task for Earl, he and Josh having learned to work well together through their labors at the Lamp Post. Josh looked forward to his time with Earl. Although Earl didn't say much, Josh told Shelby there was something inspiring about a quiet man doing a task, which she thought sounded very mature and caused her to forget about the Fire Pit incident. Katie told May Belle she'd discovered the perfect bulk-mailer assistant in Earl and assured her she'd be employing him part-time in the future, which caused May Belle to cry happy tears when she told Dorothy about it.

Since the store owners weren't going to have time to do their own browsing, Katie decided to give them each a short-stack supply of directories, not only to make them available to customers, but to pick up and read themselves should they find a spare moment or two. Of course the *Press* gave the mall opening wonderful coverage. Now that Sharon no longer had a missing person to track or an election to cover, she channeled all her energy into mall articles, including shots of the banners, interviews with the owners, stories on the rehab project itself and a picture of Katie behind her desk — which Katie hated.

Yes, the advertising bases were covered. Now, if they could all just pull themselves together before tomorrow!

Katie raved about the hallway display cases. They were her best publicity ploy ever. She told Jacob she even surprised herself with her own cleverness, but he said he doubted it — which caught her up short until she realized he was pulling her leg. His dry sense of humor was something she was becoming more accustomed to, but every once in awhile he still yanked her chain with it, which amused him no end. In the three weeks since their first official date, they'd only had time to go out to dinner once more, although she and Josh dined at Dorothy's one night, which Dorothy said didn't count since, well, "You'd hardly call it a date when you have a mother and a son as chaperones."

"To be honest," she told Jacob when they were discussing the display cases on the phone, "I can only take credit for the *idea.* Carl Jimson went above and beyond to incorporate them into the actual structure. But wait until you see what Jessica did with them! She orchestrated and created little scenes, for lack of a better word, from each store." She'd arranged a splay of books from the Word Exchange (second floor) in the display case in front of the Tea Cozy on the main floor. She showcased small glasses of candy from Alotta Chocolatta (lower level) outside A Tisket A Tasket on the main floor. Artfully arranged with each scene was calligraphy signage stating where the items could be purchased. Jessica had the best time working with owners to select the items for display. She told Katie it was like going on a personal shopping spree without having to spend any money! "Plus," she said, "it's giving me a chance to scope everything out so I know where I want to spend my winning gift certificate — although I have no doubt it will be in Baths, Boudoir and Babies because, oh, *Katie!* Did you *see* those adorable baby clothes!" It felt good, Katie thought, to hear the enthusiasm ringing in her friend's voice again.

"What do you think, May Belle?" Dorothy asked when she and Sheba stopped by hoping to snitch a double chocolate brownie or two before Earl delivered them to the Tea Cozy. "Do you think my idea's out of line? I don't want to rob anything from Katie's moment in the sun."

"I think," May Belle said, pausing to remove one batch of brownies from the oven and put in the next, "that it's brilliant and will only add to the excitement." She removed her oven mitt and gingerly sat down at the kitchen table, noticing her back tightening up again. She'd have to get the Vicks VapoRub out before she went to bed. "The problem I see isn't with Katie, though, it's with Gladys."

"How so?"

"Do you think she's really going to want to share her ribbon-cutting moment like that?"

"Oh, I didn't mean for us to do it on Saturday! But then I guess I didn't say that, did I?"

"No, ma'am, you did not."

"I'm talking about doing it Friday night while the locals are waiting to enter preview night."

"That would be perfect. Have you talked to Katie about it, though?"

"I thought I'd run it by you first."

"Well, you've got my approval."

"As if I needed it," Dorothy teased, reaching across the table and patting her friend's hand. "They'll be so surprised!"

By 6:15 p.m. people were already gathering outside the mini mall's front doors, which weren't due to open until 7. Of course Cora Davis was right up there at the front of the pack. Even Jessica, Paul and Sarah Sue, who ran late to most everything, were getting into their car already. They didn't want to miss a moment of standing beneath the Partonville Pleasantries sign in the midst of all the excitement in front of the very mall that Jessica named!

Just when Jessica snapped Sarah Sue's seat

belt, Carl Jimson surprised them by pulling into the motel lot. Even though they hadn't heard from him, and even though they assumed that likely meant he couldn't make it, they'd prepared his room anyway, just in case. They welcomed him warmly and were "honored and proud" to meet Glenda Jimson.

"You three run on ahead. We'll be along shortly," Carl said, after Jessica ran in to get them a key and told them, "You're in unit number eleven." Much to Carl and Glenda's surprise, a welcome basket awaited them, complete with a mall directory, Wednesday's *Press,* a bag of pretzels, a bottle of water, two Avon samples and a brand-new coffee mug with "Welcome to Pardon-Me-Ville" printed around it in bold blue lettering. A Tisket A Basket shop owner Jenna Olsen donated it herself after she heard who it was for.

"See, honey," Carl said to his wife as he gave her a big hug when they entered their room. "I told you! This place is a little slice of heaven."

Glenda chuckled. " 'Welcome to Pardon-Me-Ville?' You *gotta* love the spirit of a town that can laugh at itself too!"

6:55 p.m. Katie sat in the dark in her office

with her door closed, the door that now displayed the new brass MALL DIRECTOR sign Edward Showalter mounted just today. She had to laugh when he came to position it, thinking how much like Gladys it made her feel to get that name tag on just right. She was nervous, yes, but also excited and regretful. She was exhausted, grateful, overwhelmed and thankful. No wonder she wanted to cry. When she'd discovered the FAMILY OWNED AND OPERATED SINCE 1923 sign out by the trash bins yesterday, she realized she'd somehow gotten emotionally attached to the dumb thing and asked Edward Showalter to bring it up to her office and mount it on the wall behind her desk. Now she, too, was making history, but those who went before should never be forgotten.

Although several "Congratulations on your grand opening" floral arrangements had arrived and were sprinkled throughout the mall, she'd selected three of them for her desk. The mall lights shining through her office window illuminated their shadows. The huge showy arrangement of exotic flowers made her smile. The card read, "It was your turn — this time. Congratulations. Colton Craig." The dieffenbachia plant was to "Sister Katie. Hallelujah! from Delbert and family." But the small bouquet of tightly packed pink roses was the most precious on three counts: the choice of flowers, which were her favorite, the sentiment and the giver. "I'm proud of you. Jacob" It was a message that caused her many tears when it arrived, yes, because he touched her heart, but, unbeknownst to him, he'd also opened a ribbon of grief she'd been working hard to suppress since Carl Jimson's letter to the editor appeared in the paper. She rested her fingertips against the vase.

Oh, Mom, what I wouldn't give for you to be here today to see what I've helped grow in the town you fled when you got pregnant with me in order to conceal that fact. I wish I could take back all of the rude and mindless things I said to you about your beloved town, Mom. I didn't know why you loved it so much, but now I do. I'm sure I hurt you with my selfish, snide comments. Please forgive me — which I know you do. I just wish you were here so I could say it to your face and give you a hug. By now she was crying, which felt like a relief.

Thank you, Mom, for loving me. For always being so proud of my accomplishments and for telling me so. Thank you for praying for me all of those years, even when I said I didn't want to hear about your God, who I now know is my God too. But I had to come here without you to learn that. No, you didn't come back home, but I did.

There was a light rap on the door. "Ms. Durbin? You in there?" It was Edward Showalter.

"Yes."

"You okay?"

"Yes."

"It's time to open the mall. Dorothy's waiting just inside the front doors for you."

"I'll be down in a moment. You go ahead and get the surprise ready." She wiped her eyes, turned on the light and freshened her lipstick. When she stepped out into the mall, it was amazing! People stood outside their doorways buzzing with each other, waiting to greet their new customers and shouting "Good luck!" when they saw her. She made her way down the center stairs toward the front door.

"You look beautiful," Dorothy said when Katie got to the bottom of the stairs, taking note of her red puffy eyes. "This is all just so exciting, honey! I've been giving prayers of thanksgiving all the day long!"

"Thank you," Katie said, giving her a hug. "Me too."

"Do you have the glasses and the sparkling cider ready?" Katie asked, turning to Edward Showalter.

"Yes, boss lady," he said, giving her a salute. "Let me grab them!" What, Katie wondered, would she have ever done without Edward Showalter?

Katie put her hand on the door, straightened her spine and opened it wide. It looked like the whole town had turned out for the gala, but then a drawing for a prize was about to take place, she thought, chuckling to herself. *You are so clever!*

"Ladies and Gentlemen! Welcome to Partonville Pleasantries!" A loud cheer went up, which warmed her heart and caused tears to well in her eyes again. But no, she would not cry. Not now. "Thank you for coming this evening and we hope to see many of you back again tomorrow and all the days to come. After you enter, please take your time and enjoy yourselves. We'll be open until nine tonight. Look around. Talk to the owners. Make sure you enter the drawing; there are receptacles on each floor for your entries. Get a bite to eat, figure out where you want to spend your money tomorrow," she paused to let the outbreak of laughter die down, "and most of all, *celebrate* with us." The crowd started to press in, thinking she was done.

"But first, hold on a moment. Dorothy has something she'd like to say. Dorothy?"

she said, stepping aside so Dorothy could make her way out the door.

"Hello everyone. Since it's a night to celebrate, I'd just like to seize this occasion to honor and congratulate two of our own. Edward Showalter, come on out here with the 'bubbly'!" He stepped up beside her carrying the tray. "Nellie Ruth McGregor, would you please come up here and stand by your man!"

Nellie Ruth put her hand over her mouth while Edward Showalter burst out laughing. Someone had to nudge Nellie Ruth to get her to move. People started hooting and clapping as she reluctantly made her way between ES and Dorothy, where Katie directed her. After the lovebirds were situated next to each other, Katie took the tray from Edward Showalter and held it while Dorothy poured the sparkling cider into the glasses.

"Now each one of you take a glass," Dorothy told them, which they did. "Now interlock your elbows and bring your own glass back to your lips." Nellie Ruth thought she would surely die of embarrassment, but Edward Showalter was lit up brighter than a thousand-watt bulb. "Now hold it right there," she said when they were in place. "Now look into each other's eyes," which they had no trouble doing. "Now, since baseball practice is just around the corner and I'm still the Wild Musketeers' only cheerleader — due to the fact I haven't died yet," which caused everyone to laugh and Nellie Ruth to worry her shaking laughter would cause her to spill her drink, "I thought I'd just get in a little practice. Everyone, on the count of three, say, '*Congratulations on your engagement, you two!*' And a-one," she said, throwing up one finger, "and a-two, and a . . ."

"CONGRATULATIONS ON YOUR ENGAGEMENT, YOU TWO!"

While Edward Showalter and Nellie Ruth, arms still entwined, sipped from their glasses, Dorothy, eyes aglow, watched Jacob begin to make his way through the crowd. Katie had asked him if he'd serve as her escort for the evening, and he of course had said yes.

A NOTE FROM THE AUTHOR

With a sigh of relief (the type that comes at the end of all fulfilling labors), several months ago I turned in the manuscript for the book you've just read (unless you're one of those tricky types who starts at The End). Editors and copy editors had their astute way with it, and now, I've just spent the last four days (reading somewhat slowly, making a few notes, clarifying this and that) marveling at my own storytelling. It was an *amazing,* nearly *surreal* experience! I laughed and cried (same as I did while writing), page-turned with fervor and occasionally thought, OH! I hope I remember *that* prayer — that comeback, that funny line, that attitude — if the same thing ever happens to *me!* Since I'm the author, I know that might sound odd. It's just that sometimes my own storytelling seems to happen apart from me. (I do, however, know I'm typing right now. ;>))

I'm not sharing my amazement here to be a braggadocio. I'm actually in a state of *wonder.* I am amazed at what the creative process delivers if we but give ourselves over to it, become its servant, if you will. Stories — make that *any* creative tug or whisper — *often* arrive on the unsuspecting wings of grace, but far too often we don't feel ready for them, so we duck and run. This time, I'm glad I didn't take time to think, but rather *trusted* and began to write.

"How do you dream these things *up?*" I'm often asked. I even asked *myself* that after reading this book. TRUTH: I don't. I am not this clever. But the pure act of Creation is. BRAVO!

I am, however, a keen observer of life. I believe if we honor the Truth of an emotion or impulse, a bout of anger or insecurity, a moment of temptation or triumph, that we will core-connect with others. Even though I have written every word of the Welcome to Partonville series myself, I also know that I couldn't have done so if the characters (and aren't they?!) didn't "show up" in my head and lead the way — which I trusted *them* to do. And *that* wouldn't have happened without the genuine trailblazing, guts and grit of the Real Dearest Dorothy (whose hands remain on my shoulders, all the way from heaven) and my Real parents, grandparents, aunts, uncles, godparents and vibrant other oldsters) — who infused me with *their* natural spunk, Divine trust, bravery, sincere love and unquenchable zest for life.

RECAP: the Creator sets creativity in motion. I don't think; I pray to get out of my own way. I honor and serve the story that begins to unfold. I type as fast as the "movie" runs. I dare to be brave and share emotional truths. I am amazed by the outcome!

So, whatever creative act the Creator calls *you* to today, I heartily encourage you to respond. Perhaps *you* will soon enjoy the fruits of your own Amazing Experience! Write and tell me about it, okay?

Charlene Ann Baumbich
www.welcometopartonville.com
charlene@welcometopartonville.com

ABOUT THE AUTHOR

Charlene Ann Baumbich is a popular speaker, journalist, and author. Her stories, essays, and columns have appeared in numerous magazines and newspapers, including the *Chicago Tribune,* the *Chicago Sun-Times,* and *Today's Christian Woman.* She is also the author of the first five books in the Partonville series, *Dearest Dorothy, Are We There Yet?; Dearest Dorothy, Slow Down, You're Wearing Us Out!; Dearest Dorothy, Help! I've Lost Myself!; Dearest Dorothy, Who Would Have Ever Thought?!; Dearest Dorothy, Merry Everything!;* and six books of nonfiction. She lives in Glen Ellyn, Illinois. Learn more about Charlene at www .welcometopartonville.com.

The employees of Thorndike Press hope you have enjoyed this Large Print book. All our Thorndike and Wheeler Large Print titles are designed for easy reading, and all our books are made to last. Other Thorndike Press Large Print books are available at your library, through selected bookstores, or directly from us.

For information about titles, please call:
(800) 223-1244

or visit our Web site at:
http://gale.cengage.com/thorndike

To share your comments, please write:
Publisher
Thorndike Press
295 Kennedy Memorial Drive
Waterville, ME 04901